From a photograph by Pach Bros.

THE NOVELS AND STORIES OF
RICHARD HARDING DAVIS

VAN BIBBER

AND OTHERS

BY

RICHARD HARDING DAVIS

WITH AN INTRODUCTION BY
BOOTH TARKINGTON

ILLUSTRATED

NEW YORK
CHARLES SCRIBNER'S SONS
1917

PUBLISHERS' NOTE

THIS edition has been prepared in pursuance of a plan long contemplated, and on lines discussed and arranged with Mr. Davis a year or more ago. It has now been completed with what is believed to be a full knowledge of his wishes.

It has been thought of interest to preserve in connection with it some of the notable recollections and appreciations which his death called forth. They have therefore been prefixed as introductory passages to the several volumes, though in only two or three cases have they any association with special books. In a few instances they were published in periodicals and the press; those of Colonel Roosevelt, Mr. Gibson and Mr. McCutcheon appeared in *Scribner's Magazine*, and thanks are due to the *Metropolitan Magazine* and *Collier's Weekly* for permission to reprint those by Mr. Gouverneur Morris and Mr. Dunne; but most of them appear here for the first time.

SEPTEMBER, 1916.

RICHARD HARDING DAVIS

To the college boy of the early nineties Richard Harding Davis was the "beau ideal of *jeunesse dorée*," a sophisticated heart of gold. He was of that college boy's own age, but already an editor —already publishing books! His stalwart good looks were as familiar to us as were those of our own football captain; we knew his face as we knew the face of the President of the United States, but we infinitely preferred Davis's. When the Waldorf was wondrously completed, and we cut an exam. in Cuneiform Inscriptions for an excursion to see the world at lunch in its new magnificence, and Richard Harding Davis came into the Palm Room—then, oh, then, our day was radiant! That was the top of our fortune: we could never have hoped for so much. Of all the great people of every continent, this was the one we most desired to see.

The boys of those days left college to work, to raise families, to grow grizzled; but the glamour remained about Davis; *he* never grew grizzled. Youth was his great quality.

All his writing has the liveliness of springtime; it stirs with an unsuppressible gayety, and it has the attraction which companionship with him had: there is never enough. He could be sharp; he could write angrily and witheringly; but even when he was fiercest he was buoyant, and when his words were hot they were not scalding but rather of a dry, clean indignation with things which he believed could, if they would, be better. He never saw evil but as temporary.

Following him through his books, whether he wrote of home or carried his kind, stout heart far, far afield, we see an American writing to Americans. He often told us about things abroad in terms of New York; and we have all been to New York, so he made for us the pictures he wished us to see. And when he did not thus use New York for his colors he found other means as familiar to us and as suggestive; he always made us *see*. What claims our thanks in equal measure, he knew our kind of curiosity so well that he never failed to make us see what we were most anxious to see. He knew where our dark spots were, cleared up the field of vision, and left us unconfused. This discernment of our needs, and this power of enlightening and pleasuring his reader, sprang from seeds native in him. They were, as we say, gifts; for he always had them but did not make them. He was a national figure at twenty-three. He *knew how*, before he began.

Youth called to youth: all ages read him, but the

young men and young women have turned to him ever since his precocious fame made him their idol. They got many things from him, but above all they live with a happier bravery because of him. Reading the man beneath the print, they found their prophet and gladly perceived that a prophet is not always cowled and bearded, but may be a gallant young gentleman. This one called merrily to them in his manly voice; and they followed him. He bade them see that pain is negligible, that fear is a joke, and that the world is poignantly interesting, joyously lovable.

They will always follow him.

BOOTH TARKINGTON.

CONTENTS

CONTENTS

ILLUSTRATIONS

HER FIRST APPEARANCE

It was at the end of the first act of the first night of "The Sultana," and every member of the Lester Comic Opera Company, from Lester himself down to the wardrobe woman's son, who would have had to work if his mother lost her place, was sick with anxiety.

There is perhaps only one other place as feverish as it is behind the scenes on the first night of a comic opera, and that is a newspaper office on the last night of a Presidential campaign, when the returns are being flashed on the canvas outside, and the mob is howling, and the editor-in-chief is expecting to go to the Court of St. James if the election comes his way, and the office-boy is betting his wages that it won't.

Such nights as these try men's souls; but Van Bibber passed the stage-door man with as calmly polite a nod as though the piece had been running a hundred nights, and the manager was thinking up souvenirs for the one hundred and fiftieth, and the prima donna had, as usual, begun to hint for a new set of costumes. The stage-door keeper hesitated and was lost, and Van Bibber stepped into the unsuppressed excitement of the place with a pleased sniff at the familiar smell of paint and burning gas, and the dusty odor that came from the scene-lofts above.

For a moment he hesitated in the cross-lights and confusion about him, failing to recognize in their new costumes his old acquaintances of the company; but he saw Kripps, the stage-manager, in the centre of the stage, perspiring and in his shirt-sleeves as always, wildly waving an arm to some one in the flies, and beckoning with the other to the gas-man in the front entrance. The stage hands were striking the scene for the first act, and fighting with the set for the second, and dragging out a canvas floor of tessellated marble, and running a throne and a practical pair of steps over it, and aiming the high quaking walls of a palace and abuse at whoever came in their way.

"Now then, Van Bibber," shouted Kripps, with a wild glance of recognition, as the white-and-black figure came toward him, "you know you're the only man in New York who gets behind here to-night. But you can't stay. Lower it, lower it, can't you?" This to the man in the flies. "Any other night goes, but not this night. I can't have it. I— Where is the backing for the centre entrance? Didn't I tell you men——"

2

HER FIRST APPEARANCE

Van Bibber dodged two stage hands who were steering a scene at him, stepped over the carpet as it unrolled, and brushed through a group of anxious, whispering chorus people into the quiet of the star's dressing-room.

The star saw him in the long mirror before which he sat, while his dresser tugged at his boots, and threw up his hands desperately.

"Well," he cried, in mock resignation, "are we in it or are we not? Are they in their seats still or have they fled?"

"How are you, John?" said Van Bibber to the dresser. Then he dropped into a big arm-chair in the corner, and got up again with a protesting sigh to light his cigar between the wires around the gas-burner. "Oh, it's going very well. I wouldn't have come around if it wasn't. If the rest of it is as good as the first act, you needn't worry."

Van Bibber's unchallenged freedom behind the scenes had been a source of much comment and perplexity to the members of the Lester Comic Opera Company. He had made his first appearance there during one hot night of the long run of the previous summer, and had continued to be an almost nightly visitor for several weeks. At first it was supposed that he was backing the piece, that he was the "Angel," as those weak and wealthy individuals are called

3

who allow themselves to be led into supplying the finances for theatrical experiments. But as he never peered through the curtain-hole to count the house, nor made frequent trips to the front of it to look at the box sheet, but was, on the contrary, just as undisturbed on a rainy night as on those when the "standing room only" sign blocked the front entrance, this supposition was discarded as untenable. Nor did he show the least interest in the prima donna, or in any of the other pretty women of the company; he did not know them, nor did he make any effort to know them, and it was not until they inquired concerning him outside of the theatre that they learned what a figure in the social life of the city he really was. He spent most of his time in Lester's dressing-room smoking, listening to the reminiscences of Lester's dresser when Lester was on the stage; and this seclusion and his clerical attire of evening dress led the second comedian to call him Lester's father confessor, and to suggest that he came to the theatre only to take the star to task for his sins. And in this the second comedian was unknowingly not so very far wrong. Lester, the comedian, and young Van Bibber had known each other at the university, when Lester's voice and gift of mimicry had made him the leader in the college theatricals; and later, when he had gone upon the stage, and had been cut off by his family even after he had become famous, or on account of it, Van Bibber had gone to visit him, and had found him as simple and sincere and boyish as he had been in the days of his Hasty-Pudding successes. And Lester, for his part, had found Van Bibber as likable as did every one else, and welcomed his quiet voice and youthful knowledge of the world as a grateful relief to the boisterous *camaraderie* of his professional acquaintances. And he allowed Van Bibber to scold him, and to remind him of what he owed to himself, and to touch, even whether it hurt or not, upon his better side. And in time he admitted to finding his friend's occasional comments on stage matters of value as coming from the point of view of those who look on at the game; and even Kripps, the veteran, regarded him with respect after he had told him that he could turn a set of purple costumes black by throwing a red light on them. To the company, after he came to know them, he was gravely polite, and, to those who knew him if they had overheard, amusingly commonplace in his conversation. He understood them better than they did themselves, and made no mistakes. The women smiled on him, but the men were suspicious and shy of him until they saw that he was quite as shy of the women; and then they made him a confidant, and told him all their woes and troubles, and exhibited all their little jealousies and ambitions, in the innocent hope that he would repeat what they said to Lester. They were simple, unconventional, light-hearted folk, and Van Bibber found them vastly more entertaining and preferable to the silence of the deserted club, where the matting was down, and from whence the regular *habitués* had departed to the other side or to Newport. He liked the swing of the light, bright music as it came to him through the open door of the dressing-room, and the glimpse he got of the chorus people crowding and pushing for a quick charge up the iron stairway, and the feverish smell of oxygen in the air, and the picturesque disorder of Lester's wardrobe, and the wigs and swords, and the mysterious articles of make-up, all mixed together on a tray with half-finished cigars and autograph books and newspaper "notices."

And he often wished he was clever enough to be an artist with the talent to paint the unconsciously graceful groups in the sharply divided light and shadow of the wings as he saw them. The brilliantly colored, fantastically clothed girls leaning against the bare brick wall of the theatre, or whispering together in circles, with their arms close about one another, or reading apart and solitary, or working at some piece of fancy-work as soberly as though they were in a rocking-chair in their own flat, and not leaning against a scene brace, with the glare of the stage and the applause of the house just behind them. He liked to watch them coquetting with the big fireman detailed from the precinct engine-house, and clinging desperately to the curtain wire, or with one of the chorus men on the stairs, or teasing the phlegmatic scene-shifters as they tried to catch a minute's sleep on a pile of canvas. He even forgave the prima donna's smiling at him from the stage, as he stood watching her from the wings, and smiled back at her with polite cynicism, as though he did not know and she did not know that her smiles were not for him, but to disturb some more interested one in the front row. And so, in time, the company became so well accustomed to him that he moved in and about as unnoticed as the stage-manager himself, who prowled around hissing "hush" on principle, even though he was the only person who could fairly be said to be making a noise.

The second act was on, and Lester came off the stage and ran to the dressing-room and beckoned violently. "Come here," he said; "you ought to see this; the children are doing their turn. You want to hear them. They're great!''

Van Bibber put his cigar into a tumbler and stepped out into the wings. They were crowded on both sides of the stage with the members of the company; the girls were tiptoeing, with their hands on the shoulders of the men, and making futile little leaps into the air to get a better view, and others were resting on one knee that those behind might see over their shoulders. There were over a dozen children before the footlights, with the prima donna in the centre. She was singing the verses of a song, and they were following her movements, and joining in the chorus with high piping voices. They seemed entirely too much at home and too self-conscious to please Van Bibber; but there was one exception. The one exception was the smallest of them, a very, very little girl, with long auburn hair and black eyes; such a very little girl that every one in the house looked at her first, and then looked at no one else. She was apparently as unconcerned to all about her, excepting the pretty prima donna, as though she were by a piano at home practising a singing lesson. She seemed to think it was some new sort of a game. When the prima donna raised her arms, the child raised hers; when the prima donna courtesied, she stumbled into one, and straightened herself just in time to get the curls out of her eyes, and to see that the prima donna was laughing at her, and to smile cheerfully back, as if to say, "*We* are doing our best anyway, aren't we?" She had big, gentle eyes and two wonderful dimples, and in the excitement of the dancing and the singing her eyes laughed and flashed, and the dimples deepened and disappeared and reappeared again. She was as happy and innocent looking as though it were nine in the morning and she were playing school at a kindergarten. From all over the house the women were murmuring their delight, and the men were laughing and pulling their mustaches and nudging each other to "look at the littlest one."

The girls in the wings were rapturous in their enthusiasm, and were calling her absurdly extravagant titles of endearment, and making so much noise that Kripps stopped grinning at her from the entrance, and looked back over his shoulder as he looked when he threatened fines and calls for early rehearsal. And when she had finished finally, and the prima donna and the children ran off together, there was a roar from the house that went to Lester's head like wine, and seemed to leap clear across the footlights and drag the children back again.

HER FIRST APPEARANCE

"That settles it!" cried Lester, in a suppressed roar of triumph. "I knew that child would catch them."

There were four encores, and then the children and Elise Broughten, the pretty prima donna, came off jubilant and happy, with the Littlest Girl's arms full of flowers, which the management had with kindly forethought prepared for the prima donna, but which that delightful young person and the delighted leader of the orchestra had passed over to the little girl.

"Well," gasped Miss Broughten, as she came up to Van Bibber laughing, and with one hand on her side and breathing very quickly, "will you kindly tell me who is the leading woman now? Am I the prima donna, or am I not? I wasn't in it, was I?"

"You were not," said Van Bibber.

He turned from the pretty prima donna and hunted up the wardrobe woman, and told her he wanted to meet the Littlest Girl. And the wardrobe woman, who was fluttering wildly about, and as delighted as though they were all her own children, told him to come into the property-room, where the children were, and which had been changed into a dressing-room that they might be by themselves. The six little girls were in six different states of dishabille, but they were too little to mind that, and Van Bibber was too polite to observe it.

"This is the little girl, sir," said the wardrobe woman, excitedly, proud at being the means of bringing together two such prominent people. "Her name is Madeline. Speak to the gentleman, Madeline; he wants to tell you what a great big hit youse made."

The little girl was seated on one of the cushions of a double throne so high from the ground that the young woman who was pulling off the child's silk stockings and putting woollen ones on in their place did so without stooping. The young woman looked at Van Bibber and nodded somewhat doubtfully and ungraciously, and Van Bibber turned to the little girl in preference. The young woman's face was one of a type that was too familiar to be pleasant.

He took the Littlest Girl's small hand in his and shook it solemnly, and said, "I am very glad to know you. Can I sit up here beside you, or do you rule alone?"

"Yes, ma'am—yes, sir," answered the little girl.

Van Bibber put his hands on the arms of the throne and vaulted up beside the girl, and pulled out the flower in his button-hole and gave it to her.

"Now," prompted the wardrobe woman, "what do you say to the gentleman?"

"Thank you, sir," stammered the little girl.

"She is not much used to gentlemen's society," explained the woman who was pulling on the stockings.

"I see," said Van Bibber. He did not know exactly what to say next. And yet he wanted to talk to the child very much, so much more than he generally wanted to talk to most young women, who showed no hesitation in talking to him. With them he had no difficulty whatsoever. There was a doll lying on the top of a chest near them, and he picked this up and surveyed it critically. "Is this your doll?" he asked.

"No," said Madeline, pointing to one of the children, who was much taller than herself; "it's 'at 'ittle durl's. My doll he's dead."

"Dear me!" said Van Bibber. He made a mental note to get a live one in the morning, and then he said: "That's very sad. But dead dolls do come to life."

The little girl looked up at him, and surveyed him intently and critically, and then smiled, with the dimples showing, as much as to say that she understood him and approved of him entirely. Van Bibber answered this sign language by taking Madeline's hand in his and asking her how she liked being a great actress, and how soon she would begin to storm because

"Can I sit up here beside you, or do you rule
alone?"

that photographer hadn't sent the proofs. The young woman understood this, and deigned to smile at it, but Madeline yawned a very polite and sleepy yawn, and closed her eyes. Van Bibber moved up closer, and she leaned over until her bare shoulder touched his arm, and while the woman buttoned on her absurdly small shoes, she let her curly head fall on his elbow and rest there. Any number of people had shown confidence in Van Bibber—not in that form exactly, but in the same spirit—and though he was used to being trusted, he felt a sharp thrill of pleasure at the touch of the child's head on his arm, and in the warm clasp of her fingers around his. And he was conscious of a keen sense of pity and sorrow for her rising in him, which he crushed by thinking that it was entirely wasted, and that the child was probably perfectly and ignorantly happy.

"Look at that, now," said the wardrobe woman, catching sight of the child's closed eyelids; "just look at the rest of the little dears, all that excited they can't stand still to get their hats on, and she just as unconcerned as you please, and after making the hit of the piece, too."

"She's not used to it, you see," said the young woman, knowingly; "she don't know what it means. It's just that much play to her."

HER FIRST APPEARANCE

This last was said with a questioning glance at Van Bibber, in whom she still feared to find the disguised agent of a Children's Aid Society. Van Bibber only nodded in reply, and did not answer her, because he found he could not very well, for he was looking a long way ahead at what the future was to bring to the confiding little being at his side, and of the evil knowledge and temptations that would mar the beauty of her quaintly sweet face, and its strange mark of gentleness and refinement. Outside he could hear his friend Lester shouting the refrain of his new topical song, and the laughter and the hand-clapping came in through the wings and open door, broken but tumultuous.

"Does she come of professional people?" Van Bibber asked, dropping into the vernacular. He spoke softly, not so much that he might not disturb the child, but that she might not understand what he said.

"Yes," the woman answered, shortly, and bent her head to smooth out the child's stage dress across her knees.

Van Bibber touched the little girl's head with his hand and found that she was asleep, and so let his hand rest there, with the curls between his fingers. "Are—are you her mother?" he asked, with a slight inclination of his

14

head. He felt quite confident she was not; at least, he hoped not.

The woman shook her head. "No," she said. "Who is her mother?"

The woman looked at the sleeping child and then up at him almost defiantly. "Ida Clare was her mother," she said.

Van Bibber's protecting hand left the child as suddenly as though something had burned it, and he drew back so quickly that her head slipped from his arm, and she awoke and raised her eyes and looked up at him questioningly. He looked back at her with a glance of the strangest concern and of the deepest pity. Then he stooped and drew her toward him very tenderly, put her head back in the corner of his arm, and watched her in silence while she smiled drowsily and went to sleep again.

"And who takes care of her now?" he asked.

The woman straightened herself and seemed relieved. She saw that the stranger had recognized the child's pedigree and knew her story, and that he was not going to comment on it. "I do," she said. "After the divorce Ida came to me," she said, speaking more freely. "I used to be in her company when she was doing 'Aladdin,' and then when I left the stage and started to keep an actors' boarding-house, she came to me. She lived on with us a year, until she died, and she made me the guardian of the child. I train children for the stage, you know, me and my sister, Ada Dyer; you've heard of her, I guess. The courts pay us for her keep, but it isn't much, and I'm expecting to get what I spent on her from what she makes on the stage. Two of them other children are my pupils; but they can't touch Madie. She is a better dancer an' singer than any of them. If it hadn't been for the Society keeping her back, she would have been on the stage two years ago. She's great, she is. She'll be just as good as her mother was."

Van Bibber gave a little start, and winced visibly, but turned it off into a cough. "And her father," he said, hesitatingly, "does he——"

"Her father," said the woman, tossing back her head, "he looks after himself, he does. We don't ask no favors of *him*. She'll get along without him or his folks, thank you. Call him a gentleman? Nice gentleman he is!" Then she stopped abruptly. "I guess, though, you know him," she added. "Perhaps he's a friend of yourn?"

"I just know him," said Van Bibber, wearily.

He sat with the child asleep beside him while the woman turned to the others and dressed them for the third act. She explained that

She was still sleeping, and Van Bibber turned down the light in the hall, and stood looking down at her gravely while the servant went to speak to his master.

"Will you come this way, please, sir?" he said.

"You had better stay out here," said Van Bibber, "and come and tell me if she wakes."

Mr. Caruthers was standing by the mantel over the empty fireplace, wrapped in a long, loose dressing-gown which he was tying around him as Van Bibber entered. He was partly undressed, and had been just on the point of getting into bed. Mr. Caruthers was a tall, handsome man, with dark reddish hair, turning below the temples into gray; his mustache was quite white, and his eyes and face showed the signs of either dissipation or of great trouble, or of both. But even in the formless dressing-gown he had the look and the confident bearing of a gentleman, or, at least, of the man of the world. The room was very rich-looking, and was filled with the medley of a man's choice of good paintings and fine china, and papered with irregular rows of original drawings and signed etchings. The windows were open, and the lights were turned very low, so that Van Bibber could see the many gas lamps and the dark roofs of Broadway and the Avenue where they crossed a few blocks off, and the bunches of light on the Madison Square Garden, and to the lights on the boats of the East River. From below in the streets came the rattle of hurrying omnibuses and the rush of the hansom cabs. If Mr. Caruthers was surprised at this late visit, he hid it, and came forward to receive his caller as if his presence were expected.

"Excuse my costume, will you?" he said. "I turned in rather early to-night, it was so hot." He pointed to a decanter and some soda bottles on the table and a bowl of ice, and asked, "Will you have some of this?" And while he opened one of the bottles, he watched Van Bibber's face as though he were curious to have him explain the object of his visit.

"No, I think not, thank you," said the younger man. He touched his forehead with his handkerchief nervously. "Yes, it is hot," he said.

Mr. Caruthers filled a glass with ice and brandy and soda, and walked back to his place by the mantel, on which he rested his arm, while he clinked the ice in the glass and looked down into it.

"I was at the first night of 'The Sultana' this evening," said Van Bibber, slowly and uncertainly.

"Oh, yes," assented the elder man, politely,

and tasting his drink. "Lester's new piece. Was it any good?"

"I don't know," said Van Bibber. "Yes, I think it was. I didn't see it from the front. There were a lot of children in it—little ones; they danced and sang, and made a great hit. One of them had never been on the stage before. It was her first appearance."

He was turning one of the glasses around between his fingers as he spoke. He stopped, and poured out some of the soda, and drank it down in a gulp, and then continued turning the empty glass between the tips of his fingers.

"It seems to me," he said, "that it is a great pity." He looked up interrogatively at the other man, but Mr. Caruthers met his glance without any returning show of interest. "I say," repeated Van Bibber—"I say it seems a pity that a child like that should be allowed to go on in that business. A grown woman can go into it with her eyes open, or a girl who has had decent training can too. But it's different with a child. She has no choice in the matter; they don't ask her permission; and she isn't old enough to know what it means; and she gets used to it and fond of it before she grows to know what the danger is. And then it's too late. It seemed to me that if there was any one who had a right to stop it, it would be a very good thing to let that person know about her—about this child, I mean; the one who made the hit—before it was too late. It seems to me a responsibility I wouldn't care to take myself. I wouldn't care to think that I had the chance to stop it, and had let the chance go by. You know what the life is, and what the temptation a woman—" Van Bibber stopped with a gasp of concern, and added, hurriedly, "I mean we all know—every man knows."

Mr. Caruthers was looking at him with his lips pressed closely together, and his eyebrows drawn into the shape of the letter V. He leaned forward, and looked at Van Bibber intently.

"What is all this about?" he asked. "Did you come here, Mr. Van Bibber, simply to tell me this? What have you to do with it? What have I to do with it? Why did you come?"

"Because of the child."

"What child?"

"Your child," said Van Bibber.

Young Van Bibber was quite prepared for an outbreak of some sort, and mentally braced himself to receive it. He rapidly assured himself that this man had every reason to be angry, and that he, if he meant to accomplish anything, had every reason to be considerate and patient. So he faced Mr. Caruthers with shoulders squared, as though it were a physical shock he had to stand against, and in consequence he was quite unprepared for what followed. For Mr. Caruthers raised his face without a trace of feeling in it, and, with his eyes still fixed on the glass in his hand, set it carefully down on the mantel beside him, and girded himself about with the rope of his robe. When he spoke, it was in a tone of quiet politeness.

"Mr. Van Bibber," he began, "you are a very brave young man. You have dared to say to me what those who are my best friends —what even my own family would not care to say. They are afraid it might hurt me, I suppose. They have some absurd regard for my feelings; they hesitate to touch upon a subject which in no way concerns them, and which they know must be very painful to me. But you have the courage of your convictions; you have no compunctions about tearing open old wounds; and you come here, unasked and un-invited, to let me know what you think of my conduct, to let me understand that it does not agree with your own ideas of what I ought to do, and to tell me how I, who am old enough to be your father, should behave. You have rushed in where angels fear to tread, Mr. Van Bibber, to show me the error of my ways. I suppose I ought to thank you for it; but I have always said that it is not the wicked people who are to be feared in this world, or who do the most harm. We know them; we can prepare for them, and checkmate them. It is the well-meaning fool who makes all the trouble. For no one knows him until he discloses himself, and the mischief is done before he can be stopped. I think, if you will allow me to say so, that you have demonstrated my theory pretty thoroughly, and have done about as much needless harm for one evening as you can possibly wish. And so, if you will excuse me," he continued, sternly, and moving from his place, "I will ask to say good-night, and will request of you that you grow older and wiser and much more considerate before you come to see me again."

Van Bibber had flushed at Mr. Caruthers's first words, and had then grown somewhat pale, and straightened himself visibly. He did not move when the elder man had finished, but cleared his throat, and then spoke with some little difficulty. "It is very easy to call a man a fool," he said, slowly, "but it is much harder to be called a fool and not to throw the other man out of the window. But that, you see, would not do any good, and I have something to say to you first. I am quite clear in my own mind as to my position, and I am not going to allow anything you have said or can say to annoy me much until I am through. There will be time enough to resent it then. I am quite well aware that I did an unconventional thing in coming here—a bold thing or a foolish thing, as you choose—but the situation is pretty bad, and I did as I would have wished to be done by if I had had a child going to the devil and didn't know it. I should have been glad to learn of it even from a stranger. However," he said, smiling grimly, and pulling his cape about him, "there are other kindly disposed people in the world besides fathers. There is an aunt, perhaps, or an uncle or two; and sometimes, even to-day, there is the chance Samaritan."

Van Bibber picked up his high hat from the table, looked into it critically, and settled it on his head. "Good-night," he said, and walked slowly toward the door. He had his hand on the knob, when Mr. Caruthers raised his head.

"Wait just one minute, please, Mr. Van Bibber?" asked Mr. Caruthers.

Van Bibber stopped with a prompt obedience which would have led one to conclude that he might have put on his hat only to precipitate matters.

"Before you go," said Mr. Caruthers, grudgingly, "I want to say—I want you to understand my position."

HER FIRST APPEARANCE

"Oh, that's all right," said Van Bibber, lightly, opening the door.

"No, it is not all right. One moment, please. I do not intend that you shall go away from here with the idea that you have tried to do me a service, and that I have been unable to appreciate it, and that you are a much-abused and much-misunderstood young man. Since you have done me the honor to make my affairs your business, I would prefer that you should understand them fully. I do not care to have you discuss my conduct at clubs and afternoon teas with young women until you——"

Van Bibber drew in his breath sharply, with a peculiar whistling sound, and opened and shut his hands. "Oh, I wouldn't say that if I were you," he said, simply.

"I beg your pardon," the older man said, quickly. "That was a mistake. I was wrong. I beg your pardon. But you have tried me very sorely. You have intruded upon a private trouble that you ought to know must be very painful to me. But I believe you meant well. I know you to be a gentleman, and I am willing to think you acted on impulse, and that you will see to-morrow what a mistake you have made. It is not a thing I talk about; I do not speak of it to my friends, and they are far too considerate to speak of it to me. But you have put me on the defensive. You have made me out more or less of a brute, and I don't intend to be so far misunderstood. There are two sides to every story, and there is something to be said about this, even for me."

He walked back to his place beside the mantel, and put his shoulders against it, and faced Van Bibber, with his fingers twisted in the cord around his waist.

"When I married," said Mr. Caruthers, "I did so against the wishes of my people and the advice of all my friends. You know all about that. God help us! who doesn't?" he added, bitterly. "It was very rich, rare reading for you and for every one else who saw the daily papers, and we gave them all they wanted of it. I took her out of that life and married her because I believed she was as good a woman as any of those who had never had to work for their living, and I was bound that my friends and your friends should recognize her and respect her as my wife had a right to be respected; and I took her abroad that I might give all you sensitive, fine people a chance to get used to the idea of being polite to a woman who had once been a burlesque actress. It began over there in Paris. What I went through then no one knows; but when I came back—and I would never have come back if she had not made me

—it was my friends I had to consider, and not her. It was in the blood; it was in the life she had led, and in the life men like you and me had taught her to live. And it had to come out."

The muscles of Mr. Caruthers's face were moving, and beyond his control; but Van Bibber did not see this, for he was looking intently out of the window, over the roofs of the city.

"She had every chance when she married me that a woman ever had," continued the older man. "It only depended on herself. I didn't try to make a housewife of her or a drudge. She had all the healthy excitement and all the money she wanted, and she had a home here ready for her whenever she was tired of travelling about and wished to settle down. And I was—and a husband that loved her as— she had everything. Everything that a man's whole thought and love and money could bring to her. And you know what she did."

He looked at Van Bibber, but Van Bibber's eyes were still turned toward the open window and the night.

"And after the divorce—and she was free to go where she pleased, and to live as she pleased and with whom she pleased, without bringing disgrace on a husband who honestly loved her

HER FIRST APPEARANCE

—I swore to my God that I would never see her nor her child again. And I never saw her again, not even when she died. I loved the mother, and she deceived me and disgraced me and broke my heart, and I only wish she had killed me; and I was beginning to love her child, and I vowed she should not live to trick me too. I had suffered as no man I know had suffered; in a way a boy like you cannot understand, and that no one can understand who has not gone to hell and been forced to live after it. And was I to go through that again? Was I to love and care for and worship this child, and have her grow up with all her mother's vanity and animal nature, and have her turn on me some day and show me that what is bred in the bone must tell, and that I was a fool again —a pitiful fond fool? I could not trust her. I can never trust any woman or child again, and least of all that woman's child. She is as dead to me as though she were buried with her mother, and it is nothing to me what she is or what her life is. I know in time what it will be. She has begun earlier than I had supposed, that is all; but she is nothing to me." The man stopped and turned his back to Van Bibber, and hid his head in his hands, with his elbows on the mantel-piece. "I care too much," he said. "I cannot let it mean anything to me;

29

when I do care, it means so much more to me than to other men. They may pretend to laugh and to forget and to outgrow it, but it is not so with me. It means too much." He took a quick stride toward one of the arm-chairs, and threw himself into it. "Why, man," he cried, "I loved that child's mother to the day of her death. I loved that woman then, and, God help me! I love that woman still."

He covered his face with his hands, and sat leaning forward and breathing heavily as he rocked himself to and fro. Van Bibber still stood looking gravely out at the lights that picketed the black surface of the city. He was to all appearances as unmoved by the outburst of feeling into which the older man had been surprised as though it had been something in a play. There was an unbroken silence for a moment, and then it was Van Bibber who was the first to speak.

"I came here, as you say, on impulse," he said; "but I am glad I came, for I have your decisive answer now about the little girl. I have been thinking," he continued, slowly, "since you have been speaking, and before, when I first saw her dancing in front of the foot-lights, when I did not know who she was, that I could give up a horse or two, if necessary, and support this child instead. Children are worth more than horses, and a man who saves a soul, as it says"—he flushed slightly, and looked up with a hesitating, deprecatory smile—"somewhere, wipes out a multitude of sins. And it may be I'd like to try and get rid of some of mine. I know just where to send her; I know the very place. It's down in Evergreen Bay, on Long Island. They are tenants of mine there, and very nice farm sort of people, who will be very good to her. They wouldn't know anything about her, and she'd forget what little she knows of this present life very soon, and grow up with the other children to be one of them; and then, when she gets older and becomes a young lady, she could go to some school —but that's a bit too far ahead to plan for the present; but that's what I am going to do, though," said the young man, confidently, and as though speaking to himself. "That theatrical boarding-house person could be bought off easily enough," he went on, quickly, "and Lester won't mind letting her go if I ask it, and —and that's what I'll do. As you say, it's a good deal of an experiment, but I think I'll run the risk."

He walked quickly to the door and disappeared in the hall, and then came back, kicking the door open as he returned, and holding the child in his arms.

HER FIRST APPEARANCE

"This is she," he said, quietly. He did not look at or notice the father, but stood, with the child asleep in the bend of his left arm, gazing down at her. "This is she," he repeated; "this is your child."

There was something cold and satisfied in Van Bibber's tone and manner, as though he were congratulating himself upon the engaging of a new groom; something that placed the father entirely outside of it. He might have been a disinterested looker-on.

"She will need to be fed a bit," Van Bibber ran on, cheerfully. "They did not treat her very well, I fancy. She is thin and peaked and tired-looking." He drew up the loose sleeve of her jacket, and showed the bare forearm to the light. He put his thumb and little finger about it, and closed them on it gently. "It is very thin," he said. "And under her eyes, if it were not for the paint," he went on, mercilessly, "you could see how deep the lines are. This red spot on her cheek," he said, gravely, "is where Mary Vane kissed her to-night, and this is where Alma Stantley kissed her, and that Lee girl. You have heard of them, perhaps. They will never kiss her again. She is going to grow up a sweet, fine, beautiful woman—are you not?" he said, gently drawing the child higher up on his shoulder, until her face touched his, and still keeping his eyes from the face of the older man. "She does not look like her mother," he said; "she has her father's auburn hair and straight nose and finer-cut lips and chin. She looks very much like her father. It seems a pity," he added, abruptly. "She will grow up," he went on, "without knowing him, or who he is—or was, if he should die. She will never speak with him, or see him, or take his hand. She may pass him some day on the street and will not know him, and he will not know her, but she will grow to be very fond and to be very grateful to the simple, kind-hearted old people who will have cared for her when she was a little girl."

The child in his arms stirred, shivered slightly, and awoke. The two men watched her breathlessly, with silent intentness. She raised her head and stared around the unfamiliar room doubtfully, then turned to where her father stood, looking at him a moment, and passed him by; and then, looking up into Van Bibber's face, recognized him, and gave a gentle, sleepy smile, and, with a sigh of content and confidence, drew her arm up closer around his neck, and let her head fall back upon his breast.

The father sprang to his feet with a quick, jealous gasp of pain. "Give her to me!" he said, fiercely, under his breath, snatching her out of Van Bibber's arms. "She is mine; give her to me!"

Van Bibber closed the door gently behind him, and went jumping down the winding stairs of the Berkeley three steps at a time.

And an hour later, when the English servant came to his master's door, he found him still awake and sitting in the dark by the open window, holding something in his arms and looking out over the sleeping city.

"James," he said, "you can make up a place for me here on the lounge. Miss Caruthers, my daughter, will sleep in my room to-night."

VAN BIBBER'S MAN-SERVANT

VAN BIBBER's man Walters was the envy and admiration of his friends. He was English, of course, and he had been trained in the household of the Marquis Bendinot, and had travelled, in his younger days, as the valet of young Lord Upton. He was now rather well on in years, although it would have been impossible to say just how old he was. Walters had a dignified and repellent air about him, and he brushed his hair in such a way as to conceal his baldness.

And when a smirking, slavish youth with red cheeks and awkward gestures turned up in Van Bibber's livery, his friends were naturally surprised, and asked how he had come to lose Walters. Van Bibber could not say exactly, at least he could not rightly tell whether he had dismissed Walters or Walters had dismissed himself. The facts of the unfortunate separation were like this:

Van Bibber gave a great many dinners during the course of the season at Delmonico's, dinners hardly formal enough to require a private room, and yet too important to allow of his running the risk of keeping his guests standing in the hall waiting for a vacant table. So he conceived the idea of sending Walters over about half-past six to keep a table for him. As everybody knows, you can hold a table yourself at Delmonico's for any length of time until the other guests arrive, but the rule is very strict about servants. Because, as the head waiter will tell you, if servants were allowed to reserve a table during the big rush at seven o'clock, why not messenger boys? And it would certainly never do to have half a dozen large tables securely held by minute messengers while the hungry and impatient waited their turn at the door.

But Walters looked as much like a gentleman as did many of the diners; and when he seated himself at the largest table and told the waiter to serve for a party of eight or ten, he did it with such an air that the head waiter came over himself and took the orders. Walters knew quite as much about ordering a dinner as did his master; and when Van Bibber was too tired to make out the menu, Walters would look over the card himself and order the proper wines and side dishes; and with such a carelessly severe air and in such a masterly manner did he discharge this high function that the waiters looked upon him with much respect.

But respect even from your equals and the

satisfaction of having your fellow-servants mistake you for a member of the Few Hundred are not enough. Walters wanted more. He wanted the further satisfaction of enjoying the delicious dishes he had ordered; of sitting as a coequal with the people for whom he had kept a place; of completing the deception he practised only up to the point where it became most interesting.

It certainly was trying to have to rise with a subservient and unobtrusive bow and glide out unnoticed by the real guests when they arrived; to have to relinquish the feast just when the feast should begin. It would not be pleasant, certainly, to sit for an hour at a big empty table, ordering dishes fit only for epicures, and then, just as the waiters bore down with the Little Neck clams, so nicely iced and so cool and bitter-looking, to have to rise and go out into the street to a *table d'hôte* around the corner.

This was Walters's state of mind when Mr. Van Bibber told him for the hundredth time to keep a table for him for three at Delmonico's. Walters wrapped his severe figure in a frock-coat and brushed his hair, and allowed himself the dignity of a walking-stick. He would have liked to act as a substitute in an evening dress-suit, but Van Bibber would not have allowed it. So Walters walked over to Delmonico's and took a table near a window, and said that the other gentlemen would arrive later. Then he looked at his watch and ordered the dinner. It was just the sort of dinner he would have ordered had he ordered it for himself at some one else's expense. He suggested Little Neck clams first, with chablis, and pea-soup, and caviare on toast, before the oyster crabs, with Johannisberger Cabinet; then an *entrée* of calves' brains and rice; then no roast, but a bird, cold asparagus with French dressing, Camembert cheese, and Turkish coffee. As there were to be no women, he omitted the sweets and added three other wines to follow the white wine. It struck him as a particularly well-chosen dinner, and the longer he sat and thought about it the more he wished he were to test its excellence. And then the people all around him were so bright and happy, and seemed to be enjoying what they had ordered with such a refinement of zest that he felt he would give a great deal could he just sit there as one of them for a brief hour.

At that moment the servant deferentially handed him a note which a messenger boy had brought. It said:

Dinner off called out town send clothes and things after me to Young's Boston.

VAN BIBBER.

VAN BIBBER'S MAN-SERVANT

Walters rose involuntarily, and then sat still to think about it. He would have to countermand the dinner which he had ordered over half an hour before, and he would have to explain who he was to those other servants who had always regarded him as such a great gentleman. It was very hard.

And then Walters was tempted. He was a very good servant, and he knew his place as only an English servant can, and he had always accepted it, but to-night he was tempted—and he fell. He met the waiter's anxious look with a grave smile.

"The other gentlemen will not be with me to-night," he said, glancing at the note. "But I will dine here as I intended. You can serve for one."

That was perhaps the proudest night in the history of Walters. He had always felt that he was born out of his proper sphere, and to-night he was assured of it. He was a little nervous at first, lest some of Van Bibber's friends should come in and recognize him; but as the dinner progressed and the warm odor of the dishes touched his sense, and the rich wines ran through his veins, and the women around him smiled and bent and moved like beautiful birds of beautiful plumage, he became content, grandly content; and he half closed his eyes and imagined he was giving a dinner to everybody in the place. Vain and idle thoughts came to him and went again, and he eyed the others about him calmly and with polite courtesy, as they did him, and he felt that if he must later pay for this moment it was worth the paying.

Then he gave the waiter a couple of dollars out of his own pocket and wrote Van Bibber's name on the check, and walked in state into the *café*, where he ordered a green mint and a heavy, black, and expensive cigar, and seated himself at the window, where he felt that he should always have sat if the fates had been just. The smoke hung in light clouds about him, and the lights shone and glistened on the white cloths and the broad shirt-fronts of the smart young men and distinguished foreign-looking older men at the surrounding tables.

And then, in the midst of his dreamings, he heard the soft, careless drawl of his master, which sounded at that time and in that place like the awful voice of a condemning judge. Van Bibber pulled out a chair and dropped into it. His side was toward Walters, so that he did not see him. He had some men with him, and he was explaining how he had missed his train and had come back to find that one of the party had eaten the dinner without him, and he wondered who it could be; and then turning easily in his seat he saw Walters with the green mint and the cigar, trembling behind a copy of the London *Graphic*.

"Walters!" said Van Bibber, "what are you doing here?"

Walters looked his guilt and rose stiffly. He began with a feeble "If you please, sir——"

"Go back to my rooms and wait for me there," said Van Bibber, who was too decent a fellow to scold a servant in public.

Walters rose and left the half-finished cigar and the mint with the ice melting in it on the table. His one evening of sublimity was over, and he walked away, bending before the glance of his young master and the smiles of his master's friends.

When Van Bibber came back he found on his dressing-table a note from Walters stating that he could not, of course, expect to remain longer in his service, and that he left behind him the twenty-eight dollars which the dinner had cost.

"If he had only gone off with all my waistcoats and scarf-pins, I'd have liked it better," said Van Bibber, "than his leaving me cash for infernal dinner. Why, a servant like Walters is worth twenty-eight-dollar dinners—twice a day."

THE HUNGRY MAN WAS FED

Young Van Bibber broke one of his rules of life one day and came down-town. This unusual journey into the marts of trade and finance was in response to a call from his lawyer, who wanted his signature to some papers. It was five years since Van Bibber had been south of the north side of Washington Square, except as a transient traveller to the ferries on the elevated road. And as he walked through the City Hall Square he looked about him at the new buildings in the air, and the bustle and confusion of the streets, with as much interest as a lately arrived immigrant.

He rather enjoyed the novelty of the situation, and after he had completed his business at the lawyer's office he tried to stroll along lower Broadway as he did on the Avenue.

But people bumped against him, and carts and drays tried to run him down when he crossed the side streets, and those young men whom he knew seemed to be in a great hurry, and expressed such amused surprise at seeing him that he felt very much out of place indeed.

And so he decided to get back to his club window and its quiet as soon as possible.

"Hello, Van Bibber," said one of the young men who were speeding by, "what brings you here? Have you lost your way?"

"I think I have," said Van Bibber. "If you'll kindly tell me how I can get back to civilization again, be obliged to you."

"Take the elevated from Park Place," said his friend from over his shoulder, as he nodded and dived into the crowd.

The visitor from up-town had not a very distinct idea as to where Park Place was, but he struck off Broadway and followed the line of the elevated road along Church Street. It was at the corner of Vesey Street that a miserable-looking, dirty, and red-eyed object stood still in his tracks and begged Van Bibber for a few cents to buy food. "I've come all the way from Chicago," said the Object, "and I haven't tasted food for twenty-four hours."

Van Bibber drew away as though the Object had a contagious disease in his rags, and handed him a quarter without waiting to receive the man's blessing.

"Poor devil!" said Van Bibber. "Fancy going without dinner all day!" He could not fancy this, though he tried, and the impossibility of it impressed him so much that he amiably determined to go back and hunt up the Object and give him more money. Van Bibber's ideas of a dinner were rather exalted. He did not know of places where a quarter was good for a "square meal," including "one roast, three vegetables, and pie." He hardly considered a quarter a sufficiently large tip for the waiter who served the dinner, and decidedly not enough for the dinner itself. He did not see his man at first, and when he did the man did not see him. Van Bibber watched him stop three gentlemen, two of whom gave him some money, and then the Object approached Van Bibber and repeated his sad tale in a monotone. He evidently did not recognize Van Bibber, and the clubman gave him a half-dollar and walked away, feeling that the man must surely have enough by this time with which to get something to eat, if only a luncheon.

This retracing of his footsteps had confused Van Bibber, and he made a complete circuit of the block before he discovered that he had lost his bearings. He was standing just where he had started, and gazing along the line of the elevated road, looking for a station, when the familiar accents of the Object again saluted him.

When Van Bibber faced him the beggar looked uneasy. He was not sure whether or not he had approached this particular gentleman before, but Van Bibber conceived an idea of much subtlety, and deceived the Object by again putting his hand in his pocket.

"Nothing to eat for twenty-four hours! Dear me!" drawled the clubman, sympathetically. "Haven't you any money, either?"

"Not a cent," groaned the Object, "an' I'm just faint for food, sir. S'help me. I hate to beg, sir. It isn't the money I want, it's jest food. I'm starvin', sir."

"Well," said Van Bibber, suddenly, "if it is just something to eat you want, come in here with me and I'll give you your breakfast." But the man held back and began to whine and complain that they wouldn't let the likes of him in such a fine place.

"Oh, yes, they will," said Van Bibber, glancing at the bill of fare in front of the place. "It seems to be extremely cheap. Beefsteak fifteen cents, for instance. Go in," he added, and there was something in his tone which made the Object move ungraciously into the eating-house.

It was a very queer place, Van Bibber thought, and the people stared very hard at him and his gloves and the gardenia in his coat and at the tramp accompanying him.

"You ain't going to eat two breakfasts, are yer?" asked one of the very tough-looking waiters of the Object. The Object looked uneasy and Van Bibber, who stood beside his chair, smiled in triumph.

"You're mistaken," he said to the waiter. "This gentleman is starving; he has not tasted food for twenty-four hours. Give him whatever he asks for!"

The Object scowled and the waiter grinned behind his tin tray, and had the impudence to wink at Van Bibber, who recovered from this in time to give the man a half-dollar and so to make of him a friend for life. The Object ordered milk, but Van Bibber protested and ordered two beefsteaks and fried potatoes, hot rolls and two omelets, coffee, and ham with bacon.

"Holy smoke! watcher think I am?" yelled the Object, in desperation.

"Hungry," said Van Bibber, very gently. "Or else an impostor. And, you know, if you should happen to be the latter I should have to hand you over to the police."

Van Bibber leaned easily against the wall and read the signs about him, and kept one eye on a policeman across the street. The Object was choking and cursing through his breakfast. It did not seem to agree with him. Whenever he stopped Van Bibber would point with his stick to a still unfinished dish, and the Object, after

46

a husky protest, would attack it as though it were poison. The people sitting about were laughing, and the proprietor behind the desk smiling grimly.

"There, darn ye!" said the Object at last. "I've eat all I can eat for a year. You think you're mighty smart, don't ye? But if you choose to pay that high for your fun, I s'pose you can afford it. Only don't let me catch you around these streets after dark, that's all."

And the Object started off, shaking his fist.

"Wait a minute," said Van Bibber. "You haven't paid them for your breakfast."

"Haven't what?" shouted the Object. "Paid 'em! How could I pay him? Youse asked me to come in here and eat. I didn't want no breakfast, did I? Youse'll have to pay for your fun yerself, or they'll throw yer out. Don't try to be too smart."

"I gave you," said Van Bibber, slowly, "seventy-five cents with which to buy a breakfast. This check calls for eighty-five cents, and extremely cheap it is," he added, with a bow to the fat proprietor. "Several other gentlemen, on your representation that you were starving, gave you other sums to be expended on a breakfast. You have the money with you now. So pay what you owe at once, or I'll call that officer

47

across the street and tell him what I know, and have you put where you belong."

"I'll see you blowed first!" gasped the Object.

Van Bibber turned to the waiter. "Kindly beckon to that officer," said he.

The waiter ran to the door and the Object ran too, but the tough waiter grabbed him by the back of his neck and held him.

"Lemme go!" yelled the Object. "Lemme go an' I'll pay you."

Everybody in the place came up now and formed a circle around the group and watched the Object count our eighty-five cents into the waiter's hand, which left him just one dime to himself.

"You have forgotten the waiter who served you," said Van Bibber, severely pointing with his stick at the dime.

"No, you don't," groaned the Object.

"Oh, yes," said Van Bibber, "do the decent thing now, or I'll——"

The Object dropped the dime in the waiter's hand, and Van Bibber, smiling and easy, made his way through the admiring crowd and out into the street.

"I suspect," said Mr. Van Bibber later in the day, when recounting his adventure to a fellow-clubman, "that, after I left, fellow tried to get tip back from waiter, for I saw him come out of place very suddenly, you see, and without touching pavement till he lit on back of his head in gutter. He was most remarkable waiter."

VAN BIBBER AT THE RACES

Young Van Bibber had never spent a Fourth of July in the city, as he had always understood it was given over to armies of small boys on that day, who sat on all the curbstones and set off fire-crackers, and that the thermometer always showed ninety degrees in the shade, and cannon boomed and bells rang from daybreak to midnight. He had refused all invitations to join any Fourth-of-July parties at the seashore or on the Sound or at Tuxedo, because he expected his people home from Europe, and had to be in New York to meet them. He was accordingly greatly annoyed when he received a telegram saying they would sail in a boat a week later.

He finished his coffee at the club on the morning of the Fourth about ten o'clock, in absolute solitude, and with no one to expect and nothing to anticipate; so he asked for a morning paper and looked up the amusements offered for the Fourth. There were plenty of excursions with brass bands, and refreshments served on board, baseball matches by the hundred, athletic meetings and picnics by the dozen, but nothing that seemed to exactly please him.

VAN BIBBER AT THE RACES

The races sounded attractive, but then he always lost such a lot of money, and the crowd pushed so, and the sun and the excitement made his head ache between the eyes and spoiled his appetite for dinner. He had vowed again and again that he would not go to the races; but as the day wore on and the solitude of the club became oppressive and the silence of the Avenue began to tell on him, he changed his mind, and made his preparations accordingly.

First, he sent out after all the morning papers and read their tips on the probable winners. Very few of them agreed, so he took the horse which most of them seemed to think was best, and determined to back it, no matter what might happen, or what new tips he might get later. Then he put two hundred dollars in his pocket-book to bet with, and twenty dollars for expenses, and sent around for his field-glasses.

He was rather late in starting, and he made up his mind on the way to Morris Park that he would be true to the list of winners he had written out, and not make any side bets on any suggestions or inside information given him by others. He vowed a solemn vow on the rail of the boat to plunge on each of the six horses he had selected from the newspaper tips, and on no others. He hoped in this way to win something. He did not care so much to win, but he hated to lose. He always felt so flat and silly after it was over; and when it happened, as it often did, that he had paid several hundred dollars for the afternoon's sport, his sentiments did him credit.

"I shall probably, or rather certainly, be tramped on and shoved," soliloquized Van Bibber.

"I shall smoke more cigars than are good for me, and drink more than I want, owing to the unnatural excitement and heat, and I shall be late for my dinner. And for all this I shall probably pay two hundred dollars. It really seems as if I were a young man of little intellect, and yet thousands of others are going to do exactly the same thing."

The train was very late. One of the men in front said they would probably just be able to get their money up in time for the first race. A horse named Firefly was Van Bibber's choice, and he took one hundred dollars of his two hundred to put up on her. He had it already in his hand when the train reached the track, and he hurried with the rest toward the bookmakers to get his one hundred on as quickly as possible. But while he was crossing the lawn back of the stand, he heard cheers and wild yells that told him they were running the race at that moment.

VAN BIBBER AT THE RACES

"Raceland!" "Raceland!" "Raceland by a length!" shouted the crowd.

"Who's second?" a fat man shouted at another fat man.

"Firefly," called back the second, joyously, "and I've got her for a place and I win eight dollars."

"Ah!" said Van Bibber, as he slipped his one hundred dollars back in his pocket, "good thing I got here a bit late."

"What'd you win, Van Bibber?" asked a friend who rushed past him, clutching his tickets as though they were precious stones.

"I win one hundred dollars," answered Van Bibber, calmly, as he walked on up into the boxes. It was delightfully cool up there, and to his satisfaction and surprise he found several people there whom he knew. He went into Her box and accepted some *pâte* sandwiches and iced champagne, and chatted and laughed with Her so industriously, and so much to the exclusion of all else, that the horses were at the starting-post before he was aware of it, and he had to excuse himself hurriedly and run to put up his money on Bugler, the second on his list. He decided that as he had won one hundred dollars on the first race he could afford to plunge on this one, so he counted out fifty more, and putting this with the original one hundred dollars, crowded into the betting-ring and said, "A hundred and fifty on Bugler straight."

"Bugler's just been scratched," said the bookie, leaning over Van Bibber's shoulder for a greasy five-dollar bill.

"Will you play anything else?" he asked, as the young gentleman stood there irresolute.

"No, thank you," said Van Bibber, remembering his vow, and turning hastily away. "Well," he mused, "I'm one hundred and fifty dollars better off than I might have been if Bugler hadn't been scratched and hadn't won. One hundred and fifty dollars added to one hundred makes two hundred and fifty dollars. That puts me 'way ahead of the game. I am fifty dollars better off than when I left New York. I'm playing in great luck." So, on the strength of this, he bought out the man who sells bouquets, and ordered more champagne to be sent up to the box where She was sitting, and they all congratulated him on his winnings, which were suggested by his generous and sudden expenditures.

"You must have a great eye for picking a winner," said one of the older men, grudgingly.

"Y-e-s," said Van Bibber, modestly. "I know a horse when I see it, I think; and," he added to himself, "that's about all."

His horse for the third race was Rover, and

the odds were five to one against him. Van Bibber wanted very much to bet on Pirate King instead, but he remembered his vow to keep to the list he had originally prepared, whether he lost or won. This running after strange gods was always a losing business. He took one hundred dollars in five-dollar bills, and went down to the ring and put the hundred up on Rover and returned to the box. The horses had been weighed in and the bugle had sounded, and three of the racers were making their way up the track, when one of them plunged suddenly forward and went down on his knees and then stretched out dead. Van Bibber was confident it was Rover, although he had no idea which the horse was, but he knew his horse would not run. There was a great deal of excitement, and people who did not know the rule, which requires the return of all money if any accident happens to a horse on the race-track between the time of weighing in and arriving at the post, were needlessly alarmed. Van Bibber walked down to the ring and received his money back with a smile.

"I'm just one hundred dollars better off than I was three minutes ago," he said. "I've really had a most remarkable day."

Mayfair was his choice for the fourth race, and she was selling at three to one. Van Bibber determined to put one hundred and seventy-five dollars up on her, for, as he said, he had not lost on any one race yet. The girl in the box was very interesting, though, and Van Bibber found a great deal to say to her. He interrupted himself once to call to one of the messenger boys who ran with bets, and gave him one hundred and seventy-five dollars to put on Mayfair.

Several other gentlemen gave the boy large sums as well, and Van Bibber continued to talk earnestly with the girl. He raised his head to see Mayfair straggle in a bad second, and shrugged his shoulders. "How much did you lose?" she asked.

"Oh, 'bout two hundred dollars," said Van Bibber; "but it's the first time I've lost to-day, so I'm still ahead." He bent over to continue what he was saying, when a rude commotion and loud talking caused those in the boxes to raise their heads and look around. Several gentlemen were pointing out Van Bibber to one of the Pinkerton detectives, who had a struggling messenger boy in his grasp.

"These gentlemen say you gave this boy some money, sir," said the detective. "He tried to do a welsh with it, and I caught him just as he was getting over the fence. How much and on what horse, sir?"

VAN BIBBER AT THE RACES

Van Bibber showed his memoranda, and the officer handed him over one hundred and seventy-five dollars.

"Now, let me see," said Van Bibber, shutting one eye and calculating intently, "one hundred and seventy-five to three hundred and fifty dollars makes me a winner by five hundred and twenty-five dollars. That's purty good, isn't it? I'll have a great dinner at Delmonico's tonight. You'd better all come back with me!"

But She said he had much better come back with her and her party on top of the coach and take dinner in the cool country instead of the hot, close city, and Van Bibber said he would like to, only he did wish to get his one hundred dollars up on at least one race. But they said "no," they must be off at once, for the ride was a long one, and Van Bibber looked at his list and saw that his choice was Jack Frost, a very likely winner, indeed; but, nevertheless, he walked out to the enclosure with them and mounted the coach beside the girl on the back seat, with only the two coachmen behind to hear what he chose to say.

And just as they finally were all harnessed up and the horn sounded, the crowd yelled, "They're off," and Van Bibber and all of them turned on their high seats to look back.

"Magpie wins," said the whip.

"And Jack Frost's last," said another.

"And I win my one hundred dollars," said Van Bibber. "It's really very curious," he added, turning to the girl. "I started out with two hundred dollars to-day, I spent only twenty-five dollars on flowers, I won six hundred and twenty-five dollars, and I have only one hundred and seventy-five dollars to show for it, and yet I've had a very pleasant Fourth."

AN EXPERIMENT IN ECONOMY

OF course, Van Bibber lost all the money he saved at the races on the Fourth of July. He went to the track the next day, and he saw the whole sum melt away, and in his vexation tried to "get back," with the usual result. He plunged desperately, and when he had reached his rooms and run over his losses, he found he was a financial wreck, and that he, as his sporting friends expressed it, "would have to smoke a pipe" for several years to come, instead of indulging in Regalias. He could not conceive how he had come to make such a fool of himself, and he wondered if he would have enough confidence to spend a dollar on luxuries again.

It was awful to contemplate the amount he had lost. He felt as if it were sinful extravagance to even pay his car-fare up-town, and he contemplated giving his landlord the rent with keen distress. It almost hurt him to part with five cents to the conductor, and as he looked at the hansoms dashing by with lucky winners inside he groaned audibly.

"I've got to economize," he soliloquized. "No use talking; must economize. I'll begin

59

to-morrow morning and keep it up for a month. Then I'll be on my feet again. Then I can stop economizing, and enjoy myself. But no more races; never, never again."

He was delighted with this idea of economizing. He liked the idea of self-punishment that it involved, and as he had never denied himself anything in his life, the novelty of the idea charmed him. He rolled over to sleep, feeling very much happier in his mind than he had been before his determination was taken, and quite eager to begin on the morrow. He arose very early, about ten o'clock, and recalled his idea of economy for a month, as a saving clause to his having lost a month's spending money.

He was in the habit of taking his coffee and rolls and a parsley omelet, at Delmonico's, every morning. He decided that he would start out on his road of economy by omitting the omelet and ordering only a pot of coffee. By some rare intuition he guessed that there were places up-town where things were cheaper than at his usual haunt, only he did not know where they were. He stumbled into a restaurant on a side street finally, and ordered a cup of coffee and some rolls.

The waiter seemed to think that was a very poor sort of breakfast, and suggested some nice chops or a bit of steak or "ham and eggs, sah," all of which made Van Bibber shudder. The waiter finally concluded that Van Bibber was poor and couldn't afford any more, which, as it happened to be more or less true, worried that young gentleman; so much so, indeed, that when the waiter brought him a check for fifteen cents, Van Bibber handed him a half-dollar and told him to "keep the change."

The satisfaction he felt in this wore off very soon when he appreciated that, while he had economized in his breakfast, his vanity had been very extravagantly pampered, and he felt how absurd it was when he remembered he would not have spent more if he had gone to Delmonico's in the first place. He wanted one of those large black Regalias very much, but they cost entirely too much. He went carefully through his pockets to see if he had one with him, but he had not, and he determined to get a pipe. Pipes are always cheap.

"What sort of a pipe, sir?" said the man behind the counter.

"A cheap pipe," said Van Bibber.

"But what sort?" persisted the man.

Van Bibber thought a brier pipe, with an amber mouth-piece and a silver band, would about suit his fancy. The man had just such a pipe, with trade-marks on the brier and hall-marks and "Sterling" on the silver band. It

61

lay in a very pretty silk box, and there was another mouth-piece you could screw in, and a cleaner and top piece with which to press the tobacco down. It was most complete, and only five dollars. "Isn't that a good deal for a pipe?" asked Van Bibber. The man said, being entirely unprejudiced, that he thought not. It was cheaper, he said, to get a good thing at the start. It lasted longer. And cheap pipes bite your tongue. This seemed to Van Bibber most excellent reasoning. Some Oxford-Cambridge mixture attracted Van Bibber on account of its name. This cost one dollar more. As he left the shop he saw a lot of pipes, brier and corn-cob and Sallie Michaels, in the window marked, "Any of these for a quarter." This made him feel badly, and he was conscious he was not making a success of his economy. He started back to the club, but it was so hot that he thought he would faint before he got there; so he called a hansom, on the principle that it was cheaper to ride and keep well than to walk and have a sunstroke.

He saw some people that he knew going by in a cab with a pile of trunks on the top of it, and that reminded him that they had asked him to come down and see them off when the steamer left that afternoon. So he waved his hand when they passed, and bowed to them,

and cried, "See you later," before he counted
the consequences. He did not wish to arrive
empty-handed, so he stopped in at a florist's
and got a big basket of flowers and another of
fruit, and piled them into the hansom.

When he came to pay the driver he found the
trip from Thirty-fifth Street to the foot of Liberty was two dollars and a half, and the fruit
and flowers came to twenty-two dollars. He
was greatly distressed over this, and could not
see how it had happened. He rode back in the
elevated for five cents, and felt much better.
Then some men just back from a yachting trip
joined him at the club and ordered a great many
things to drink, and of course he had to do the
same, and seven dollars were added to his
economy fund. He argued that this did not
matter, because he signed a check for it, and
that he would not have to pay for it until the
end of the month, when the necessity of economizing would be over.

Still, his conscience did not seem convinced,
and he grew very desperate. He felt he was
not doing it at all properly, and he determined
that he would spend next to nothing on his dinner. He remembered with a shudder the place
he had taken the tramp to dinner, and he vowed
that before he would economize as rigidly as
that he would starve; but he had heard of the

table d'hôte places on Sixth Avenue, so he went there and wandered along the street until he found one that looked clean and nice.´ He began with a heavy soup, shoved a rich, fat, fried fish over his plate, and followed it with a queer *entrée* of spaghetti with a tomato dressing that satisfied his hunger and killed his appetite as if with the blow of a lead pipe. But he went through with the rest of it, for he felt it was the truest economy to get his money's worth, and the limp salad in bad oil and the ice-cream of sour milk made him feel that eating was a positive pain rather than a pleasure; and in this state of mind and body, drugged and disgusted, he lighted his pipe and walked slowly toward the club along Twenty-sixth Street.

He looked in at the *café* at Delmonico's with envy and disgust, and, going disheartenedly on, passed the dining-room windows that were wide open and showed the heavy white linen, the silver, and the women coolly dressed and everybody happy.

And then there was a wild waving of arms inside, and white hands beckoning him, and he saw with mingled feelings of regret that the whole party of the Fourth of July were inside and motioning to him. They made room for him, and the captain's daughter helped him to olives, and the chaperon told how they had come into town for the day, and had been telegraphing for him and Edgar and Fred and "dear Bill," and the rest said they were so glad to see him because they knew he could appreciate a good dinner if any one could.

But Van Bibber only groaned, and the awful memories of the lead-like spaghetti and the bad oil and the queer cheese made him shudder, and turned things before him into a Tantalus feast of rare cruelty. There were Little Neck clams, delicious cold consommé, and white fish, and French chops with a dressing of truffles, and Roman punch and woodcock to follow, and crisp lettuce and toasted crackers-and-cheese, with a most remarkable combination of fruits and ices; and Van Bibber could eat nothing, and sat unhappily looking at his plate and shaking his head when the waiter urged him gently. "Economy!" he said, with disgusted solemnity. "It's all tommy rot. It wouldn't have cost me a cent to have eaten this dinner, and yet I've paid half a dollar to make myself ill so that I can't. If you know how to economize, it may be all right; but if you don't understand it, you must leave it alone. It's dangerous. I'll economize no more."

And he accordingly broke his vow by taking the whole party up to see the lady who would not be photographed in tights, and put them in a box where they were gagged by the comedian, and where the soubrette smiled on them and all went well.

MR. TRAVERS'S FIRST HUNT

YOUNG Travers, who had been engaged to a girl down on Long Island for the last three months, only met her father and brother a few weeks before the day set for the wedding. The brother is a master of hounds near Southampton, and shared the expense of importing a pack from England with Van Bibber. The father and son talked horse all day and until one in the morning; for they owned fast thoroughbreds, and entered them at the Sheepshead Bay and other race-tracks. Old Mr. Paddock, the father of the girl to whom Travers was engaged, had often said, that when a young man asked him for his daughter's hand he would ask him in return, not if he had lived straight, but if he could ride straight. And on his answering this question in the affirmative depended his gaining her parent's consent. Travers had met Miss Paddock and her mother in Europe, while the men of the family were at home. He was invited to their place in the fall when the hunting season opened, and spent the evening most pleasantly and satisfactorily with his *fiancée* in a corner of the drawing-room. But as soon as the women had gone, young Paddock joined him and said, "You ride, of course?" Travers had never ridden; but he had been prompted how to answer by Miss Paddock, and so said there was nothing he liked better. As he expressed it, he would rather ride than sleep.

"That's good," said Paddock. "I'll give you a mount on Satan to-morrow morning at the meet. He is a bit nasty at the start of the season; and ever since he killed Wallis, the second groom, last year, none of us care much to ride him. But you can manage him, no doubt. He'll just carry your weight."

Mr. Travers dreamed that night of taking large, desperate leaps into space on a wild horse that snorted forth flames, and that rose at solid stone walls as though they were hayricks.

He was tempted to say he was ill in the morning—which was, considering his state of mind, more or less true—but concluded that, as he would have to ride sooner or later during his visit, and that if he did break his neck it would be in a good cause, he determined to do his best. He did not want to ride at all, for two excellent reasons—first, because he wanted to live for Miss Paddock's sake, and, second, because he wanted to live for his own.

The next morning was a most forbidding and doleful-looking morning, and young Travers had great hopes that the meet would be declared off; but, just as he lay in doubt, the servant knocked at his door with his riding things and his hot water.

He came down-stairs looking very miserable indeed. Satan had been taken to the place where they were to meet, and Travers viewed him on his arrival there with a sickening sense of fear, as he saw him pulling three grooms off their feet.

Travers decided that he would stay with his feet on solid earth just as long as he could, and when the hounds were thrown off and the rest had started at a gallop he waited, under the pretense of adjusting his gaiters, until they were all well away. Then he clinched his teeth, crammed his hat down over his ears, and scrambled up on to the saddle. His feet fell quite by accident into the stirrups, and the next instant he was off after the others, with an indistinct feeling that he was on a locomotive that was jumping the ties. Satan was in among and had passed the other horses in less than five minutes, and was so close on the hounds that the whippers-in gave a cry of warning. But Travers could as soon have pulled a boat back from going over the Niagara Falls as Satan, and it was only because the hounds were well ahead that saved them from having Satan ride them down. Travers had taken hold of the saddle with his left hand to keep himself down, and sawed and swayed on the reins with his right. He shut his eyes whenever Satan jumped, and never knew how he happened to stick on; but he did stick on, and was so far ahead that no one could see in the misty morning just how badly he rode. As it was, for daring and speed he led the field, and not even young Paddock was near him from the start. There was a broad stream in front of him, and a hill just on its other side. No one had ever tried to take this at a jump. It was considered more of a swim than anything else, and the hunters always crossed it by the bridge, toward the left. Travers saw the bridge and tried to jerk Satan's head in that direction; but Satan kept right on as straight as an express train over the prairie. Fences and trees and furrows passed by and under Travers like a panorama run by electricity, and he only breathed by accident. They went on at the stream and the hill beyond as though they were riding at a stretch of turf, and, though the whole field set up a shout of warning and dismay, Travers could only gasp and shut his eyes. He remembered the fate of the second groom and shivered. Then the horse rose like a rocket, lifting Travers so high in the air that he thought Satan would never come down again; but he did come down, with his feet bunched, on the opposite side of the stream. The next instant he was up and over the hill, and had stopped panting in the very centre of the pack that were snarling and snapping around the fox. And then Travers showed that he was a thoroughbred, even though he could not ride, for he hastily fumbled for his cigar-case, and when the field came pounding up over the bridge and around the hill, they saw him seated nonchalantly on his saddle, puffing critically at a cigar and giving Satan patronizing pats on the head.

"My dear girl," said old Mr. Paddock to his daughter as they rode back, "if you love that young man of yours and want to keep him, make him promise to give up riding. A more reckless and more brilliant horseman I have never seen. He took that double jump at the gate and that stream like a centaur. But he will break his neck sooner or later, and he ought to be stopped." Young Paddock was so delighted with his prospective brother-in-law's great riding that that night in the smoking-room he made him a present of Satan before all the men.

"No," said Travers, gloomily, "I can't take him. Your sister has asked me to give up what is dearer to me than anything next to herself, and that is my riding. You see, she is absurdly anxious for my safety, and she has asked me to promise never to ride again, and I have given my word."

A chorus of sympathetic remonstrance rose from the men.

"Yes, I know," said Travers to her brother, "it is rough, but it just shows what sacrifices a man will make for the woman he loves."

LOVE ME, LOVE MY DOG

YOUNG Van Bibber had been staying with some people at Southampton, L. I., where, the fall before, his friend Travers made his reputation as a cross-country rider. He did this, it may be remembered, by shutting his eyes and holding on by the horse's mane and letting the horse go as it pleased. His recklessness and courage are still spoken of with awe; and the place where he cleared the water jump that every one else avoided is pointed out as Travers's Leap to visiting horsemen, who look at it gloomily and shake their heads. Miss Arnett, whose mother was giving the house-party, was an attractive young woman, with an admiring retinue of youths who gave attention without intention, and for none of whom Miss Arnett showed particular preference. Her whole interest, indeed, was centred in a dog, a Scotch collie called Duncan. She allowed this dog every liberty, and made a decided nuisance of him for every one around her. He always went with her when she walked, or trotted beside her horse when she rode. He stretched himself before the fire in the dining-room, and startled

73

people at table by placing his cold nose against their hands or putting his paws on their gowns. He was generally voted a most annoying adjunct to the Arnett household; but no one dared hint so to Miss Arnett, as she only loved those who loved the dog, or pretended to do it. On the morning of the afternoon on which Van Bibber and his bag arrived, the dog disappeared and could not be recovered. Van Bibber found the household in a state of much excitement in consequence, and his welcome was necessarily brief. The arriving guest was not to be considered at all with the departed dog. The men told Van Bibber, in confidence, that the general relief among the guests was something ecstatic, but this was marred later by the gloom of Miss Arnett and her inability to think of anything else but the finding of the lost collie. Things became so feverish that for the sake of rest and peace the house-party proposed to contribute to a joint purse for the return of the dog, as even, nuisance as it was, it was not so bad as having their visit spoiled by Miss Arnett's abandonment to grief and crossness.

"I think," said the young woman, after luncheon, "that some of you men might be civil enough to offer to look for him. I'm sure he can't have gone far, or, if he has been stolen, the men who took him couldn't have gone very far away either. Now which of you will volunteer? I'm sure you'll do it to please me. Mr. Van Bibber, now: you say you're so clever. We're all the time hearing of your adventures. Why don't you show how full of expedients you are and rise to the occasion?" The suggestion of scorn in this speech nettled Van Bibber.

"I'm sure I never posed as being clever," he said, "and finding a lost dog with all Long Island to pick and choose from isn't a particularly easy thing to pull off successfully, I should think."

"I didn't suppose you'd take a dare like that, Van Bibber," said one of the men. "Why, it's just the sort of thing you do so well."

"Yes," said another, "I'll back you to find him if you try."

"Thanks," said Van Bibber, dryly. "There seems to be a disposition on the part of the young men present to turn me into a dog-catcher. I doubt whether this is altogether unselfish. I do not say that they would rather remain indoors and teach the girls how to play billiards, but I quite appreciate their reasons for not wishing to roam about in the snow and whistle for a dog. However, to oblige the despondent mistress of this valuable member of the household, I will risk pneumonia, and I will, at the same time, in order to make the event interesting to all concerned, back myself to bring that dog back by eight o'clock. Now, then, if any of you unselfish youths have any sporting blood, you will just name the sum."

They named one hundred dollars, and arranged that Van Bibber was to have the dog back by eight o'clock, or just in time for dinner; for Van Bibber said he wouldn't miss his dinner for all the dogs in the two hemispheres, unless the dogs happened to be his own.

Van Bibber put on his great-coat and told the man to bring around the dog-cart; then he filled his pockets with cigars and placed a flask of brandy under the seat, and wrapped the robes around his knees.

"I feel just like a relief expedition to the North Pole. I think I ought to have some lieutenants," he suggested.

"Well," cried one of the men, "suppose we make a pool and each chip in fifty dollars, and the man who brings the dog back in time gets the whole of it?"

"That bet of mine stands, doesn't it?" asked Van Bibber.

The men said it did, and went off to put on their riding things, and four horses were saddled and brought around from the stable. Each of the four explorers was furnished with a long rope to tie to Duncan's collar, and with which he was to be led back if they found him. They were cheered ironically by the maidens they had deserted on compulsion, and were smiled upon severally by Miss Arnett. Then they separated and took different roads. It was snowing gently, and was very cold. Van Bibber drove aimlessly ahead, looking to the right and left and scanning each back yard and side street. Every now and then he hailed some passing farm wagon and asked the driver if he had seen a stray collie dog, but the answer was invariably in the negative. He soon left the village in the rear, and plunged out over the downs. The wind was bitter cold, and swept from the water with a chill that cut through his clothes.

"Oh, this is great," said Van Bibber to the patient horse in front of him; "this *is* sport, this is. The next time I come to this part of the world I'll be dragged here with a rope. Nice, hospitable people those Arnetts, aren't they? Ask you to make yourself at home chasing dogs over an ice fjord. Don't know when I've enjoyed myself so much." Every now and then he stood up and looked all over the hills and valleys to see if he could not distinguish a black object running over the white surface of the snow, but he saw nothing like a dog, not even the track of one.

Twice he came across one of the other men,

shivering and swearing from his saddle, and
with teeth chattering.

"Well," said one of them, shuddering, "you
haven't found that dog yet, I see."

"No," said Van Bibber. "Oh, no. I've
given up looking for the dog. I'm just driving
around enjoying myself. The air's so invigorat-
ing, and I like to feel the snow settling between
my collar and the back of my neck."

At four o'clock Van Bibber was about as
nearly frozen as a man could be after he had
swallowed half a bottle of brandy. It was so
cold that the ice formed on his cigar when he
took it from his lips, and his feet and the dash-
board seemed to have become stuck together.

"I think I'll give it up," he said, finally, as he
turned the horse's head toward Southampton.
"I hate to lose three hundred and fifty dollars
as much as any man; but I love my fair young
life, and I'm not going to turn into an equestrian
statue in ice for anybody's collie dog."

He drove the cart to the stable and unhar-
nessed the horse himself, as all the grooms were
out scouring the country, and then went up-
stairs unobserved and locked himself in his
room, for he did not care to have the others
know that he had given out so early in the
chase. There was a big open fire in his room,
and he put on his warm things and stretched

out before it in a great easy-chair, and smoked and sipped the brandy and chuckled with delight as he thought of the four other men racing around in the snow.

"They may have more nerve than I," he soliloquized, "and I don't say they have not; but they can have all the credit and rewards they want, and I'll be satisfied to stay just where I am."

At seven he saw the four riders coming back dejectedly, and without the dog. As they passed his room he heard one of the men ask if Van Bibber had got back yet, and another say yes, he had, as he had left the cart in the stable, but that one of the servants had said that he had started out again on foot.

"He has, has he?" said the voice. "Well, he's got sporting blood, and he'll need to keep it at fever heat if he expects to live. I'm frozen so that I can't bend my fingers."

Van Bibber smiled, and moved comfortably in the big chair; he had dozed a little, and was feeling very contented. At half-past seven he began to dress, and at five minutes to eight he was ready for dinner and stood looking out of the window at the moonlight on the white lawn below. The snow had stopped falling, and everything lay quiet and still as though it were cut in marble. And then suddenly, across the lawn, came a black, bedraggled object on four legs, limping painfully, and lifting its feet as though there were lead on them.

"Great heavens!" cried Van Bibber, "it's the dog!" He was out of the room in a moment and down into the hall. He heard the murmur of voices in the drawing-room, and the sympathetic tones of the women who were pitying the men. Van Bibber pulled on his overshoes and a great-coat that covered him from his ears to his ankles, and dashed out into the snow. The dog had just enough spirit left to try and dodge him, and with a leap to one side went off again across the lawn. It was, as Van Bibber knew, but three minutes to eight o'clock, and have the dog he must and would. The collie sprang first to one side and then to the other, and snarled and snapped; but Van Bibber was keen with the excitement of the chase, so he plunged forward recklessly and tackled the dog around the body, and they both rolled over and over together. Then Van Bibber scrambled to his feet and dashed up the steps and into the drawing-room just as the people were in line for dinner, and while the minute-hand stood at a minute to eight o'clock.

"How is this?" shouted Van Bibber, holding up one hand and clasping the dog under his other arm.

LOVE ME, LOVE MY DOG

Miss Arnett flew at the collie and embraced it, wet as it was, and ruined her gown, and all the men glanced instinctively at the clock and said:

"You've won, Van."

"But you must be frozen to death," said Miss Arnett, looking up at him with gratitude in her eyes.

"Yes, yes," said Van Bibber, beginning to shiver. "I've had a terrible long walk, and I had to carry him all the way. If you'll excuse me, I'll go change my things."

He reappeared again in a suspiciously short time for one who had to change outright, and the men admired his endurance and paid up the bet.

"Where did you find him, Van?" one of them asked.

"Oh, yes," they all chorussed. "Where was he?"

"That," said Mr. Van Bibber, "is a thing known to only two beings, Duncan and myself. Duncan can't tell, and I won't. If I did, you'd say I was trying to make myself out clever, and I never boast about the things I do."

A LEANDER OF THE EAST RIVER

"Hefty" Burke was one of the best swimmers in the East River. There was no regular way open for him to prove this, as the gentlemen of the Harlem boat-clubs, under whose auspices the annual races were given, called him a professional and would not swim against him. "They won't keep company with me on land," Hefty complained, bitterly, "and they can't keep company with me in the water; so I lose both ways." Young Burke held these gentlemen of the rowing clubs in great contempt, and their outriggers and low-necked and picturesque rowing clothes as well. They were fond of lying out of the current, with the oars pulled across at their backs for support, smoking and commenting audibly upon the other oarsmen who passed them by perspiring uncomfortably, and conscious that they were being criticised. Hefty said that these amateur oarsmen and swimmers were only pretty boys, and that he could give them two hundred yards' start in a mile of rough or smooth water and pass them as easily as a tug passes a lighter.

He was quite right in this latter boast; but, as they would call him a professional and would not swim against him, there was no way for him to prove it. His idea of a race and their idea of a race differed. They had a committee to select prizes and open a book for entries, and when the day of the races came they had a judges' boat with gay bunting all over it, and a badly frightened referee and a host of reporters, and police boats to keep order. But when Hefty swam, his two backers, who had challenged some other young man through a sporting paper, rowed in a boat behind him and yelled and swore directions, advice, warnings, and encouragement at him, and in their excitement drank all of the whiskey that had been intended for him. And the other young man's backers, who had put up ten dollars on him, and a tugboat filled with other rough young men, kegs of beer, and three Italians with two fiddles and one harp, followed close in the wake of the swimmers. It was most exciting, and though Hefty never had any prizes to show for it, he always came in first, and so won a great deal of local reputation. He also gained renown as a life-saver; for if it had not been for him many a venturesome lad would have ended his young life in the waters of the East River.

For this he received ornate and very thin gold medals, with very little gold spread over a large extent of medal, from grateful parents and admiring friends. These were real medals, and given to him, and not paid for by himself, as were "Rags" Raegan's, who always bought himself a medal whenever he assaulted a reputable citizen and the case was up before the Court of General Sessions. It was the habit of Mr. Raegan's friends to fall overboard for him whenever he was in difficulty of this sort, and allow themselves to be saved, and to present Raegan with the medal he had prepared; and this act of heroism would get into the papers, and Raegan's lawyer would make the most of it before the judges. Rags had been Hefty's foremost rival among the swimmers of the East Side, but since the retirement of the former into reputable and private life Hefty was the acknowledged champion of the river front.

Hefty was not at all a bad young man—that is, he did not expect his people to support him —and he worked occasionally, especially about election time, and what he made in bets and in backing himself to swim supplied him with small change. Then he fell in love with Miss Casey, and the trouble and happiness of his life came to him hand and hand together; and as this human feeling does away with class distinctions, I need not feel I must apologize for him any longer, but just tell his story.

He met her at the Hon. P. C. McGovern's

Fourth Ward Association's excursion and picnic, at which he was one of the twenty-five vice-presidents. On this occasion Hefty had jumped overboard after one of the Rag Gang whom the members of the Half-Hose Social Club had, in a spirit of merriment, dropped over the side of the boat. This action and the subsequent rescue and ensuing intoxication of the half-drowned member of the Rag Gang had filled Miss Casey's heart with admiration, and she told Hefty he was a good one and ought to be proud of himself.

On the following Sunday he walked out Avenue A to Tompkins Square with Mary, and he also spent a great deal of time every day on her stoop when he was not working, for he was working now and making ten dollars a week as an assistant to an ice-driver. They had promised to give him fifteen dollars a week and a seat on the box if he proved steady. He had even dreamed of wedding Mary in the spring. But Casey was a particularly objectionable man for a father-in-law, and his objections to Hefty were equally strong. He honestly thought the young man no fit match for his daughter, and would only promise to allow him to "keep company" with Mary on the condition of his living steadily.

So it became Hefty's duty to behave himself. He found this a little hard to do at first, but he confessed that it grew easier as he saw more of Miss Casey. He attributed his reform to her entirely. She had made the semi-political, semi-social organizations to which he belonged appear stupid, and especially so when he lost his money playing poker in the club-room (for the club had only one room), when he might have put it away for her. He liked to talk with her about the neighbors in the tenement, and his chance of political advancement to the position of a watchman at the Custom-house Wharf, and hear her play "Mary and John" on the melodeon. He boasted that she could make it sound as well as it did on the barrel-organ.

He was very polite to her father and very much afraid of him, for he was a most particular old man from the North of Ireland, and objected to Hefty because he was a good Catholic and fond of street fights. He also asked pertinently how Hefty expected to support a wife by swimming from one pier to another on the chance of winning ten dollars, and pointed out that even this precarious means of livelihood would be shut off when the winter came. He much preferred "Patsy" Moffat as a prospective son-in-law, because Moffat was one of the proprietors in a local express company with a capital stock of three wagons and two horses. Miss Casey herself, so it seemed to

86

Hefty, was rather fond of Moffat; but he could not tell for whom she really cared, for she was very shy, and would as soon have thought of speaking a word of encouragement as of speaking with unkindness.

There was to be a ball at the Palace Garden on Wednesday night, and Hefty had promised to call for Mary at nine o'clock. She told him to be on time, and threatened to go with her old love, Patsy Moffat, if he were late.

On Monday night the foreman at the livery stable of the ice company appointed Hefty a driver, and, as his wages would now be fifteen dollars a week, he concluded to ask Mary to marry him on Wednesday night at the dance.

He was very much elated and very happy.

His fellow-workmen heard of his promotion and insisted on his standing treat, which he did several times, until the others became flippant in their remarks and careless in their conduct. In this innocent but somewhat noisy state they started home, and on the way were injudicious enough to say, "Ah there!" to a policeman as he issued from the side door of a saloon. The policeman naturally pounded the nearest of them on the head with his club, and as Hefty happened to be that one, and as he objected, he was arrested. He gave a false name, and next morning pleaded not guilty to the charge of "assaulting an officer and causing a crowd to collect."

His sentence was thirty days in default of three hundred dollars, and by two o'clock he was on the boat to the Island, and by three he had discarded the blue shirt and red suspenders of an iceman for the gray stiff cloth of a prisoner. He took the whole trouble terribly to heart. He knew that if Old Man Casey, as he called him, heard of it there would be no winning his daughter with his consent, and he feared that the girl herself would have grave doubts concerning him. He was especially cast down when he thought of the dance on Wednesday night, and of how she would go off with Patsy Moffat. And what made it worse was the thought that if he did not return he would lose his position at the ice company's stable, and then marriage with Mary would be quite impossible. He grieved over this all day, and speculated as to what his family would think of him. His circle of friends was so well known to other mutual friends that he did not dare to ask any of them to bail him out, for this would have certainly come to Casey's ears.

He could do nothing but wait. And yet thirty days was a significant number to his friends, and an absence of that duration would be hard to explain. On Wednesday morning, two days after his arrest, he was put to work with a gang of twenty men breaking stone on the roadway that leads from the insane quarters to the penitentiary. It was a warm, sunny day, and the city, lying just across the narrow channel, never looked more beautiful. It seemed near enough for him to reach out his hand and touch it. And the private yachts and big excursion-boats that passed, banging out popular airs and alive with bunting, made Hefty feel very bitter. He determined that when he got back he would go look up the policeman who had assaulted him and break his head with a brick in a stocking. This plan cheered him somewhat, until he thought again of Mary Casey at the dance that night with Patsy Moffat, and this excited him so that he determined madly to break away and escape. His first impulse was to drop his crowbar and jump into the river on the instant, but his cooler judgment decided him to wait.

At the northern end of the Island the grass runs high, and there are no houses of any sort upon it. It reaches out into a rocky point, where it touches the still terribly swift eddies of Hell Gate, and its sharp front divides the water and directs it toward Astoria on the east and the city on the west. Hefty determined to walk off from the gang of workmen until he could drop into this grass and to lie there until night. This would be easy, as there was only one man to watch them, for they were all there for only ten days or one month, and the idea that they should try to escape was hardly considered. So Hefty edged off farther from the gang, and then, while the guard was busy lighting his pipe, dropped into the long grass and lay there quietly, after first ridding himself of his shoes and jacket. At six o'clock a bell tolled and the guard marched away, with his gang shambling after him. Hefty guessed they would not miss him until they came to count heads at supper-time; but even now it was already dark, and lights were showing on the opposite bank. He had selected the place he meant to swim for—a green bank below a row of new tenements, a place where a few bushes still stood, and where the boys of Harlem hid their clothes when they went in swimming.

At half-past seven it was quite dark, so dark, in fact, that the three lanterns which came tossing toward him told Hefty that his absence had been discovered. He rose quickly and stepped cautiously, instead of diving, into the river, for he was fearful of hidden rocks. The current was much stronger than he had imagined, and he hesitated for a moment, with the water pulling at his knees, but only for a moment; for the men were hunting for him in the grass.

He drew the gray cotton shirt from his shoulders, and threw it back of him with an exclamation of disgust, and of relief at being a free man again, and struck his broad, bare chest and the biceps of his arms with a little gasp of pleasure in their perfect strength, and then bent forward and slid into the river.

The current from the opening at Hell Gate caught him up as though he had been a plank. It tossed him and twisted him and sucked him down. He beat his way for a second to the surface and gasped for breath and was drawn down again, striking savagely at the eddies which seemed to twist his limbs into useless, heavy masses of flesh and muscle. Then he dived down and down, seeking a possibly less rapid current at the muddy bottom of the river; but the current drew him up again until he reached the top, just in time, so it seemed to him, to breathe the pure air before his lungs split with the awful pressure. He was gloriously and fiercely excited by the unexpected strength of his opponent and the probably fatal outcome of his adventure. He stopped struggling, that he might gain fresh strength, and let the current bear him where it would, until he saw that it was carrying him swiftly to the shore and to the rocks of the Island. And then he dived again and beat his way along the bottom, clutching with his hands at the soft, thick mud, and rising only to gasp for breath and sink again. His eyes were smarting hotly, and his head and breast ached with pressure that seemed to come from the inside and threatened to burst its way out. His arms had grown like lead and had lost their strength, and his legs were swept and twisted away from his control and were numb and useless. He assured himself fiercely that he could not have been in the water for more than five minutes at the longest, and reminded himself that he had often before lived in it for hours, and that this power, which was so much greater than his own, could not outlast him. But there was no sign of abatement in the swift, cruel uncertainty of its movement, and it bore him on and down or up as it pleased. The lights on the shore became indistinct, and he finally confused the two shores, and gave up hope of reaching the New York side, except by accident, and hoped only to reach some solid land alive. He did not go over all of his past life, but the vision of Mary Casey did come to him, and how she would not know that he had been innocent. It was a little thing to distress himself about at such a time, but it hurt him keenly. And then the lights grew blurred, and he felt that he was making heavy mechanical strokes that barely kept his lips above the water-line. He felt the current slacken perceptibly, but he was too much exhausted to take advantage of it, and drifted forward with it, splashing feebly like a dog, and holding his head back with a desperate effort. A huge, black shadow, only a shade blacker than the water around him, loomed up suddenly on his right, and he saw a man's face appear in the light of a hatchway and disappear again.

"Help!" he cried, "help!" but his voice sounded far away and barely audible. He struck out desperately against the current, and turned on his back and tried to keep himself afloat where he was. "Help!" he called again, feebly, grudging the strength it took to call even that. "Help! Quick, for God's sake! help me!"

Something heavy, black, and wet struck him sharply in the face and fell with a splash on the water beside him. He clutched for it quickly, and clasped it with both hands and felt it grow taut, and then gave up thinking, and they pulled him on board.

When he came to himself, the captain of the canal-boat stooped and took a fold of the gray trousers between his thumb and finger. Then he raised his head and glanced across at the big black Island, where lights were still moving about on the shore, and whistled softly. But Hefty looked at him so beseechingly that he arose and came back with a pair of old boots and a suit of blue jeans.

"Will you send these back to me to-morrow?" he asked.

"Sure," said Hefty.

"And what'll I do with these?" said the captain, holding up the gray trousers.

"Anything you want, except to wear 'em," said Mr. Burke, feebly, with a grin.

One hour later Miss Casey was standing up with Mr. Patsy Moffat for the grand march of the grand ball of the Jolly Fellows' Pleasure Club of the Fourteenth Ward, held at the Palace Garden. The band was just starting the "Boulanger March," and Mr. Moffat was saying wittily that it was warm enough to eat ice, when Mr. Hefty Burke shouldered in between him and Miss Casey. He was dressed in his best suit of clothes, and his hair was conspicuously damp.

"Excuse me, Patsy," said Mr. Burke, as he took Miss Casey's arm in his, "but this march is promised to me. I'm sorry I was late, and

I'm sorry to disappoint you; but you're like the lad that drives the hansom cab, see?—you're not in it."

"But, indeed," said Miss Casey, later, "you shouldn't have kept me a-waiting. It wasn't civil."

"I know," assented Hefty, gloomily, "but I came as soon as I could. I even went widout me supper so's to get here; an' they wuz expectin' me to stay to supper, too."

HOW HEFTY BURKE GOT EVEN

Hefty Burke was once clubbed by a policeman named McCluire, who excused the clubbing to his Honor by swearing that Hefty had been drunk and disorderly, which was not true. Hefty got away from the Island by swimming the East River, and swore to get even with the policeman. This story tells how he got even.

Mr. Carstairs was an artist who had made his first great success by painting figures and landscapes in Brittany. He had a studio at Fifty-eighth Street and Sixth Avenue, and was engaged on an historical subject in which there were three figures. One was a knight in full armor, and the other was a Moor, and the third was the figure of a woman. The suit of armor had been purchased by Mr. Carstairs in Paris, and was believed to have been worn by a brave nobleman, one of whose extravagant descendants had sold everything belonging to his family in order to get money with which to play baccarat. Carstairs was at the sale and paid a large price for the suit of armor which the Marquis de Neuville had worn, and set it up in a corner of his studio. It was in eight or a dozen pieces, and quite heavy, but was wonderfully carved and inlaid with silver, and there were dents on it that showed where a Saracen's scimitar had been dulled and many a brave knight's spear had struck. Mr. Carstairs had paid so much for it that he thought he ought to make a better use of it, if possible, than simply to keep it dusted and show it off to his friends. So he began this historical picture, and engaged Hefty Burke to pose as the knight and wear the armor. Hefty's features were not exactly the sort of features you would imagine a Marquis de Neuville would have; but as his visor was down in the picture, it did not make much material difference; and as his figure was superb, he answered very well. Hefty drove an ice-wagon during business hours, and, as a personal favor to Mr. Carstairs, agreed to pose for him, for a consideration, two afternoons of each week, and to sleep in the studio at night, for it was filled with valuable things.

The armor was a never-ending source of amazement and bewilderment to Hefty. He could not understand why a man would wear such a suit, and especially when he went out to fight. It was the last thing in the world he would individually have selected in which to make war.

"Ef I was goin' to scrap wid anybody," he

said to Mr. Carstairs, "I'd as lief tie meself up wid dumb-bells as take to carry all this stuff on me. A man wid a baseball bat and swimmin' tights on could dance all around youse and knock spots out of one of these things. The other lad wouldn't be in it. Why, before he could lift his legs or get his hands up you cud hit him on his helmet, and he wouldn't know what killed him. They must hev sat down to fight in them days."

Mr. Carstairs painted on in silence and smiled grimly.

"I'd like to have seen a go with the parties fixed out in a pair of these things," continued Hefty. "I'd bet on the lad that got in the first whack. He wouldn't have to do nothing but shove the other one over on his back and fall on him. Why, I guess this weighs half a ton if it weighs an ounce!"

For all his contempt, Hefty had a secret admiration for the ancient marquis who had worn this suit, and had been strong enough to carry its weight and demolish his enemies besides. The marks on the armor interested him greatly, and he was very much impressed one day when he found what he declared to be blood-stains on the lining of the helmet.

"I guess the old feller that wore this was a sport, eh?" he said, proudly, shaking the pieces on his arms until they rattled. "I guess he done 'em up pretty well for all these handicaps. I'll bet when he got to falling around on 'em and butting 'em with this fire helmet he made 'em purty tired. Don't youse think so?"

Young Carstairs said he didn't doubt it for a moment.

The Small Hours Social Club was to give a prize masquerade ball at the Palace Garden on New Year's Night, and Hefty had decided to go. Every gentleman dancer was to get a white silk badge with a gold tassel, and every committeeman received a blue badge with "Committee" written across it in brass letters. It cost three dollars to be a committeeman, but only one dollar "for self and lady." There were three prizes. One of a silver water-pitcher for the "handsomest-costumed lady dancer," an accordion for the "best-dressed gent," and a cake for the most original idea in costume, whether worn by "gent or lady." Hefty, as well as many others, made up his mind to get the accordion, if it cost him as much as seven dollars, which was half of his week's wages. It wasn't the prize he wanted so much, but he thought of the impression it would make on Miss Casey, whose father was the well-known janitor of that name. They had been engaged for some time, but the engagement hung fire, and Hefty thought that a becoming and appropriate costume might hasten matters a little. He was undecided as to whether he should go as an Indian or as a courtier of the time of Charles II. Auchmuty Stein, of the Bowery, who supplies costumes and wigs at reasonable rates, was of the opinion that a neat sailor suit of light blue silk and decorated with white anchors was about the "brettiest thing in the shop, and sheap at fife dollars"; but Hefty said he never saw a sailor in silk yet, and he didn't think they ever wore it. He couldn't see how they could keep the tar and salt-water from ruining it.

The Charles II. court suit was very handsome, and consisted of red cotton tights, blue velveteen doublet, and a blue cloak lined with pale pink silk. A yellow wig went with this, and a jewelled sword which would not come out of the scabbard. It could be had for seven dollars a night. Hefty was still in doubt about it and was much perplexed. Auchmuty Stein told him Charlie Macklin, the Third Avenue ticket-chopper, was after the same suit, and that he had better take it while he could get it. But Hefty said he'd think about it. The next day was his day for posing, and as he stood arrayed in the Marquis de Neuville's suit of mail he chanced to see himself in one of the long mir-

rors, and was for the first time so struck with
the ferocity of his appearance that he determined to see if old man Stein had not a suit of
imitation armor, which would not be so heavy
and would look as well. But the more Hefty
thought of it, the more he believed that only
the real suit would do. Its associations, its
blood-stains, and the real silver tracings haunted
him, and he half decided to ask Mr. Carstairs
to lend it to him.

But then he remembered overhearing Carstairs tell a brother-artist that he had paid two
thousand francs for it, and, though he did not
know how much a franc might be, two thousand of anything was too much to wear around
at a masquerade ball. But the thing haunted
him. He was sure if Miss Casey saw him in
that suit she would never look at Charlie Macklin again.

"They wouldn't be in the same town with
me," said Hefty. "And I'd get two of the
prizes, sure."

He was in great perplexity, when good luck or
bad luck settled it for him.

"Burke," said Mr. Carstairs, "Mrs. Carstairs
and I are going out of town for New Year's
Day, and will be gone until Sunday. Take a
turn through the rooms each night, will you? as
well as the studio, and see that everything is

all right." That clinched the matter for Hefty. He determined to go as far as the Palace Garden as the Marquis de Neuville, and say nothing whatever to Mr. Carstairs about it.

Stuff McGovern, who drove a night-hawk and who was a particular admirer of Hefty's, even though as a cabman he was in a higher social scale than the driver of an ice-cart, agreed to carry Hefty and his half-ton of armor to the Garden, and call for him when the ball was over.

"Holee smoke!" gasped Mr. McGovern, as Hefty stumbled heavily across the pavement with an overcoat over his armor and his helmet under his arm. "Do you expect to do much dancing in that sheet-iron?"

"It's the looks of the thing I'm gambling on," said Hefty. "I look like a locomoteeve when I get this stovepipe on me head."

Hefty put on his helmet in the cab and pulled down the visor, and when he alighted the crowd around the door was too greatly awed to jeer, but stood silent with breathless admiration. He had great difficulty in mounting the somewhat steep flight of stairs which led to the dancing-room, and considered gloomily that in the event of a fire he would have a very small chance of getting out alive. He made so much noise coming up that the committeemen thought some one was rolling some one else down the stairs, and came out to see the fight. They observed Hefty's approach with whispered awe and amazement.

"Wot are you?" asked the man at the door. "Youse needn't give your real name," he explained, politely. "But you've got to give something if youse are trying for a prize, see?"

"I'm the Black Knight," said Hefty in a hoarse voice, "the Marquis de Newveal; and when it comes to scrappin' wid der perlice, I'm de best in der business."

This last statement was entirely impromptu, and inspired by the presence of Policeman Mc-Cluire, who, with several others, had been detailed to keep order. McCluire took this challenge calmly, and looked down and smiled at Hefty's feet.

"He looks like a stove on two legs," he said to the crowd. The crowd, as a matter of policy, laughed.

"You'll look like a fool standing on his head in a snow-bank if you talk impudent to me," said Hefty, epigrammatically, from behind the barrier of his iron mask. What might have happened next did not happen, because at that moment the music sounded for the grand march, and Hefty and the policeman were swept apart by the crowd of Indians, Mexicans, courtiers, negro minstrels, and clowns. Hefty stamped across the waxed floor about as lightly as a safe could do it if a safe could walk. He found Miss Casey after the march and disclosed his identity. She promised not to tell, and was plainly delighted and flattered at being seen with the distinct sensation of the ball. "Say, Hefty," she said, "they just ain't in it with you. You'll take the two prizes sure. How do I look?"

"Out o' sight," said Hefty. "Never saw you lookin' better."

"That's good," said Miss Casey, simply, and with a sigh of satisfaction.

Hefty was undoubtedly a great success. The men came around him and pawed him, and felt the dents in the armor, and tried the weight of it by holding up one of his arms, and handled him generally as though he were a freak in a museum. "Let 'em alone," said Hefty to Miss Casey, "I'm not sayin' a word. Let the judges get on to the sensation I'm a-makin', and I'll walk off with the prizes. The crowd is wid me sure."

At midnight the judges pounded on a table for order, and announced that after much debate they gave the first prize to Miss Lizzie Cannon, of Hester Street, for "having the most handsomest costume on the floor, that of Columbia." The fact that Mr. "Buck" Masters, who was one of the judges, and who was engaged to Miss Cannon, had said that he would pound things out of the other judges if they gave the prize elsewhere was not known, but the decision met with as general satisfaction as could well be expected.

"The second prize," said the judges, "goes to the gent calling himself the Black Knight—him in the iron leggings—and the other prize for the most original costume goes to him, too." Half the crowd cheered at this, and only one man hissed. Hefty, filled with joy and with the anticipation of the elegance the ice-pitcher would lend to his flat when he married Miss Casey, and how conveniently he could fill it, turned on this gentleman and told him that only geese hissed.

The gentleman, who had spent much time on his costume, and who had been assured by each judge on each occasion that evening when he had treated him to beer that he would get the prize, told Hefty to go lie down. It has never been explained just what horrible insult lies back of this advice, but it is a very dangerous thing to tell a gentleman to do. Hefty lifted one foot heavily and bore down on the disappointed masker like an ironclad in a heavy sea. But before he could reach him Policeman McCluire, mindful of the insult put upon him by this stranger, sprang between them and said: "Here, now, no scrapping here; get out of this," and shoved Hefty back with his hand. Hefty uttered a mighty howl of wrath and long-cherished anger, and lurched forward, but before he could reach his old-time enemy three policemen had him around the arms and by the leg, and he was as effectually stopped as though he had been chained to the floor.

"Let go o' me," said Hefty, wildly. "You're smotherin' me. Give me a fair chance at him."

But they would not give him any sort of a chance. They rushed him down the steep stairs, and while McCluire ran ahead two more pushed back the crowd that had surged uncertainly forward to the rescue. If Hefty had declared his identity the police would have had a very sad time of it; but that he must not get Mr. Carstairs's two-thousand-franc suit into trouble was all that filled Hefty's mind, and all that he wanted was to escape. Three policemen walked with him down the street. They said they knew where he lived, and that they were only going to take him home. They said this because they were afraid the crowd would interfere if it imagined Hefty was being led to the precinct station-house.

HOW HEFTY BURKE GOT EVEN

But Hefty knew where he was going as soon as he turned the next corner and was started off in the direction of the station-house. There was still quite a small crowd at his heels, and Stuff McGovern was driving along at the side anxious to help, but fearful to do anything, as Hefty had told him not to let any one know who his fare had been and that his incognito must be preserved.

The blood rushed to Hefty's head like hot liquor. To be arrested for nothing, and by that thing McCluire, and to have the noble coat-of-mail of the Marquis de Neuville locked up in a dirty cell and probably ruined, and to lose his position with Carstairs, who had always treated him so well, it was terrible! It could not be! He looked through his visor; to the right and to the left a policeman walked on each side of him with his hand on his iron sleeve, and McCluire marched proudly before. The dim lamps of McGovern's night-hawk shone at the side of the procession and showed the crowd trailing on behind. Suddenly Hefty threw up his visor. "Stuff," he cried, "are youse with me?"

He did not wait for any answer, but swung back his two iron arms and then brought them forward with a sweep on to the back of the necks of the two policemen. They went down and forward as if a lamp-post had fallen on them, but were up again in a second. But before they could rise Hefty set his teeth, and with a gurgle of joy butted his iron helmet into McCluire's back and sent him flying forward into a snowbank. Then he threw himself on him and buried him under three hundred pounds of iron and flesh and blood, and beat him with his mailed hand over the head and choked the snow and ice down into his throat and nostrils.

"You'll club me again, will you?" he cried. "You'll send me to the Island?" The two policemen were pounding him with their nightsticks as effectually as though they were rapping on a door-step; and the crowd, seeing this, fell on them from behind, led by Stuff McGovern with his whip, and rolled them in the snow and tried to tear off their coat-tails, which means money out of the policeman's own pocket for repairs, and hurts more than broken ribs, as the Police Benefit Society pays for them.

"Now then, boys, get me into a cab," cried Hefty. They lifted him in and obligingly blew out the lights so that the police could not see its number, and Stuff drove Hefty proudly home. "I guess I'm even with that cop now," said Hefty as he stood at the door of the studio building, perspiring and happy; "but if them cops ever find out who the Black Knight was, I'll go away for six months on the Island. I guess," he added, thoughtfully, "I'll have to give them two prizes up."

VAN BIBBER AND THE
SWAN-BOATS

It was very hot in the Park, and young Van Bibber, who has a good heart and a great deal more money than good-hearted people generally get, was cross and somnolent. He had told his groom to bring a horse he wanted to try to the Fifty-ninth Street entrance at ten o'clock and the groom had not appeared. Hence Van Bibber's crossness.

He waited as long as his dignity would allow, and then turned off into a by-lane and dropped on a bench and looked gloomily at the Lohengrin swans with the paddle-wheel attachment that circle around the lake. They struck him as the most idiotic inventions he had ever seen, and he pitied, with the pity of a man who contemplates crossing the ocean to be measured for his fall clothes, the people who could find delight in having some one paddle them around an artificial lake.

Two little girls from the East Side, with a lunch basket, and an older girl with her hair down her back, sat down on a bench beside him and gazed at the swans.

The place was becoming too popular, and

VAN BIBBER AND THE SWAN-BOATS

Van Bibber decided to move on. But the bench on which he sat was in the shade, and the asphalt walk leading to the street was in the sun, and his cigarette was soothing, so he ignored the near presence of the three little girls, and remained where he was.

"I s'pose," said one of the two little girls, in a high, public school voice, "there's lots to see from those swan-boats that youse can't see from the banks."

"Oh, lots," assented the girl with long hair.

"If you walked all round the lake, clear all the way round, you could see all there is to see," said the third, "except what there's in the middle where the island is."

"I guess it's mighty wild on that island," suggested the youngest.

"Eddie Case he took a trip around the lake on a swan-boat the other day. He said that it was grand. He said youse could see fishes and ducks, and that it looked just as if there were snakes and things on the island."

"What sort of things?" asked the other one, in a hushed voice.

"Well, wild things," explained the elder, vaguely; "bears and animals like that, that grow in wild places."

Van Bibber lit a fresh cigarette, and settled himself comfortably and unreservedly to listen.

"My, but I'd like to take a trip just once," said the youngest, under her breath. Then she clasped her fingers together and looked up anxiously at the elder girl, who glanced at her with severe reproach.

"Why, Mame!" she said; "ain't you ashamed! Ain't you having a good time 'nuff without wishing for everything you set your eyes on?"

Van Bibber wondered at this—why humans should want to ride around on the swans in the first place, and why, if they had such a wild desire, they should not gratify it.

"Why, it costs more'n it costs to come all the way up-town in an open car," added the elder girl, as if in answer to his unspoken question.

The younger girl sighed at this, and nodded her head in submission, but blinked longingly at the big swans and the parti-colored awning and the red seats.

"I beg your pardon," said Van Bibber, addressing himself uneasily to the eldest girl with long hair, "but if the little girl would like to go around in one of those things, and—and hasn't brought the change with her, you know, I'm sure I should be very glad if she'd allow me to send her around."

"Oh! will you?" exclaimed the little girl, with a jump, and so sharply and in such a shrill voice that Van Bibber shuddered. But the elder girl objected.

"I'm afraid maw wouldn't like our taking money from any one we didn't know," she said with dignity; "but if you're going anyway and want company——"

"Oh! my, no," said Van Bibber, hurriedly. He tried to picture himself riding around the lake behind a tin swan with three little girls from the East Side, and a lunch basket.

"Then," said the head of the trio, "we can't go."

There was such a look of uncomplaining acceptance of this verdict on the part of the two little girls, that Van Bibber felt uncomfortable. He looked to the right and to the left, and then said desperately, "Well, come along." The young man in a blue flannel shirt, who did the paddling, smiled at Van Bibber's riding-breeches, which were so very loose at one end and so very tight at the other, and at his gloves and crop. But Van Bibber pretended not to care. The three little girls placed the awful lunch basket on the front seat and sat on the middle one, and Van Bibber cowered in the back. They were hushed in silent ecstasy when it started, and gave little gasps of pleasure when it careened slightly in turning. It was shady under the awning, and the motion was pleasant enough, but Van Bibber was so afraid some one would see him that he failed to enjoy it.

But as soon as they passed into the narrow straits and were shut in by the bushes and were out of sight of the people, he relaxed, and began to play the host. He pointed out the fishes among the rocks at the edges of the pool, and the sparrows and robins bathing and ruffling their feathers in the shallow water, and agreed with them about the possibility of bears, and even tigers, in the wild part of the island, although the glimpse of the gray helmet of a Park policeman made such a supposition doubtful.

And it really seemed as though they were enjoying it more than he ever enjoyed a trip up the Sound on a yacht or across the ocean on a record-breaking steamship. It seemed long enough before they got back to Van Bibber, but his guests were evidently but barely satisfied. Still, all the goodness in his nature would not allow him to go through that ordeal again.

He stepped out of the boat eagerly and helped out the girl with long hair as though she had been a princess and tipped the rude young man who had laughed at him, but who was perspiring now with the work he had done; and then as he turned to leave the dock he came face to face with A Girl He Knew and Her brother.

Her brother said, "How're you, Van Bibber? Been taking a trip around the world in eighty minutes?" And added in a low voice, "Introduce me to your young lady friends from Hester Street."

"Ah, how're you—quite a surprise!" gasped Van Bibber, while his late guests stared admiringly at the pretty young lady in the riding-habit, and utterly refused to move on. "Been taking ride on the lake," stammered Van Bibber; "most exhilarating. Young friends of mine—these young ladies never rode on lake, so I took 'em. Did you see me?"

"Oh, yes, we saw you," said Her brother, dryly, while she only smiled at him, but so kindly and with such perfect understanding that Van Bibber grew red with pleasure and bought three long strings of tickets for the swans at some absurd discount, and gave each little girl a string.

"There," said Her brother to the little ladies from Hester Street, "now you can take trips for a week without stopping. Don't try to smuggle in any laces, and don't forget to fee the smoking-room steward."

The Girl He Knew said they were walking over to the stables, and that he had better go get his other horse and join her, which was to be his reward for taking care of the young ladies. And the three little girls proceeded to use up the yards of tickets so industriously that they were sunburned when they reached the tenement, and went to bed dreaming of a big white swan, and a beautiful young gentleman in patent-leather riding-boots and baggy breeches.

VAN BIBBER'S BURGLAR

THERE had been a dance up-town, but as Van Bibber could not find Her there, he accepted young Travers's suggestion to go over to Jersey City and see a "go" between "Dutchy" Mack and a colored person professionally known as the Black Diamond. They covered up all signs of their evening dress with their great-coats, and filled their pockets with cigars, for the smoke which surrounds a "go" is trying to sensitive nostrils, and they also fastened their watches to both key-chains. Alf Alpin, who was acting as master of ceremonies, was greatly pleased and flattered at their coming, and boisterously insisted on their sitting on the platform. The fact was generally circulated among the spectators that the "two gents in high hats" had come in a carriage, and this and their patent-leather boots made them objects of keen interest. It was even whispered that they were the "parties" who were putting up the money to back the Black Diamond against the "Hester Street Jackson." This in itself entitled them to respect. Van Bibber was asked to hold the watch, but he wisely declined the honor, which was given to Andy Spielman, the sporting reporter of the *Track and Ring*, whose watch-case was covered with diamonds, and was just the sort of a watch a timekeeper should hold.

It was two o'clock before "Dutchy" Mack's backer threw the sponge into the air, and three before they reached the city. They had another reporter in the cab with them besides the gentleman who had bravely held the watch in the face of several offers to "do for" him; and as Van Bibber was ravenously hungry, and as he doubted that he could get anything at that hour at the club, they accepted Spielman's invitation and went for a porterhouse steak and onions at the Owl's Nest, Gus McGowan's all-night restaurant on Third Avenue.

It was a very dingy, dirty place, but it was as warm as the engine-room of a steamboat, and the steak was perfectly done and tender. It was too late to go to bed, so they sat around the table, with their chairs tipped back and their knees against its edge. The two club men had thrown off their great-coats, and their wide shirt fronts and silk facings shone grandly in the smoky light of the oil lamps and the red glow from the grill in the corner. They talked about the life the reporters led, and the Philistines asked foolish questions, which the gentle-

man of the press answered without showing
them how foolish they were.

"And I suppose you have all sorts of curious
adventures," said Van Bibber, tentatively.

"Well, no, not what I would call adventures,"
said one of the reporters. "I have never seen
anything that could not be explained or attributed directly to some known cause, such as
crime or poverty or drink. You may think at
first that you have stumbled on something
strange and romantic, but it comes to nothing.
You would suppose that in a great city like this
one would come across something that could
not be explained away—something mysterious
or out of the common, like Stevenson's Suicide
Club. But I have not found it so. Dickens
once told James Payn that the most curious
thing he ever saw in his rambles around London
was a ragged man who stood crouching under
the window of a great house where the owner
was giving a ball. While the man hid beneath
a window on the ground floor, a woman wonderfully dressed and very beautiful raised the sash
from the inside and dropped her bouquet down
into the man's hand, and he nodded and stuck
it under his coat and ran off with it.

"I call that, now, a really curious thing to
see. But I have never come across anything
like it, and I have been in every part of this

big city, and at every hour of the night and morning, and I am not lacking in imagination either, but no captured maidens have ever beckoned to me from barred windows nor 'white hands waved from a passing hansom.' Balzac and De Musset and Stevenson suggest that they have had such adventures, but they never come to me. It is all commonplace and vulgar, and always ends in a police court or with a 'found drowned' in the North River."

McGowan, who had fallen into a doze behind the bar, woke suddenly and shivered and rubbed his shirt-sleeves briskly. A woman knocked at the side door and begged for a drink "for the love of heaven," and the man who tended the grill told her to be off. They could hear her feeling her way against the wall and cursing as she staggered out of the alley. Three men came in with a hack driver and wanted everybody to drink with them, and became insolent when the gentlemen declined, and were in consequence hustled out one at a time by McGowan, who went to sleep again immediately, with his head resting among the cigar boxes and pyramids of glasses at the back of the bar, and snored.

"You see," said the reporter, "it is all like this. Night in a great city is not picturesque and it is not theatrical. It is sodden, sometimes brutal, exciting enough until you get used to it, but it runs in a groove. It is dramatic, but the plot is old and the motives and characters always the same."

The rumble of heavy market wagons and the rattle of milk carts told them that it was morning, and as they opened the door the cold fresh air swept into the place and made them wrap their collars around their throats and stamp their feet. The morning wind swept down the cross-street from the East River and the lights of the street lamps and of the saloon looked old and tawdry. Travers and the reporter went off to a Turkish bath, and the gentleman who held the watch, and who had been asleep for the last hour, dropped into a night-hawk and told the man to drive home. It was almost clear now and very cold, and Van Bibber determined to walk. He had the strange feeling one gets when one stays up until the sun rises, of having lost a day somewhere, and the dance he had attended a few hours before seemed to have come off long ago, and the fight in Jersey City was far back in the past.

The houses along the cross-street through which he walked were as dead as so many blank walls, and only here and there a lace curtain waved out of the open window where some honest citizen was sleeping. The street was quite deserted; not even a cat or a policeman moved on it and Van Bibber's footsteps sounded brisk on the sidewalk. There was a great house at the corner of the avenue and the cross-street on which he was walking. The house faced the avenue and a stone wall ran back to the brown stone stable which opened on the side street. There was a door in this wall, and as Van Bibber approached it on his solitary walk it opened cautiously, and a man's head appeared in it for an instant and was withdrawn again like a flash, and the door snapped to. Van Bibber stopped and looked at the door and at the house and up and down the street. The house was tightly closed, as though some one was lying inside dead, and the streets were still empty.

Van Bibber could think of nothing in his appearance so dreadful as to frighten an honest man, so he decided the face he had had a glimpse of must belong to a dishonest one. It was none of his business, he assured himself, but it was curious, and he liked adventure, and he would have liked to prove his friend the reporter, who did not believe in adventure, in the wrong. So he approached the door silently, and jumped and caught at the top of the wall and stuck one foot on the handle of the door, and, with the other on the knocker, drew himself up and looked cautiously down

on the other side. He had done this so lightly
that the only noise he made was the rattle of
the door-knob on which his foot had rested,
and the man inside thought that the one outside was trying to open the door, and placed
his shoulder to it and pressed against it heavily.
Van Bibber, from his perch on the top of the
wall, looked down directly on the other's head
and shoulders. He could see the top of the
man's head only two feet below, and he also
saw that in one hand he held a revolver and
that two bags filled with projecting articles of
different sizes lay at his feet.

It did not need explanatory notes to tell
Van Bibber that the man below had robbed the
big house on the corner, and that if it had not
been for his having passed when he did the burglar would have escaped with his treasure. His
first thought was that he was not a policeman,
and that a fight with a burglar was not in his
line of life; and this was followed by the thought
that though the gentleman who owned the
property in the two bags was of no interest to
him, he was, as a respectable member of society,
more entitled to consideration than the man
with the revolver.

The fact that he was now, whether he liked
it or not, perched on the top of the wall like
Humpty Dumpty, and that the burglar might

see him and shoot him the next minute, had also an immediate influence on his movements. So he balanced himself cautiously and noiselessly and dropped upon the man's head and shoulders, bringing him down to the flagged walk with him and under him. The revolver went off once in the struggle, but before the burglar could know how or from where his assailant had come, Van Bibber was standing up over him and had driven his heel down on his hand and kicked the pistol out of his fingers. Then he stepped quickly to where it lay and picked it up and said, "Now, if you try to get up I'll shoot at you." He felt an unwarranted and ill-timedly humorous inclination to add, "and I'll probably miss you," but subdued it. The burglar, much to Van Bibber's astonishment, did not attempt to rise, but sat up with his hands locked across his knees and said: "Shoot ahead. I'd a damned sight rather you would."

His teeth were set and his face desperate and bitter, and hopeless to a degree of utter hopelessness that Van Bibber had never imagined.

"Go ahead," reiterated the man, doggedly, "I won't move. Shoot me."

It was a most unpleasant situation. Van Bibber felt the pistol loosening in his hand, and he was conscious of a strong inclination to lay it down and ask the burglar to tell him all about it.

"You haven't got much heart," said Van Bibber, finally. "You're a pretty poor sort of a burglar, I should say."

"What's the use?" said the man, fiercely. "I won't go back—I won't go back there alive. I've served my time forever in that hole. If I have to go back again—s'help me if I don't do for a keeper and die for it. But I won't serve there no more."

"Go back where?" asked Van Bibber, gently, and greatly interested; "to prison?"

"To prison, yes!" cried the man, hoarsely: "to a grave. That's where. Look at my face," he said, "and look at my hair. That ought to tell you where I've been. With all the color gone out of my skin, and all the life out of my legs. You needn't be afraid of me. I couldn't hurt you if I wanted to. I'm a skeleton and a baby, I am. I couldn't kill a cat. And now you're going to send me back again for another lifetime. For twenty years, this time, into that cold, forsaken hole, and after I done my time so well and worked so hard." Van Bibber shifted the pistol from one hand to the other and eyed his prisoner doubtfully.

"How long have you been out?" he asked,

seating himself on the steps of the kitchen and holding the revolver between his knees. The sun was driving the morning mist away, and he had forgotten the cold.

"I got out yesterday," said the man.

Van Bibber glanced at the bags and lifted the revolver. "You didn't waste much time," he said.

"No," answered the man, sullenly, "no, I didn't. I knew this place and I wanted money to get West to my folks, and the Society said I'd have to wait until I earned it, and I couldn't wait. I haven't seen my wife for seven years, nor my daughter. Seven years, young man; think of that—seven years. Do you know how long that is? Seven years without seeing your wife or your child! And they're straight people, they are," he added, hastily. "My wife moved West after I was put away and took another name, and my girl never knew nothing about me. She thinks I'm away at sea. I was to join 'em. That was the plan. I was to join 'em, and I thought I could lift enough here to get the fare, and now," he added, dropping his face in his hands, "I've got to go back. And I had meant to live straight after I got West— God help me, but I did! Not that it makes much difference now. An' I don't care whether you believe it or not neither," he added, fiercely.

VAN BIBBER'S BURGLAR

"I didn't say whether I believed it or not," answered Van Bibber, with grave consideration.

He eyed the man for a brief space without speaking, and the burglar looked back at him, doggedly and defiantly, and with not the faintest suggestion of hope in his eyes, or of appeal for mercy. Perhaps it was because of this fact, or perhaps it was the wife and child that moved Van Bibber, but whatever his motives were, he acted on them promptly. "I suppose, though," he said, as though speaking to himself, "that I ought to give you up."

"I'll never go back alive," said the burglar, quietly.

"Well, that's bad, too," said Van Bibber. "Of course I don't know whether you're lying or not, and as to your meaning to live honestly, I very much doubt it; but I'll give you a ticket to wherever your wife is, and I'll see you on the train. And you can get off at the next station and rob my house to-morrow night, if you feel that way about it. Throw those bags inside that door where the servant will see them before the milkman does, and walk on out ahead of me, and keep your hands in your pockets, and don't try to run. I have your pistol, you know."

The man placed the bags inside the kitchen door; and, with a doubtful look at his custodian, stepped out into the street, and walked, as he was directed to do, toward the Grand Central station. Van Bibber kept just behind him, and kept turning the question over in his mind as to what he ought to do. He felt very guilty as he passed each policeman, but he recovered himself when he thought of the wife and child who lived in the West, and who were "straight."

"Where to?" asked Van Bibber, as he stood at the ticket-office window. "Helena, Montana," answered the man with, for the first time, a look of relief. Van Bibber bought the ticket and handed it to the burglar. "I suppose you know," he said, "that you can sell that at a place down-town for half the money." "Yes, I know that," said the burglar. There was a half-hour before the train left, and Van Bibber took his charge into the restaurant and watched him eat everything placed before him, with his eyes glancing all the while to the right or left. Then Van Bibber gave him some money and told him to write to him, and shook hands with him. The man nodded eagerly and pulled off his hat as the car drew out of the station; and Van Bibber came down-town again with the shop girls and clerks going to work, still wondering if he had done the right thing.

He went to his rooms and changed his clothes, took a cold bath, and crossed over to Delmonico's for his breakfast, and, while the waiter laid the cloth in the café, glanced at the headings in one of the papers. He scanned first with polite interest the account of the dance on the night previous and noticed his name among those present. With greater interest he read of the fight between "Dutchy" Mack and the "Black Diamond," and then he read carefully how "Abe" Hubbard, alias "Jimmie the Gent," a burglar, had broken jail in New Jersey, and had been traced to New York. There was a description of the man, and Van Bibber breathed quickly as he read it. "The detectives have a clew of his whereabouts," the account said; "if he is still in the city they are confident of recapturing him. But they fear that the same friends who helped him to break jail will probably assist him from the country or to get out West."

"They may do that," murmured Van Bibber to himself, with a smile of grim contentment; "they probably will."

Then he said to the waiter, "Oh, I don't know. Some bacon and eggs and green things and coffee."

VAN BIBBER AS BEST MAN

Young Van Bibber came up to town in June from Newport to see his lawyer about the preparation of some papers that needed his signature. He found the city very hot and close, and as dreary and as empty as a house that has been shut up for some time while its usual occupants are away in the country.

As he had to wait over for an afternoon train, and as he was down-town, he decided to lunch at a French restaurant near Washington Square, where some one had told him you could get particular things particularly well cooked. The tables were set on a terrace with plants and flowers about them, and covered with a tri-colored awning. There were no jangling horse-car bells nor dust to disturb him, and almost all the other tables were unoccupied. The waiters leaned against these tables and chatted in a French *argot;* and a cool breeze blew through the plants and billowed the awning, so that, on the whole, Van Bibber was glad he had come.

There was, beside himself, an old Frenchman scolding over his late breakfast; two young artists with Van Dyke beards, who ordered the most remarkable things in the same French *argot* that the waiters spoke; and a young lady and a young gentleman at the table next to his own. The young man's back was toward him, and he could only see the girl when the youth moved to one side. She was very young and very pretty, and she seemed in a most excited state of mind from the tip of her wide-brimmed, pointed French hat to the points of her patent-leather ties. She was strikingly well-bred in appearance, and Van Bibber wondered why she should be dining alone with so young a man.

"It wasn't my fault," he heard the youth say earnestly. "How could I know he would be out of town? and anyway it really doesn't matter. Your cousin is not the only clergyman in the city."

"Of course not," said the girl, almost tearfully, "but they're not my cousins and he is, and that would have made it so much, oh, so very much different. I'm awfully frightened!"

"Runaway couple," commented Van Bibber. "Most interesting. Read about 'em often; never seen 'em. Most interesting."

He bent his head over an entrée, but he could not help hearing what followed, for the young runaways were indifferent to all around them, and though he rattled his knife and fork in a most vulgar manner, they did not heed him nor lower their voices.

"Well, what are you going to do?" said the girl, severely but not unkindly. ".It doesn't seem to me that you are exactly rising to the occasion."

"Well, I don't know," answered the youth, easily. "We're safe here anyway. Nobody we know ever comes here, and if they did they are out of town now. You go on and eat something, and I'll get a directory and look up a lot of clergymen's addresses, and then we can make out a list and drive around in a cab until we find one who has not gone off on his vacation. We ought to be able to catch the Fall River boat back at five this afternoon; then we can go right on to Boston from Fall River to-morrow morning and run down to Narragansett during the day."

"They'll never forgive us," said the girl.

"Oh, well, that's all right," exclaimed the young man, cheerfully. "Really, you're the most uncomfortable young person I ever ran away with. One might think you were going to a funeral. You were willing enough two days ago, and now you don't help me at all. Are you sorry?" he asked, and then added, "but please don't say so, even if you are."

"No, not sorry, exactly," said the girl; "but,

indeed, Ted, it is going to make so much talk.
If we only had a girl with us, or if you had a
best man, or if we had witnesses, as they do in
England, and a parish registry, or something
of that sort; or if Cousin Harold had only been
at home to do the marrying."

The young gentleman called Ted did not look,
judging from the expression of his shoulders, as
if he were having a very good time.

He picked at the food on his plate gloomily,
and the girl took out her handkerchief and then
put it resolutely back again and smiled at him.
The youth called the waiter and told him to
bring a directory, and as he turned to give the
order Van Bibber recognized him and he recognized Van Bibber. Van Bibber knew him for
a very nice boy, of a very good Boston family
named Standish, and the younger of two sons.
It was the elder who was Van Bibber's particular friend. The girl saw nothing of this mutual
recognition, for she was looking with startled
eyes at a hansom that had dashed up the side
street and was turning the corner.

"Ted, O Ted!" she gasped. "It's your
brother. There! In that hansom. I saw him
perfectly plainly. Oh, how did he find us?
What shall we do?"

Ted grew very red and then very white.

"Standish," said Van Bibber, jumping up

133

and reaching for his hat, "pay this chap for these things, will you, and I'll get rid of your brother."

Van Bibber descended the steps lighting a cigar as the elder Standish came up them on a jump.

"Hello, Standish!" shouted the New Yorker. "Wait a minute; where are you going? Why, it seems to rain Standishes to-day! First see your brother; then I see you. What's on?"

"You've seen him?" cried the Boston man, eagerly. "Yes, and where is he? Was she with him? Are they married? Am I in time?"

Van Bibber answered these different questions to the effect that he had seen young Standish and Mrs. Standish not half an hour before, and that they were just then taking a cab for Jersey City, whence they were to depart for Chicago.

"The driver who brought them here, and who told me where they were, said they could not have left this place by the time I would reach it," said the elder brother, doubtfully.

"That's so," said the driver of the cab, who had listened curiously. "I brought 'em here not more'n half an hour ago. Just had time to get back to the depot. They can't have gone long."

"Yes, but they have," said Van Bibber.

"However, if you get over to Jersey City in time for the 2.30, you can reach Chicago almost as soon as they do. They are going to the Palmer House, they said."

"Thank you, old fellow," shouted Standish, jumping back into his hansom. "It's a terrible business. Pair of young fools. Nobody objected to the marriage, only too young, you know. Ever so much obliged."

"Don't mention it," said Van Bibber, politely.

"Now, then," said that young man, as he approached the frightened couple trembling on the terrace, "I've sent your brother off to Chicago. I do not know why I selected Chicago as a place where one would go on a honeymoon. But I'm not used to lying, and I'm not very good at it. Now, if you will introduce me, I'll see what can be done toward getting you two babes out of the woods."

Standish said, "Miss Cambridge, this is Mr. Cortlandt Van Bibber, of whom you have heard my brother speak," and Miss Cambridge said she was very glad to meet Mr. Van Bibber even under such peculiarly trying circumstances.

"Now what you two want to do," said Van Bibber, addressing them as though they were just about fifteen years old and he were at least forty, "is to give this thing all the publicity you can."

VAN BIBBER AS BEST MAN

"What?" chorussed the two runaways, in violent protest.

"Certainly," said Van Bibber. "You were about to make a fatal mistake. You were about to go to some unknown clergyman of an unknown parish, who would have married you in a back room, without a certificate or a witness, just like any eloping farmer's daughter and lightning-rod agent. Now it's different with you two. Why you were not married respectably in church I don't know, and I do not intend to ask, but a kind Providence has sent me to you to see that there is no talk nor scandal, which is such bad form, and which would have got your names into all the papers. I am going to arrange this wedding properly, and you will kindly remain here until I send a carriage for you. Now just rely on me entirely and eat your luncheon in peace. It's all going to come out right—and allow me to recommend the salad, which is especially good."

Van Bibber first drove madly to the Little Church Around the Corner, where he told the kind old rector all about it, and arranged to have the church open and the assistant organist in her place, and a district-messenger boy to blow the bellows, punctually at three o'clock. "And now," he soliloquized, "I must get some names. It doesn't matter much whether they happen to know the high contracting parties or not, but they must be names that everybody knows. Whoever is in town will be lunching at Delmonico's, and the men will be at the clubs." So he first went to the big restaurant, where, as good luck would have it, he found Mrs. "Regy" Van Arnt and Mrs. "Jack" Peabody, and the Misses Brookline, who had run up the Sound for the day on the yacht *Minerva* of the Boston Yacht Club, and he told them how things were and swore them to secrecy, and told them to bring what men they could pick up.

At the club he pressed four men into service who knew everybody and whom everybody knew, and when they protested that they had not been properly invited and that they only knew the bride and groom by sight, he told them that made no difference, as it was only their names he wanted. Then he sent a messenger boy to get the biggest suite of rooms on the Fall River boat, and another one for flowers, and then he put Mrs. "Regy" Van Arnt into a cab and sent her after the bride, and, as best man, he got into another cab and carried off the groom.

"I have acted either as best man or usher forty-two times now," said Van Bibber, as they drove to the church, "and this is the first time I ever appeared in either capacity in Russia-leather shoes and a blue serge yachting suit. But then," he added, contentedly, "you ought to see the other fellows. One of them *is* in a striped flannel."

Mrs. "Regy" and Miss Cambridge wept a great deal on the way up-town, but the bride was smiling and happy when she walked up the aisle to meet her prospective husband, who looked exceedingly conscious before the eyes of the men, all of whom he knew by sight or by name, and not one of whom he had ever met before. But they all shook hands after it was over, and the assistant organist played the Wedding March, and one of the club men insisted in pulling a cheerful and jerky peal on the church bell in the absence of the janitor, and then Van Bibber hurled an old shoe and a handful of rice—which he had thoughtfully collected from the chef at the club—after them as they drove off to the boat.

"Now," said Van Bibber, with a proud sigh of relief and satisfaction, "I will send that to the papers, and when it is printed to-morrow it will read like one of the most orthodox and one of the smartest weddings of the season. And yet I can't help thinking——"

"Well?" said Mrs. "Regy," as he paused doubtfully.

"Well, I can't help thinking," continued Van

138

Bibber, "of Standish's older brother racing around Chicago with the thermometer at 102 in the shade. I wish I had only sent him to Jersey City. It just shows," he added, mournfully, "that when a man is not practised in lying, he should leave it alone."

AN ASSISTED EMIGRANT

GUIDO stood on the curb-stone in Fourteenth
Street, between Fifth Avenue and Sixth Avenue,
with a row of plaster figures drawn up on the
sidewalk in front of him. It was snowing, and
they looked cold in consequence, especially the
Night and Morning. A line of men and boys
stretched on either side of Guido all along the
curb-stone, with toys and dolls, and guns that
shot corks into the air with a loud report, and
glittering dressings for the Christmas-trees. It
was the day before Christmas. The man who
stood next in line to Guido had hideous black
monkeys that danced from the end of a rubber
string. The man danced up and down too,
very much, so Guido thought, as the monkeys
did, and stamped his feet on the icy pavement,
and shouted: "Here yer are, lady, for five cents.
Take them home to the children." There were
hundreds and hundreds of ladies and little girls
crowding by all of the time; some of them were
a little cross and a little tired, as if Christmas
shopping had told on their nerves, but the
greater number were happy-looking and warm,
and some stopped and laughed at the monkeys

dancing on the rubber strings, and at the man with the frost on his mustache, who jumped too, and cried, "Only five cents, lady—nice Christmas presents for the children."

Sometimes the ladies bought the monkeys, but no one looked at the cold plaster figures of St. Joseph, and Diana, and Night and Morning, nor at the heads of Mars and Minerva—not even at the figure of the Virgin, with her two hands held out, which Guido pressed in his arms against his breast.

Guido had been in New York city just one month. He was very young—so young that he had never done anything at home but sit on the wharfs and watch the ships come in and out of the great harbor of Genoa. He never had wished to depart with these ships when they sailed away, nor wondered greatly as to where they went. He was content with the wharfs and with the narrow streets near by, and to look up from the bulkheads at the sailors working in the rigging, and the 'longshoremen rolling the casks on board, or lowering great square boxes into the holds.

He would have liked, could he have had his way, to live so for the rest of his life; but they would not let him have his way, and coaxed him on a ship to go to the New World to meet his uncle. He was not a real uncle, but only a make-believe one, to satisfy those who objected to assisted immigrants, and who wished to be assured against having to support Guido, and others like him. But they were not half so anxious to keep Guido at home as he himself was to stay there.

The new uncle met him at Ellis Island, and embraced him affectionately, and put him in an express wagon, and drove him with a great many more of his countrymen to where Mulberry Street makes a bend and joins Hester. And in the Bend Guido found thousands of his fellows sleeping twenty in a room and overcrowded into the street; some who had but just arrived, and others who had already learned to swear in English, and had their street-cleaning badges and their pedler's licenses, to show that they had not been overlooked by the kindly society of Tammany, which sees that no free and independent voter shall go unrewarded.

New York affected Guido like a bad dream. It was cold and muddy, and the snow when it fell turned to mud so quickly that Guido believed they were one and the same. He did not dare to think of the place he knew as home. And the sight of the colored advertisements of the steamship lines that hung in the windows of the Italian bankers hurt him as the sound of traffic on the street cuts to the heart of a prisoner in the Tombs. Many of his countrymen bade good-by to Mulberry Street and sailed away; but they had grown rich through obeying the padrones, and working night and morning sweeping the Avenue up-town, and by living on the refuse from the scows at Canal Street. Guido never hoped to grow rich, and no one stopped to buy his uncle's wares.

The electric lights came out, and still the crowd passed and thronged before him, and the snow fell and left no mark on the white figures. Guido was growing cold, and the bustle of the hurrying hundreds which had entertained him earlier in the day had ceased to interest him, and his amusement had given place to the fear that no one of them would ever stop, and that he would return to his uncle empty-handed. He was hungry now, as well as cold, and though there was not much rich food in the Bend at any time, to-day he had had nothing of any quality to eat since early morning. The man with the monkeys turned his head from time to time, and spoke to him in a language that he could not understand; although he saw that it was something amusing and well meant that the man said, and so smiled back and nodded. He felt it to be quite a loss when the man moved away.

Guido thought very slowly, but he at last

began to feel a certain contempt for the stiff statues and busts which no one wanted, and buttoned the figure of the one of the woman with her arms held out inside of his jacket, and tucked his scarf in around it, so that it might not be broken, and also that it might not bear the ignominy with the others of being over-looked. Guido was a gentle, slow-thinking boy, and could not have told you why he did this, but he knew that this figure was of different clay from the others. He had seen it placed high in the cathedrals at home, and he had been told that if you ask certain things of it it will listen to you.

The women and children began to disappear from the crowd, and the necessity of selling some of his wares impressed itself more urgently upon him as the night grew darker and possible customers fewer. He decided that he had taken up a bad position, and that instead of waiting for customers to come to him, he ought to go seek for them. With this purpose in his mind he gathered the figures together upon his tray, and, resting it upon his shoulder, moved further along the street, to Broadway, where the crowd was greater and the shops more brilliantly lighted. He had good cause to be watchful, for the sidewalks were slippery with ice, and the people rushed and hurried and brushed past him without noticing the burden he carried on one shoulder. He wished now that he knew some words of this new language, that he might call his wares and challenge the notice of the passers-by, as did the other men who shouted so continually and vehemently at the hurrying crowds. He did not know what might happen if he failed to sell one of his statues; it was a possibility so awful that he did not dare conceive of its punishment. But he could do nothing, and so stood silent, dumbly presenting his tray to the people near him.

His wanderings brought him to the corner of a street, and he started to cross it, in the hope of better fortune in untried territory. There was no need of his hurrying to do this, although a car was coming toward him, so he stepped carefully but surely. But as he reached the middle of the track a man came toward him from the opposite pavement; they met and hesitated, and then both jumped to the same side, and the man's shoulder struck the tray and threw the white figures flying to the track, where the horses tramped over them on their way. Guido fell backward, frightened and shaken, and the car stopped, and the driver and the conductor leaned out anxiously from each end.

There seemed to be hundreds of people all

around Guido, and some of them picked him up and asked him questions in a very loud voice, as though that would make the language they spoke more intelligible. Two men took him by each arm and talked with him in earnest tones, and punctuated their questions by shaking him gently. He could not answer them, but only sobbed, and beat his hands softly together, and looked about him for a chance to escape. The conductor of the car jerked the strap violently, and the car went on its way. Guido watched the conductor, as he stood with his hands in his pockets looking back at him. Guido had a confused idea that the people on the car might pay him for the plaster figures which had been scattered in the slush and snow, so that the heads and arms and legs lay on every side or were ground into heaps of white powder. But when the car disappeared into the night he gave up this hope, and pulling himself free from his captor, slipped through the crowd and ran off into a side street. A man who had seen the accident had been trying to take up a collection in the crowd, which had grown less sympathetic and less numerous in consequence, and had gathered more than the plaster casts were worth; but Guido did not know this, and when they came to look for him he was gone, and the bareheaded gentleman, with his hat full of coppers and dimes, was left in much embarrassment.

Guido walked to Washington Square, and sat down on a bench to rest, and then curled over quickly, and, stretching himself out at full length, wept bitterly. When any one passed he held his breath and pretended to be asleep. He did not know what he was to do or where he was to go. Such a calamity as this had never entered into his calculations of the evils which might overtake him, and it overwhelmed him utterly. A policeman touched him with his night-stick, and spoke to him kindly enough, but the boy only backed away from the man until he was out of his reach, and then ran on again, slipping and stumbling on the ice and snow. He ran to Christopher Street, through Greenwich Village, and on to the wharfs.

It was quite late, and he had recovered from his hunger, and only felt a sick tired ache at his heart. His feet were heavy and numb, and he was very sleepy. People passed him continually, and doors opened into churches and into noisy, glaring saloons and crowded shops, but it did not seem possible to him that there could be any relief from any source for the sorrow that had befallen him. It seemed too awful, and as impossible to mend as it would be to bring the crushed plaster into shape again. He

147

considered dully that his uncle would miss him
and wait for him, and that his anger would increase with every moment of his delay. He
felt that he could never return to his uncle again.

Then he came to another park, opening into
a square, with lighted saloons on one side, and
on the other great sheds, with ships lying beside
them, and the electric lights showing their spars
and masts against the sky. It had ceased snowing, but the air from the river was piercing and
cold, and swept through the wires overhead
with a ceaseless moaning. The numbness had
crept from his feet up over the whole extent of
his little body, and he dropped upon a flight of
steps back of a sailors' boarding-house, and
shoved his hands inside of his jacket for possible
warmth. His fingers touched the figure he had
hidden there and closed upon it lightly, and
then his head dropped back against the wall,
and he fell into a heavy sleep. The night
passed on and grew colder, and the wind came
across the ice-blocked river with shriller, sharper
blasts, but Guido did not hear it.

"Chuckey" Martin, who blacked boots in
front of the corner saloon in summer and swept
out the barroom in winter, came out through
the family entrance and dumped a pan of hot
ashes into the snow-bank, and then turned into
the house with a shiver. He saw a mass of

something lying curled up on the steps of the next house, and remembered it after he had closed the door of the family entrance behind him and shoved the pan under the stove. He decided at last that it might be one of the saloon's customers, or a stray sailor with loose change in his pockets, which he would not miss when he awoke. So he went out again, and picking Guido up, brought him in in his arms and laid him out on the floor.

There were over thirty men in the place; they had been celebrating the coming of Christmas; and three of them pushed each other out of the way in their eagerness to pour very bad brandy between Guido's teeth. "Chuckey" Martin felt a sense of proprietorship in Guido, by the right of discovery, and resented this, pushing them away, and protesting that the thing to do was to rub his feet with snow.

A fat, oily chief engineer of an Italian tramp steamer dropped on his knees beside Guido and beat the boy's hands, and with unsteady fingers tore open his scarf and jacket, and as he did this the figure of the plaster Virgin with her hands stretched out looked up at him from its bed on Guido's chest.

Some of the sailors drew their hands quickly across their breasts, and others swore in some alarm, and the barkeeper drank the glass of whiskey he had brought for Guido at a gulp, and then readjusted his apron to show that nothing had disturbed his equanimity. Guido sat up, with his head against the chief engineer's knees, and opened his eyes, and his ears were greeted with words in his own tongue. They gave him hot coffee and hot soup and more brandy, and he told his story in a burst of words that flowed like a torrent of tears—how he had been stolen from his home at Genoa, where he used to watch the boats from the stone pier in front of the custom-house, at which the sailors nodded, and how the padrone, who was not his uncle, finding he could not black boots nor sell papers, had given him these plaster casts to sell, and how he had whipped him when people would not buy them, and how at last he had tripped and broken them all except this one hidden in his breast, and how he had gone to sleep, and he asked now why had they wakened him, for he had no place to go.

Guido remembered telling them this, and following them by their gestures as they retold it to the others in a strange language, and then the lights began to spin, and the faces grew distant, and he reached out his hand for the fat chief engineer, and felt his arms tightening around him.

A cold wind woke Guido, and the sound of

something throbbing and beating like a great clock. He was very warm and tired and lazy, and when he raised his head he touched the ceiling close above him, and when he opened his eyes he found himself in a little room with a square table covered with oilcloth in the centre, and rows of beds like shelves around the walls. The room rose and fell as the streets did when he had had nothing to eat, and he scrambled out of the warm blankets and crawled fearfully up a flight of narrow stairs. There was water on either side of him, beyond and behind him—water blue and white and dancing in the sun, with great blocks of dirty ice tossing on its surface.

And behind him lay the odious city of New York, with its great bridge and high buildings, and before him the open sea. The chief engineer crawled up from the engine-room and came toward him, rubbing the perspiration from his face with a dirty towel.

"Good-morning," he called out. "You are feeling pretty well?"

"Yes."

"It is Christmas day. Do you know where you are going? You are going to Italy, to Genoa. It is over there," he said, pointing with his finger. "Go back to your bed and keep warm."

AN ASSISTED EMIGRANT

He picked Guido up in his arms, and ran with him down the companion-way, and tossed him back into his berth. Then he pointed to the shelf at one end of the little room, above the sheet-iron stove. The plaster figure that Guido had wrapped in his breast had been put there and lashed to its place.

"That will bring us good luck and a quick voyage," said the chief engineer.

Guido lay quite still until the fat engineer had climbed up the companion-way again and permitted the sunlight to once more enter the cabin. Then he crawled out of his berth and dropped on his knees, and raised up his hands to the plaster figure which no one would buy.

MY DISREPUTABLE FRIEND,
MR. RAEGEN

RAGS RAEGEN was out of his element. The water was his proper element—the water of the East River by preference. And when it came to "running the roofs," as he would have himself expressed it, he was "not in it."

On those other occasions when he had been followed by the police, he had raced them toward the river front and had dived boldly in from the wharf, leaving them staring blankly and in some alarm as to his safety. Indeed, three different men in the precinct, who did not know of young Raegen's aquatic prowess, had returned to the station-house and seriously reported him to the sergeant as lost, and regretted having driven a citizen into the river, where he had been unfortunately drowned. It was even told how, on one occasion, when hotly followed, young Raegen had dived off Wakeman's Slip, at East Thirty-third Street, and had then swum back under water to the landing-steps, while the policeman and a crowd of stevedores stood watching for him to reappear where he had sunk. It is further related that

153

he had then, in a spirit of recklessness, and in the possibility of the policeman's failing to recognize him, pushed his way through the crowd from the rear and plunged in to rescue the supposedly drowned man. And that after two or three futile attempts to find his own corpse, he had climbed up on the dock and told the officer that he had touched the body sticking in the mud. And, as a result of this fiction, the river-police dragged the river-bed around Wakeman's Slip with grappling irons for four hours, while Rags sat on the wharf and directed their movements.

But on this present occasion the police were standing between him and the river, and so cut off his escape in that direction, and as they had seen him strike McGonegal and had seen McGonegal fall, he had to run for it and seek refuge on the roofs. What made it worse was that he was not in his own hunting-grounds, but in McGonegal's, and while any tenement on Cherry Street would have given him shelter, either for love of him or fear of him, these of Thirty-third Street were against him and "all that Cherry Street gang," while "Pike" McGonegal was their darling and their hero. And, if Rags had known it, any tenement on the block was better than Case's, into which he first turned, for Case's was empty and untenanted, save in one or two rooms, and the opportunities for dodging from one to another were in consequence very few. But he could not know this, and so he plunged into the dark hallway and sprang up the first four flights of stairs, three steps at a jump, with one arm stretched out in front of him, for it was very dark and the turns were short. On the fourth floor he fell headlong over a bucket with a broom sticking in it, and cursed whoever left it there. There was a ladder leading from the sixth floor to the roof, and he ran up this and drew it after him as he fell forward out of the wooden trap that opened on the flat tin roof like a companionway of a ship. The chimneys would have hidden him, but there was a policeman's helmet coming up from another companion-way, and he saw that the Italians hanging out of the windows of the other tenements were pointing at him and showing him to the officer. So he hung by his hands and dropped back again. It was not much of a fall, but it jarred him, and the race he had already run had nearly taken his breath from him. For Rags did not live a life calculated to fit young men for sudden trials of speed.

He stumbled back down the narrow stairs, and, with a vivid recollection of the bucket he had already fallen upon, felt his way cautiously with his hands and with one foot stuck out in front of him. If he had been in his own baili-wick, he would have rather enjoyed the tense excitement of the chase than otherwise, for there he was at home and knew all the cross-cuts and where to find each broken paling in the roof-fences, and all the traps in the roofs. But here he was running in a maze, and what looked like a safe passage-way might throw him head on into the outstretched arms of the officers.

And while he felt his way his mind was ter-ribly acute to the fact that as yet no door on any of the landings had been thrown open to him, either curiously or hospitably as offering a place of refuge. He did not want to be taken, but in spite of this he was quite cool, and so, when he heard quick, heavy footsteps beating up the stairs, he stopped himself suddenly by placing one hand on the side of the wall and the other on the banister and halted, panting. He could distinguish from below the high voices of women and children and excited men in the street, and as the steps came nearer he heard some one lowering the ladder he had thrown upon the roof to the sixth floor and preparing to descend. "Ah!" snarled Raegen, panting and desperate, "youse think you have me now, sure, don't you?" It rather frightened him to find the house so silent, for, save the footsteps of the officers, descending and ascending upon him, he seemed to be the only living person in all the dark, silent building.

He did not want to fight.

He was under heavy bonds already to keep the peace, and this last had surely been in self-defense, and he felt he could prove it. What he wanted now was to get away, to get back to his own people and to lie hidden in his own cellar or garret, where they would feed and guard him until the trouble was over. And still, like the two ends of a vise, the representatives of the law were closing in upon him. He turned the knob of the door opening to the landing on which he stood, and tried to push it in, but it was locked. Then he stepped quickly to the door on the opposite side and threw his shoulder against it. The door opened, and he stumbled forward sprawling. The room in which he had taken refuge was almost bare, and very dark; but in a little room leading from it he saw a pile of tossed-up bedding on the floor, and he dived at this as though it was water, and crawled far under it until he reached the wall beyond, squirming on his face and stomach, and flattening out his arms and legs. Then he lay motionless, holding back his breath, and listening to the beating of his heart and to

the footsteps on the stairs. The footsteps
stopped on the landing leading to the outer
room, and he could hear the murmur of voices
as the two men questioned one another. Then
the door was kicked open, and there was a long
silence, broken sharply by the click of a revolver.

"Maybe he's in there," said a bass voice.
The men stamped across the floor leading into
the dark room in which he lay, and halted at
the entrance. They did not stand there over a
moment before they turned and moved away
again; but to Raegen, lying with blood-vessels
choked, and with his hand pressed across his
mouth, it seemed as if they had been contem-
plating and enjoying his agony for over an
hour. "I was in this place not more than
twelve hours ago," said one of them easily. "I
come in to take a couple out for fighting. They
were yelling 'murder' and 'police,' and breaking things; but they went quiet enough. The
man is a stevedore, I guess, and him and his
wife used to get drunk regular and carry on
up here every night or so. They got thirty days
on the Island."

"Who's taking care of the rooms?" asked the
bass voice. The first voice said he guessed "no
one was," and added: "There ain't much to
take care of, that I can see." "That's so,"
assented the bass voice. "Well," he went on

briskly, "he's not here; but he's in the building, sure, for he put back when he seen me coming over the roof. And he didn't pass me, neither, I know that, anyway," protested the bass voice. Then the bass voice said that he must have slipped into the flat below, and added something that Raegen could not hear distinctly, about Schaffer on the roof, and their having him safe enough, as that red-headed cop from the Eighteenth Precinct was watching on the street. They closed the door behind them, and their footsteps clattered down the stairs, leaving the big house silent and apparently deserted. Young Raegen raised his head, and let his breath escape with a great gasp of relief, as when he had been a long time under water, and cautiously rubbed the perspiration out of his eyes and from his forehead. It had been a cruelly hot, close afternoon, and the stifling burial under the heavy bedding, and the excitement, had left him feverishly hot and trembling. It was already growing dark outside, although he could not know that until he lifted the quilts an inch or two and peered up at the dirty window-panes. He was afraid to rise, as yet, and flattened himself out with an impatient sigh, as he gathered the bedding over his head again and held back his breath to listen. There may have been a minute or more of absolute silence in which he lay there, and then his blood froze to ice in his veins, his breath stopped, and he heard, with a quick gasp of terror, the sound of something crawling toward him across the floor of the outer room. The instinct of self-defense moved him first to leap to his feet, and to face and fight it, and then followed as quickly a foolish sense of safety in his hiding-place; and he called upon his greatest strength, and, by his mere brute will alone, forced his forehead down to the bare floor and lay rigid, though his nerves jerked with unknown, un-reasoning fear. And still he heard the sound of this living thing coming creeping toward him until the instinctive terror that shook him over-came his will, and he threw the bed-clothes from him with a hoarse cry, and sprang up trembling to his feet, with his back against the wall, and with his arms thrown out in front of him wildly, and with the willingness in them and the power in them to do murder.

The room was very dark, but the windows of the one beyond let in a little stream of light across the floor, and in this light he saw mov-ing toward him on its hands and knees a little baby who smiled and nodded at him with a pleased look of recognition and kindly welcome.

The fear upon Raegen had been so strong and the reaction was so great that he dropped to a

He sprang up trembling to his feet.

sitting posture on the heap of bedding and laughed long and weakly, and still with a feeling in his heart that this apparition was something strangely unreal and menacing.

But the baby seemed well pleased with his laughter, and stopped to throw back its head and smile and coo and laugh gently with him, as though the joke was a very good one which they shared in common. Then it struggled solemnly to its feet and came pattering toward him on a run, with both bare arms held out, and with a look of such confidence in him, and welcome in its face, that Raegen stretched out his arms and closed the baby's fingers fearfully and gently in his own.

He had never seen so beautiful a child. There was dirt enough on its hands and face, and its torn dress was soiled with streaks of coal and ashes. The dust of the floor had rubbed into its bare knees, but the face was like no other face that Rags had ever seen. And then it looked at him as though it trusted him, and just as though they had known each other at some time long before, but the eyes of the baby somehow seemed to hurt him so that he had to turn his face away, and when he looked again it was with a strangely new feeling of dissatisfaction with himself and of wishing to ask pardon. They were wonderful eyes, black and rich, and with a deep superiority of knowledge in them, a knowledge that seemed to be above the knowledge of evil; and when the baby smiled at him, the eyes smiled too with confidence and tenderness in them that in some way frightened Rags and made him move uncomfortably. "Did you know that youse scared me so that I was going to kill you?" whispered Rags, apologetically, as he carefully held the baby from him at arm's length. "Did you?" But the baby only smiled at this and reached out its hand and stroked Rags's cheek with its fingers. There was something so wonderfully soft and sweet in this that Rags drew the baby nearer and gave a quick, strange gasp of pleasure as it threw its arms around his neck and brought the face up close to his chin and hugged him tightly. The baby's arms were very soft and plump, and its cheek and tangled hair were warm and moist with perspiration, and the breath that fell on Raegen's face was sweeter than anything he had ever known. He felt wonderfully and for some reason uncomfortably happy, but the silence was oppressive.

"What's your name, little 'un?" said Rags.

The baby ran its arms more closely around Raegen's neck and did not speak, unless its cooing in Raegen's ear was an answer. "What did you say your name was?" persisted Raegen, in a whisper. The baby frowned at this and stopped cooing long enough to say: "Marg'ret," mechanically and without apparently associating the name with herself or anything else. "Margaret, eh!" said Raegen, with grave consideration. "It's a very pretty name," he added, politely, for he could not shake off the feeling that he was in the presence of a superior being. "An' what did you say your dad's name was?" asked Raegen, awkwardly. But this was beyond the baby's patience or knowledge, and she waived the question aside with both arms and began to beat a tattoo gently with her two closed fists on Raegen's chin and throat. "You're mighty strong now, ain't you?" mocked the young giant, laughing. "Perhaps you don't know, Missie," he added, gravely, "that your dad and mar are doing time on the Island, and you won't see 'em again for a month." No, the baby did not know this nor care apparently; she seemed content with Rags and with his company. Sometimes she drew away and looked at him long and dubiously, and this cut Rags to the heart, and he felt guilty, and unreasonably anxious until she smiled reassuringly again and ran back into his arms, nestling her face against his and stroking his rough chin wonderingly with her little fingers.

MR. RAEGEN

Rags forgot the lateness of the night and the darkness that fell upon the room in the interest of this strange entertainment, which was so much more absorbing, and so much more innocent than any other he had ever known. He almost forgot the fact that he lay in hiding, that he was surrounded by unfriendly neighbors, and that at any moment the representatives of local justice might come in and rudely lead him away. For this reason he dared not make a light, but he moved his position so that the glare from an electric lamp on the street outside might fall across the baby's face, as it lay alternately dozing and awakening, to smile up at him in the bend of his arm. Once it reached inside the collar of his shirt and pulled out the scapular that hung around his neck, and looked at it so long, and with such apparent seriousness, that Rags was confirmed in his fear that this kindly visitor was something more or less of a superhuman agent, and his efforts to make this supposition coincide with the fact that the angel's parents were on Blackwell's Island, proved one of the severest struggles his mind had ever experienced. He had forgotten to feel hungry, and the knowledge that he was acutely so, first came to him with the thought that the baby must obviously be in greatest need of food herself. This pained him greatly, and he laid his burden down upon the bedding, and after slipping off his shoes, tiptoed his way across the room on a foraging expedition after something she could eat. There was a half of a ham-bone, and a half loaf of hard bread in a cupboard, and on the table he found a bottle quite filled with wretched whiskey. That the police had failed to see the baby had not appealed to him in any way, but that they should have allowed this last find to remain unnoticed pleased him intensely, not because it now fell to him, but because they had been cheated of it. It really struck him as so humorous that he stood laughing silently for several minutes, slapping his thigh with every outward exhibition of the keenest mirth. But when he found that the room and cupboard were bare of anything else that might be eaten he sobered suddenly. It was very hot, and though the windows were open, the perspiration stood upon his face, and the foul close air that rose from the court and street below made him gasp and pant for breath. He dipped a wash rag in the water from the spigot in the hall, and filled a cup with it and bathed the baby's face and wrists. She woke and sipped up the water from the cup eagerly, and then looked up at him, as if to ask for something more. Rags soaked the crusty bread in the water, and put

it to the baby's lips, but after nibbling at it
eagerly she shook her head and looked up at
him again with such reproachful pleading in her
eyes, that Rags felt her silence more keenly
than the worst abuse he had ever received.

It hurt him so, that the pain brought tears
to his eyes.

"Deary girl," he cried, "I'd give you anything you could think of if I had it. But I
can't get it, see? It ain't that I don't want to
—good Lord, little 'un, you don't think that, do
you?"

The baby smiled at this, just as though she
understood him, and touched his face as if to
comfort him, so that Rags felt that same ex-
quisite content again, which moved him so
strangely whenever the child caressed him, and
which left him soberly wondering. Then the
baby crawled up onto his lap and dropped
asleep, while Rags sat motionless and fanned
her with a folded newspaper, stopping every
now and then to pass the damp cloth over her
warm face and arms. It was quite late now.
Outside he could hear the neighbors laughing
and talking on the roofs, and when one group
sang hilariously to an accordion, he cursed them
under his breath for noisy, drunken fools, and
in his anger lest they should disturb the child
in his arms, expressed an anxious hope that

they would fall off and break their useless necks. It grew silent and much cooler as the night ran out, but Rags still sat immovable, shivering slightly every now and then, and cautiously stretching his stiff legs and body. The arm that held the child grew stiff and numb with the light burden, but he took a fierce pleasure in the pain, and became hardened to it, and at last fell into an uneasy slumber from which he awoke to pass his hands gently over the soft yielding body, and to draw it slowly and closer to him. And then, from very weariness, his eyes closed and his head fell back heavily against the wall, and the man and the child in his arms slept peacefully in the dark corner of the deserted tenement.

The sun rose hissing out of the East River, a broad, red disk of heat. It swept the cross-streets of the city as pitilessly as the search-light of a man-of-war sweeps the ocean. It blazed brazenly into open windows, and changed beds into gridirons on which the sleepers tossed and turned and woke unrefreshed and with throats dry and parched. Its glare awakened Rags into a startled belief that the place about him was on fire, and he stared wildly until the child in his arms brought him back to the knowledge of where he was. He ached in every joint and limb, and his eyes smarted with the dry heat, but the baby concerned him most, for she was breathing with hard, long, irregular gasps, her mouth was open and her absurdly small fists were clinched, and around her closed eyes were deep blue rings. Rags felt a cold rush of fear and uncertainty come over him as he stared about him helplessly for aid. He had seen babies look like this before, in the tenements; they were like this when the young doctors of the Health Board climbed to the roofs to see them, and they were like this, only quiet and still, when the ambulance came clattering up the narrow streets, and bore them away. Rags carried the baby into the outer room, where the sun had not yet penetrated, and laid her down gently on the coverlets; then he let the water in the sink run until it was fairly cool, and with this bathed the baby's face and hands and feet, and lifted a cup of the water to her open lips. She woke at this and smiled again, but very faintly, and when she looked at him he felt fearfully sure that she did not know him, and that she was looking through and past him at something he could not see.

He did not know what to do, and he wanted to do so much. Milk was the only thing he was quite sure babies cared for, but in want of this he made a mess of bits of the dry ham and crumbs of bread, moistened with the raw whiskey, and put it to her lips on the end of a spoon. The baby tasted this, and pushed his hand away, and then looked up and gave a feeble cry, and seemed to say, as plainly as a grown woman could have said or written, "It isn't any use, Rags. You are very good to me, but, indeed, I cannot do it. Don't worry, please; I don't blame you."

"Great Lord," gasped Rags, with a queer choking in his throat, "but ain't she got grit." Then he bethought him of the people who he still believed inhabited the rest of the tenement, and he concluded that as the day was yet so early they might still be asleep, and that while they slept, he could "lift"—as he mentally described the act—whatever they might have laid away for breakfast. Excited with this hope, he ran noiselessly down the stairs in his bare feet, and tried the doors of the different landings. But each he found open and each room bare and deserted. Then it occurred to him that at this hour he might even risk a sally into the street. He had money with him, and the milk-carts and bakers' wagons must be passing every minute. He ran back to get the money out of his coat, delighted with the chance and chiding himself for not having dared to do it sooner. He stood over the baby a moment before he left the room, and flushed like a girl

as he stooped and kissed one of the bare arms.
"I'm going out to get you some breakfast," he
said. "I won't be gone long, but if I should,"
he added, as he paused and shrugged his shoulders, "I'll send the sergeant after you from the
station-house. If I only wasn't under bonds,"
he muttered, as he slipped down the stairs.
"If it wasn't for that they couldn't give me
more'n a month at the most, even knowing all
they do of me. It was only a street fight, anyway, and there was some there that must have
seen him pull his pistol." He stopped at the
top of the first flight of stairs and sat down to
wait. He could see below the top of the open
front door, the pavement and a part of the
street beyond, and when he heard the rattle of
an approaching cart he ran on down and then,
with an oath, turned and broke up-stairs again.
He had seen the ward detectives standing together on the opposite side of the street.

"Wot are they doing out a bed at this hour?"
he demanded angrily. "Don't they make trouble enough through the day, without prowling
around before decent people are up? I wonder, now, if they're after me." He dropped on
his knees when he reached the room where the
baby lay, and peered cautiously out of the window at the detectives, who had been joined by
two other men, with whom they were talking

earnestly. Raegen knew the new-comers for two of McGonegal's friends, and concluded, with a momentary flush of pride and self-importance, that the detectives were forced to be up at this early hour solely on his account. But this was followed by the afterthought that he must have hurt McGonegal seriously, and that he was wanted in consequence very much. This disturbed him most, he was surprised to find, because it precluded his going forth in search of food. "I guess I can't get you that milk I was looking for," he said, jocularly, to the baby, for the excitement elated him. "The sun outside isn't good for me health." The baby settled herself in his arms and slept again, which sobered Rags, for he argued it was a bad sign, and his own ravenous appetite warned him how the child suffered. When he again offered her the mixture he had prepared for her, she took it eagerly, and Rags breathed a sigh of satisfaction. Then he ate some of the bread and ham himself and swallowed half the whiskey, and stretched out beside the child and fanned her while she slept. It was something strangely incomprehensible to Rags that he should feel so keen a satisfaction in doing even this little for her, but he gave up wondering, and forgot everything else in watching the strange beauty of the sleeping baby and in the

171

odd feeling of responsibility and self-respect she had brought to him.

He did not feel it coming on, or he would have fought against it, but the heat of the day and the sleeplessness of the night before, and the fumes of the whiskey on his empty stomach, drew him unconsciously into a dull stupor, so that the paper fan slipped from his hand, and he sank back on the bedding into a heavy sleep. When he awoke it was nearly dusk and past six o'clock, as he knew by the newsboys calling the sporting extras on the street below. He sprang up, cursing himself, and filled with bitter remorse.

"I'm a drunken fool, that's what I am," said Rags, savagely. "I've let her lie here all day in the heat with no one to watch her." Margaret was breathing so softly that he could hardly discern any life at all, and his heart almost stopped with fear. He picked her up and fanned and patted her into wakefulness again and then turned desperately to the window and looked down. There was no one he knew or who knew him as far as he could tell on the street, and he determined recklessly to risk another sortie for food.

"Why, it's been near two days that child's gone without eating," he said, with keen self-reproach, "and here you've let her suffer to save yourself a trip to the Island. You're a hulking big loafer, you are," he ran on, muttering, "and after her coming to you and taking notice of you and putting her face to yours like an angel." He slipped off his shoes and picked his way cautiously down the stairs.

As he reached the top of the first flight a newsboy passed, calling the evening papers, and shouted something which Rags could not distinguish. He wished he could get a copy of the paper. It might tell him, he thought, something about himself. The boy was coming nearer, and Rags stopped and leaned forward to listen.

"Extry! Extry!" shouted the newsboy, running. "*Sun, World,* and *Mail.* Full account of the murder of Pike McGonegal by Ragsey Raegen."

The lights in the street seemed to flash up suddenly and grow dim again, leaving Rags blind and dizzy.

"Stop," he yelled, "stop. Murdered, no, by God, no," he cried, staggering half-way down the stairs; "stop, stop!" But no one heard Rags, and the sound of his own voice halted him. He sank back weak and sick upon the top step of the stairs and beat his hands together upon his head.

"It's a lie, it's a lie," he whispered, thickly.

173

"I struck him in self-defense, s'help me. I struck him in self-defense. He drove me to it. He pulled his gun on me. I done it in self-defense."

And then the whole appearance of the young tough changed, and the terror and horror that had showed on his face turned to one of low sharpness and evil cunning. His lips drew together tightly and he breathed quickly through his nostrils, while his fingers locked and unlocked around his knees. All that he had learned on the streets and wharfs and roof-tops, all that pitiable experience and dangerous knowledge that had made him a leader and a hero among the thieves and bullies of the river-front he called to his assistance now. He faced the fact flatly and with the cool consideration of an uninterested counsellor. He knew that the history of his life was written on Police Court blotters from the day that he was ten years old, and with pitiless detail; that what friends he had he held more by fear than by affection, and that his enemies, who were many, only wanted just such a chance as this to revenge injuries long suffered and bitterly cherished, and that his only safety lay in secret and instant flight. The ferries were watched, of course; he knew that the depots, too, were covered by the men whose only duty was to watch the coming and to halt the departing criminal. But he knew of one old man who was too wise to ask questions and who would row him over the East River to Astoria, and of another on the west side whose boat was always at the disposal of silent white-faced young men who might come at any hour of the night or morning, and whom he would pilot across to the Jersey shore and keep well away from the lights of the passing ferries and the green lamp of the police boat. And once across, he had only to change his name and write for money to be forwarded to that name, and turn to work until the thing was covered up and forgotten. He rose to his feet in his full strength again, and intensely and agreeably excited with the danger, and possibly fatal termination of his adventure, and then there fell upon him, with the suddenness of a blow, the remembrance of the little child lying on the dirty bedding in the room above.

"I can't do it," he muttered fiercely; "I can't do it," he cried, as if he argued with some other presence. "There's a rope around me neck, and the chances are all against me; it's every man for himself and no favor." He threw his arms out before him as if to push the thought away from him and ran his fingers through his hair and over his face. All of his old self rose in him and mocked him for a weak fool, and showed him just how great his personal danger was, and so he turned and dashed forward on a run, not only to the street, but as if to escape from the other self that held him back. He was still without his shoes, and in his bare feet, and he stopped as he noticed this and turned to go up-stairs for them, and then he pictured to himself the baby lying as he had left her, weakly unconscious and with dark rims around her eyes, and he asked himself excitedly what he would do, if, on his return, she should wake and smile and reach out her hands to him.

"I don't dare go back," he said, breathlessly. "I don't dare do it; killing's too good for the likes of Pike McGonegal, but I'm not fighting babies. An' maybe, if I went back, maybe I wouldn't have the nerve to leave her; I can't do it," he muttered, "I don't dare go back." But still he did not stir, but stood motionless, with one hand trembling on the stair-rail and the other clinched beside him, and so fought it on alone in the silence of the empty building.

The lights in the stores below came out one by one, and the minutes passed into half-hours, and still he stood there with the noise of the streets coming up to him below speaking of escape and of a long life of ill-regulated pleasures, and up above him the baby lay in the darkness and reached out her hands to him in her sleep.

The surly old sergeant of the Twenty-first Precinct station-house had read the evening papers through for the third time and was dozing in the fierce lights of the gas-jet over the high desk when a young man with a white, haggard face came in from the street with a baby in his arms.

"I want to see the woman thet look after the station-house—quick," he said.

The surly old sergeant did not like the peremptory tone of the young man nor his general appearance, for he had no hat, nor coat, and his feet were bare; so he said, with deliberate dignity, that the char-woman was up-stairs lying down, and what did the young man want with her? "This child," said the visitor, in a queer thick voice, "she's sick. The heat's come over her, and she ain't had anything to eat for two days, an' she's starving. Ring the bell for the matron, will yer, and send one of your men around for the house surgeon." The sergeant leaned forward comfortably on his elbows, with his hands under his chin so that the gold lace on his cuffs shone effectively in the gas-light. He believed he had a sense of humor and he chose this unfortunate moment to exhibit it.

"Did you take this for a dispensary, young man?" he asked; "or," he continued, with added facetiousness, "a foundling hospital?"

The young man made a savage spring at the barrier in front of the high desk. "Damn you," he panted, "ring that bell, do you hear me, or I'll pull you off that seat and twist your heart out."

The baby cried at this sudden outburst, and Rags fell back, patting it with his hand and muttering between his closed teeth. The sergeant called to the men of the reserve squad in the reading-room beyond, and to humor this desperate visitor, sounded the gong for the janitress. The reserve squad trooped in leisurely with the playing-cards in their hands and with their pipes in their mouths.

"This man," growled the sergeant, pointing with the end of his cigar to Rags, "is either drunk, or crazy, or a bit of both."

The char-woman came down-stairs majestically, in a long, loose wrapper, fanning herself with a palm-leaf fan, but when she saw the child, her majesty dropped from her like a cloak, and she ran toward her and caught the baby up in her arms. "You poor little thing," she murmured, "and, oh, how beautiful!" Then she whirled about on the men of the reserve squad: "You, Conners," she said, "run up to my room and get the milk out of my ice-chest; and, Moore, put on your coat and go around and tell the surgeon I want to see him. And one of you crack some ice up fine in a towel. Take it out of the cooler. Quick, now."

Raegen came up to her fearfully. "Is she very sick?" he begged; "she ain't going to die, is she?"

"Of course not," said the woman, promptly, "but she's down with the heat, and she hasn't been properly cared for; the child looks half-starved. Are you her father?" she asked, sharply. But Rags did not speak, for at the moment she had answered his question and had said the baby would not die, he had reached out swiftly, and taken the child out of her arms and held it hard against his breast, as though he had lost her and some one had been just giving her back to him.

His head was bending over hers, and so he did not see Wade and Heffner, the two ward detectives, as they came in from the street, looking hot, and tired, and anxious. They gave a careless glance at the group, and then stopped with a start, and one of them gave a long, low whistle.

"Well," exclaimed Wade, with a gasp of surprise and relief. "So, Raegen, you're here, after all, are you? Well, you did give us a chase, you did. Who took you?"

The men of the reserve squad, when they heard the name of the man for whom the whole force had been looking for the past two days, shifted their positions slightly, and looked curiously at Rags, and the woman stopped pouring out the milk from the bottle in her hand, and stared at him in frank astonishment. Raegen threw back his head and shoulders, and ran his eyes coldly over the faces of the semicircle of men around him.

"Who took me?" he began, defiantly, with a swagger of braggadocio, and then, as though it were hardly worth while, and as though the presence of the baby lifted him above everything else, he stopped, and raised her until her cheek touched his own. It rested there a moment, while Rags stood silent.

"Who took me?" he repeated, quietly, and without lifting his eyes from the baby's face. "Nobody took me," he said. "I gave myself up."

One morning, three months later, when Raegen had stopped his ice-cart in front of my door, I asked him whether at any time he had ever regretted what he had done.

"She'd reach out her hands and kiss me."

MR. RAEGEN

"Well, sir," he said, with easy superiority, "seeing that I've shook the gang, and that the Society's decided her folks ain't fit to take care of her, we can't help thinking we are better off, see?

"But, as for my ever regretting it, why, even when things was at the worst, when the case was going dead against me, and before that cop, you remember, swore to McGonegal's drawing the pistol, and when I used to sit in the Tombs expecting I'd have to hang for it, well, even then, they used to bring her to see me every day, and when they'd lift her up, and she'd reach out her hands and kiss me through the bars, why—they could have took me out and hung me, and been damned to 'em, for all I'd have cared."

A WALK UP THE AVENUE

HE came down the steps slowly, and pulling mechanically at his gloves.

He remembered afterward that some woman's face had nodded brightly to him from a passing brougham, and that he had lifted his hat through force of habit, and without knowing who she was.

He stopped at the bottom of the steps, and stood for a moment uncertainly, and then turned toward the north, not because he had any definite goal in his mind, but because the other way led toward his rooms, and he did not want to go there yet.

He was conscious of a strange feeling of elation, which he attributed to his being free, and to the fact that he was his own master again in everything. And with this he confessed to a distinct feeling of littleness, of having acted meanly or unworthily of himself or of her.

And yet he had behaved well, even quixotically. He had tried to leave the impression with her that it was her wish, and that she had broken with him, not he with her.

He held a man who threw a girl over as some-

182

thing contemptible, and he certainly did not want to appear to himself in that light; or, for her sake, that people should think he had tired of her, or found her wanting in any one particular. He knew only too well how people would talk. How they would say he had never really cared for her; that he didn't know his own mind when he had proposed to her; and that it was a great deal better for her as it is than if he had grown out of humor with her later. As to their saying she had jilted him, he didn't mind that. He much preferred they should take that view of it, and he was chivalrous enough to hope she would think so too.

He was walking slowly, and had reached Thirtieth Street. A great many young girls and women had bowed to him or nodded from the passing carriages, but it did not tend to disturb the measure of his thoughts. He was used to having people put themselves out to speak to him; everybody made a point of knowing him, not because he was so very handsome and well-looking, and an over-popular youth, but because he was as yet unspoiled by it.

But, in any event, he concluded, it was a miserable business. Still, he had only done what was right. He had seen it coming on for a month now, and how much better it was that they should separate now than later, or that they should have had to live separated in all but location for the rest of their lives! Yes, he had done the right thing—decidedly the only thing to do.

He was still walking up the Avenue, and had reached Thirty-second Street, at which point his thoughts received a sudden turn. A half-dozen men in a club window nodded to him, and brought to him sharply what he was going back to. He had dropped out of their lives as entirely of late as though he had been living in a distant city. When he had met them he had found their company uninteresting and unprofitable. He had wondered how he had ever cared for that sort of thing, and where had been the pleasure of it. Was he going back now to the gossip of that window, to the heavy discussions of traps and horses, to late breakfasts and early suppers? Must he listen to their congratulations on his being one of them again, and must he guess at their whispered conjectures as to how soon it would be before he again took up the chains and harness of their fashion? He struck the pavement sharply with his stick. No, he was not going back.

She had taught him to find amusement and occupation in many things that were better and higher than any pleasures or pursuits he had known before, and he could not give them up.

A WALK UP THE AVENUE

He had her to thank for that at least. And he would give her credit for it, too, and gratefully. He would always remember it, and he would show in his way of living the influence and the good effects of these three months in which they had been continually together.

He had reached Forty-second Street now.

Well, it was over with, and he would get to work at something or other. This experience had shown him that he was not meant for marriage; that he was intended to live alone. Because, if he found that a girl as lovely as she undeniably was palled on him after three months, it was evident that he would never live through life with any other one. Yes, he would always be a bachelor. He had lived his life, had told his story at the age of twenty-five, and would wait patiently for the end, a marked and gloomy man. He would travel now and see the world. He would go to that hotel in Cairo she was always talking about, where they were to have gone on their honeymoon; or he might strike further into Africa, and come back bronzed and worn with long marches and jungle fever, and with his hair prematurely white. He even considered himself, with great self-pity, returning and finding her married and happy, of course. And he enjoyed, in anticipation, the secret doubts she would have of her later choice when she heard on all sides praise of this distinguished traveller.

And he pictured himself meeting her reproachful glances with fatherly friendliness, and presenting her husband with tiger-skins, and buying her children extravagant presents.

This was at Forty-fifth Street.

Yes, that was decidedly the best thing to do. To go away and improve himself, and study up all those painters and cathedrals with which she was so hopelessly conversant.

He remembered how out of it she had once made him feel, and how secretly he had admired her when she had referred to a modern painting as looking like those in the long gallery of the Louvre. He thought he knew all about the Louvre, but he would go over again and locate that long gallery, and become able to talk to her understandingly about it.

And then it came over him like a blast of icy air that he could never talk over things with her again. He had reached Fifty-fifth Street now, and the shock brought him to a standstill on the corner, where he stood gazing blankly before him. He felt rather weak physically, and decided to go back to his rooms, and then he pictured how cheerless they would look, and how little of comfort they contained. He had used them only to dress and sleep in of late, and the distaste with which he regarded the idea that he must go back to them to read and sit and live in them, showed him how utterly his life had become bound up with the house on Twenty-seventh Street.

"Where was he to go in the evening?" he asked himself, with pathetic hopelessness, "or in the morning or afternoon for that matter?" Were there to be no more of those journeys to picture-galleries and to the big publishing houses, where they used to hover over the new book counter and pull the books about, and make each other innumerable presents of daintily bound volumes, until the clerks grew to know them so well that they never went through the form of asking where the books were to be sent? And those tête-à-tête luncheons at her house when her mother was up-stairs with a headache or a dressmaker, and the long rides and walks in the Park in the afternoon, and the rush down-town to dress, only to return to dine with them, ten minutes late always, and always with some new excuse, which was allowed if it was clever, and frowned at if it was commonplace—was all this really over?

Why, the town had only run on because she was in it, and as he walked the streets the very shop windows had suggested her to him—florists only existed that he might send her

flowers, and gowns and bonnets in the milliners'
windows were only pretty as they would become
her; and as for the theatres and the newspapers,
they were only worth while as they gave her
pleasure. And he had given all this up, and for
what, he asked himself, and why?

He could not answer that now. It was simply because he had been surfeited with too
much content, he replied, passionately. He had
not appreciated how happy he had been. She
had been too kind, too gracious. He had never
known until he had quarrelled with her and
lost her how precious and dear she had been
to him.

He was at the entrance to the Park now, and
he strode on along the walk, bitterly upbraiding
himself for being worse than a criminal—a fool,
a common blind mortal to whom a goddess had
stooped.

He remembered with bitter regret a turn off
the drive into which they had wandered one
day, a secluded, pretty spot with a circle of box
around it, and into the turf of which he had
driven his stick, and claimed it for them both
by the right of discovery. And he recalled how
they had used to go there, just out of sight of
their friends in the ride, and sit and chatter on
a green bench beneath a bush of box, like any
nursery maid and her young man, while her

groom stood at the brougham door in the bridle-path beyond. He had broken off a sprig of the box one day and given it to her, and she had kissed it foolishly, and laughed, and hidden it in the folds of her riding-skirt, in burlesque fear lest the guards should arrest them for breaking the much-advertised ordinance.

And he remembered with a miserable smile how she had delighted him with her account of her adventure to her mother, and described them as fleeing down the Avenue with their treasure, pursued by a squadron of mounted policemen.

This and a hundred other of the foolish, happy fancies they had shared in common came back to him, and he remembered how she had stopped one cold afternoon just outside of this favorite spot, beside an open iron grating sunk in the path, into which the rain had washed the autumn leaves, and pretended it was a steam radiator, and held her slim gloved hands out over it as if to warm them.

How absurdly happy she used to make him, and how light-hearted she had been! He determined suddenly and sentimentally to go to that secret place now, and bury the engagement ring she had handed back to him under that bush as he had buried his hopes of happiness, and he pictured how some day when he was

dead she would read of this in his will, and go
and dig up the ring, and remember and forgive
him. He struck off from the walk across the
turf straight toward this dell, taking the ring
from his waistcoat pocket and clinching it in
his hand. He was walking quickly with rapt
interest in this idea of abnegation when he
noticed, unconsciously at first and then with
a start, the familiar outlines and colors of her
brougham drawn up in the drive not twenty
yards from their old meeting-place. He could
not be mistaken; he knew the horses well
enough, and there was old Wallis on the box
and young Wallis on the path.

He stopped breathlessly, and then tipped on
cautiously, keeping the encircling line of bushes
between him and the carriage. And then he
saw through the leaves that there was some
one in the place, and that it was she. He
stopped, confused and amazed. He could not
comprehend it. She must have driven to the
place immediately on his departure. But why?
And why to that place of all others?

He parted the bushes with his hands, and
saw her lovely and sweet-looking as she had
always been, standing under the box bush beside the bench, and breaking off one of the
green branches. The branch parted and the
stem flew back to its place again, leaving a

green sprig in her hand. She turned at that moment directly toward him, and he could see from his hiding-place how she lifted the leaves to her lips, and that a tear was creeping down her cheek.

Then he dashed the bushes aside with both arms, and with a cry that no one but she heard sprang toward her.

Young Van Bibber stopped his mail phaeton in front of the club, and went inside to recuperate, and told how he had seen them driving home through the Park in her brougham and unchaperoned.

"Which I call very bad form," said the punctilious Van Bibber, "even though they are engaged."

CINDERELLA

THE servants of the Hotel Salisbury, which is so called because it is situated on Broadway and conducted on the American plan by a man named Riggs, had agreed upon a date for their annual ball and volunteer concert, and had announced that it would eclipse every other annual ball in the history of the hotel. As the Hotel Salisbury had been only two years in existence, this was not an idle boast, and it had the effect of inducing many people to buy the tickets, which sold at a dollar apiece, and were good for "one gent and a lady," and entitled the bearer to a hat-check without extra charge.

In the flutter of preparation all ranks were temporarily levelled, and social barriers taken down with the mutual consent of those separated by them; the night-clerk so far unbent as to personally request the colored hall-boy Number Eight to play a banjo-solo at the concert, which was to fill in the pauses between the dances, and the chamber-maids timidly consulted with the lady telegraph-operator and the lady in charge of the telephone, as to whether or not they intended to wear hats.

CINDERELLA

And so every employee on every floor of the hotel was working individually for the success of the ball, from the engineers in charge of the electric-light plant in the cellar to the night-watchman on the ninth story, and the elevator-boys, who belonged to no floor in particular.

Miss Celestine Terrell, who was Mrs. Grahame West in private life, and young Grahame West, who played the part opposite to hers in the Gilbert and Sullivan Opera that was then in the third month of its New York run, were among the honored patrons of the Hotel Salisbury. Miss Terrell, in her utter inability to adjust the American coinage to English standards, and also in the kindness of her heart, had given too generous tips to all of the hotel waiters, and some of this money had passed into the gallery window of the Broadway Theatre, where the hotel waiters had heard her sing and seen her dance, and had failed to recognize her young husband in the Lord Chancellor's wig and black silk court-dress. So they knew that she was a celebrated personage, and they urged the *maître d'hôtel* to invite her to the ball, and then persuade her to take a part in their volunteer concert.

Paul, the head-waiter, or "Pierrot," as Grahame West called him, because it was shorter, as he explained, hovered over the two young

English people one night at supper, and served them lavishly with his own hands.

"Miss Terrell," said Paul, nervously—"I beg pardon, Madam, Mrs. Grahame West, I should say—I would like to make an invitation to you."

Celestine looked at her husband inquiringly, and bowed her head for Paul to continue.

"The employees of the Salisbury give the annual ball and concert on the sixteenth of December, and the committee have inquired and requested of me, on account of your kindness, to ask you would you be so polite as to sing a little song for us at the night of our ball?"

The head-waiter drew a long breath and straightened himself with a sense of relief at having done his part, whether the Grahame Wests did theirs or not.

As a rule, Miss Terrell did not sing in private, and had only broken this rule twice, when the inducements which led her to do so were forty pounds for each performance, and the fact that her beloved Princess of Wales was to be present. So she hesitated for an instant.

"Why, you are very good," she said, doubtfully. "Will there be any other people there— any one not an employee, I mean?"

Paul misunderstood her and became a servant again.

"No, I am afraid there will be only the employees, Madam," he said.

"Oh, then, I should be very glad to come," murmured Celestine, sweetly. "But I never sing out of the theatre, so you mustn't mind if it is not good."

The head-waiter played a violent tattoo on the back of the chair in his delight, and balanced and bowed.

"Ah, we are very proud and pleased that we can induce Madam to make so great exceptions," he declared. "The committee will be most happy. We will send a carriage for Madam, and a bouquet for Madam also," he added, grandly, as one who was not to be denied the etiquette to which he plainly showed he was used.

"Will we come?" cried Van Bibber, incredulously, as he and Travers sat watching Grahame make up in his dressing-room. "I should say we would come. And you must all take supper with us first, and we will get Letty Chamberlain from the Gaiety Company and Lester to come, too, and make them each do a turn."

"And we can dance on the floor ourselves, can't we?" asked Grahame West, "as they do at home Christmas-eve in the servants' hall, when her ladyship dances in the same set with the butler, and the men waltz with the cook."

"Well, over here," said Van Bibber, "you'll have to be careful that you're properly presented to the cook first, or she'll appeal to the floor committee and have you thrown out."

"The interesting thing about that ball," said Travers, as he and Van Bibber walked home that night, "is the fact that those hotel people are getting a galaxy of stars to amuse them for nothing who wouldn't exhibit themselves at a Fifth Avenue dance for all the money in Wall Street. And the joke of it is going to be that the servants will vastly prefer the banjo-solo by hall-boy Number Eight."

Lyric Hall lies just this side of the Forty-second Street station along the line of the Sixth Avenue Elevated road, and you can look into its windows from the passing train. It was after one o'clock when the invited guests and their friends pushed open the storm-doors and were recognized by the anxious committee-men who were taking tickets at the top of the stairs. The committee-men fled in different directions, shouting for Mr. Paul, and Mr. Paul arrived beaming with delight and moisture, and presented a huge bouquet to Mrs. West, and welcomed her friends with hospitable warmth.

Mrs. West and Miss Chamberlain took off

their hats and the men gave up their coats, not
without misgivings, to a sleepy young man who
said pleasantly, as he dragged them into the
coat-room window, "that they would be playing in great luck if they ever saw them
again."

"I don't need to give you no checks," he explained; "just ask for the coats with real fur on
'em. Nobody else has any."

There was a balcony overhanging the floor,
and the invited guests were escorted to it, and
given seats where they could look down upon
the dancers below, and the committee-men, in
dangling badges with edges of silver fringe,
stood behind their chairs and poured out champagne for them lavishly, and tore up the wine-
check which the barkeeper brought with it,
with princely hospitality.

The entrance of the invited guests created
but small interest, and neither the beauty of
the two English girls nor Lester's well-known
features, which smiled from shop-windows and
on every ash-barrel in the New York streets,
aroused any particular comment. The employees were much more occupied with the lancers
then in progress and with the joyful actions of
one of their number who was playing blind-
man's-buff with himself, and swaying from set
to set in search of his partner, who had given

him up as hopeless and retired to the supper-room for crackers and beer.

Some of the ladies wore bonnets, and others wore flowers in their hair, and a half-dozen were in gowns which were obviously intended for dancing and nothing else. But none of them were in *décolleté* gowns. A few wore gloves. They had copied the fashions of their richer sisters with the intuitive taste of the American girl of their class, and they waltzed quite as well as the ladies whose dresses they copied, and many of them were exceedingly pretty. The costumes of the gentlemen varied from the clothes they wore nightly when waiting on the table, to cutaway coats with white satin ties, and the regular blue and brass-buttoned uniform of the hotel.

"I am going to dance," said Van Bibber, "if Mr. Pierrot will present me to one of the ladies."

Paul introduced him to a lady in a white cheese-cloth dress and black walking-shoes, with whom no one else would dance, and the musicians struck up "The Band Played On," and they launched out upon a slippery floor.

Van Bibber was conscious that his friends were applauding him in dumb show from the balcony, and when his partner asked who they were, he repudiated them altogether, and said he could not imagine, but that he guessed from

their bad manners they were professional enter-
tainers hired for the evening.

The music stopped abruptly, and as he saw
Mrs. West leaving the balcony, he knew that
his turn had come, and as she passed him he
applauded her vociferously, and as no one else
applauded even slightly, she grew very red.

Her friends knew that they formed the audience which she dreaded, and she knew that they
were rejoicing in her embarrassment, which the
head of the down-stairs department, as Mr. Paul
described him, increased to an hysterical point
by introducing her as "Miss Ellen Terry, the
great English actress, who would now oblige
with a song."

The man had seen the name of the wonderful
English actress on the bill-boards in front of
Abbey's Theatre, and he had been told that
Miss Terrell was English, and confused the two
names. As he passed Van Bibber he drew his
waistcoat into shape with a proud shrug of his
shoulders, and said, anxiously, "I gave your
friend a good introduction, anyway, didn't I?"

"You did, indeed," Van Bibber answered.
"You couldn't have surprised her more; and it
made a great hit with me, too."

No one in the room listened to the singing.
The gentlemen had crossed their legs comfortably and were expressing their regret to their

partners that so much time was wasted in sand-wiching songs between the waltzes, and the ladies were engaged in criticising Celestine's hair, which she wore in a bun. They thought that it might be English, but it certainly was not their idea of good style.

Celestine was conscious of the fact that her husband and Lester were hanging far over the balcony, holding their hands to their eyes as though they were opera-glasses, and exclaiming with admiration and delight; and when she had finished the first verse, they pretended to think that the song was over, and shouted, "Bravo, encore!" and applauded frantically, and then, apparently overcome with confusion at their mistake, sank back entirely from sight.

"I think Miss Terrell's an elegant singer," Van Bibber's partner said to him. "I seen her at the hotel frequently. She has such a pleas-ant way with her, quite lady-like. She's the only actress I ever saw that has retained her timidity. She acts as though she were shy, don't she?"

Van Bibber, who had spent a month on the Thames the summer before with the Grahame Wests, surveyed Celestine with sudden interest, as though he had never seen her before until that moment, and agreed that she did look shy, one might almost say frightened to death. Mrs.

West rushed through the second verse of the song, bowed breathlessly, and ran down the steps of the stage and back to the refuge of the balcony, while the audience applauded with perfunctory politeness and called clamorously to the musicians to "Let her go!"

"And that is the song," commented Van Bibber, "that gets six encores and three calls every night on Broadway!"

Grahame West affected to be greatly chagrined at his wife's failure to charm the chambermaids and porters with her little love-song, and when his turn came, he left them with alacrity, assuring them that they would now see the difference, as he would sing a song better suited to their level.

But the song that had charmed London and captured the unprotected coast-town of New York, fell on heedless ears; and, except the evil ones in the gallery, no one laughed and no one listened, and Lester declared with tears in his eyes that he would not go through such an ordeal for the receipts of an Actors' Fund Benefit.

Van Bibber's partner caught him laughing at Grahame West's vain efforts to amuse, and said, tolerantly, that Mr. West was certainly comical, but that she had a lady friend with her who could recite pieces which were that comic that you'd die of laughing. She presented her friend to Van Bibber, and he said he hoped that they were going to hear her recite, as laughing must be a pleasant death. But the young lady explained that she had had the misfortune to lose her only brother that summer, and that she had given up everything but dancing in consequence. She said she did not think it looked right to see a girl in mourning recite comic monologues.

Van Bibber struggled to be sympathetic, and asked what her brother had died of. She told him that "he died of a Thursday," and the conversation came to an embarrassing pause.

Van Bibber's partner had another friend in a gray corduroy waistcoat and tan shoes, who was of Hebraic appearance. He also wore several very fine rings, and officiated with what was certainly religious tolerance at the M. E. Bethel Church. She said he was an elegant or—gan—ist, putting the emphasis on the second syllable, which made Van Bibber think that she was speaking of some religious body to which he belonged. But the organist made his profession clear by explaining that the committee had just invited him to oblige the company with a solo on the piano, but that he had been hitting the champagne so hard that he doubted if he could tell the keys from the pedals, and he added that if they'd excuse him he would go to sleep, which he immediately did with his head on the shoulder of the lady recitationist, who tactfully tried not to notice that he was there.

They were all waltzing again, and as Van Bibber guided his partner for a second time around the room, he noticed a particularly handsome girl in a walking-dress, who was doing some sort of a fancy step with a solemn, grave-faced young man in the hotel livery. They seemed by their manner to know each other very well, and they had apparently practised the step that they were doing often before.

The girl was much taller than the man, and was superior to him in every way. Her movements were freer and less conscious, and she carried her head and shoulders as though she had never bent them above a broom. Her complexion was soft and her hair of the finest, deepest auburn. Among all the girls upon the floor she was the most remarkable, even if her dancing had not immediately distinguished her.

The step which she and her partner were exhibiting was one that probably had been taught her by a professor of dancing at some East Side academy, at the rate of fifty cents per hour, and which she no doubt believed was the latest step danced in the gilded halls of the Few Hundred. In this waltz the two dancers held each other's hands, and the man swung his partner behind him, and then would turn and take up the step with her where they had dropped it; or they swung around and around each other several times, as people do in fancy skating, and sometimes he spun her so quickly one way that the skirt of her walking-dress was wound as tightly around her legs and ankles as a cord around a top, and then as he swung her in the opposite direction, it unwound again, and wrapped about her from the other side. They varied this when it pleased them with balancings and steps and posturings that were not sufficiently extravagant to bring any comment from the other dancers, but which were so full of grace and feeling for time and rhythm, that Van Bibber continually reversed his partner so that he might not for an instant lose sight of the girl with auburn hair.

"She is a very remarkable dancer," he said at last, apologetically. "Do you know who she is?"

His partner had observed his interest with increasing disapproval, and she smiled triumphantly now at the chance that his question gave her.

"She is the seventh-floor chambermaid," she said. "I," she added in a tone which marked the social superiority, "am a checker and marker."

CINDERELLA

"Really?" said Van Bibber, with a polite accent of proper awe.

He decided that he must see more of this Cinderella of the Hotel Salisbury; and dropping his partner by the side of the lady recitationist, he bowed his thanks and hurried to the gallery for a better view.

When he reached it he found his professional friends hanging over the railing, watching every movement which the girl made with an intense and unaffected interest.

"Have you noticed that girl with red hair?" he asked, as he pulled up a chair beside them.

But they only nodded and kept their eyes fastened on the opening in the crowd through which she had disappeared.

"There she is!" Grahame West cried, excitedly, as the girl swept out from the mass of dancers into the clear space. "Now you can see what I mean, Celestine," he said. "Where he turns her like that. We could do it in the shadow-dance in the second act. It's very pretty. She lets go his right hand and then he swings her and balances backward until she takes up the step again, when she faces him. It is very simple and very effective. Isn't it, George?"

Lester nodded and said, "Yes, very. She's a born dancer. You can teach people steps, but you can't teach them to be graceful."

CINDERELLA

"She reminds me of Sylvia Grey," said Miss Chamberlain. "There's nothing violent about it, or faked, is there? It's just the poetry of motion, without any tricks."

Lester, who was a trick-dancer himself, and Grahame West, who was one of the best eccentric dancers in England, assented to this cheerfully.

Van Bibber listened to the comments of the authorities and smiled grimly. The contrast which their lives presented to that of the young girl whom they praised so highly, struck him as being most interesting. Here were two men who had made comic dances a profound and serious study, and the two women who had lifted dancing to the plane of a fine art, all envying and complimenting a girl who was doing for her own pleasure that which was to them hard work and a livelihood. But while they were going back the next day to be applauded and petted and praised by a friendly public, she was to fly like Cinderella, to take up her sweeping and dusting and the making of beds, and the answering of peremptory summonses from electric buttons.

"A good teacher could make her worth one hundred dollars a week in six lessons," said Lester, dispassionately. "I'd be willing to make her an offer myself, if I hadn't too many dancers in the piece already."

CINDERELLA

"A hundred dollars—that's twenty pounds," said Mrs. Grahame West. "You do pay such prices over here! But I quite agree that she is very graceful; and she is so unconscious, too, isn't she?"

The interest in Cinderella ceased when the waltzing stopped, and the attention of those in the gallery was riveted with equal intensity upon Miss Chamberlain and Travers, who had faced each other in a quadrille, Miss Chamberlain having accepted the assistant barkeeper for a partner, while Travers contented himself with a tall, elderly female, who in business hours had entire charge of the linen department. The barkeeper was a melancholy man with a dyed mustache, and when he asked the English dancer from what hotel she came, and she, thinking he meant at what hotel was she stopping, told him, he said that that was a slow place, and that if she would let him know when she had her night off, he would be pleased to meet her at the Twenty-third Street station of the Sixth Avenue road on the up-town side, and would take her to the theatre, for which, he explained, he was able to obtain tickets for nothing, as so many men gave him their return checks for drinks.

Miss Chamberlain told him in return that she just doted on the theatre, and promised to meet him the very next evening. She sent him anonymously instead two seats in the front row for her performance. She had much delight the next night in watching his countenance when, after arriving somewhat late and cross, he recognized the radiant beauty on the stage as the young person with whom he had condescended to dance.

When the quadrille was over she introduced him to Travers, and Travers told him he mixed drinks at the Knickerbocker Club, and that his greatest work was a Van Bibber cocktail. And when the barkeeper asked for the recipe and promised to "push it along," Travers told him he never made it twice the same, as it depended entirely on his mood.

Mrs. Grahame West and Lester were scandalized at the conduct of these two young people and ordered the party home, and as the dance was growing somewhat noisy and the gentlemen were smoking as they danced, the invited guests made their bows to Mr. Paul and went out into cold, silent streets, followed by the thanks and compliments of seven bareheaded and swaying committee-men.

The next week Lester went on the road with his comic opera company; the Grahame Wests sailed to England; Letty Chamberlain and the other "Gee Gees," as Travers called the Gaiety

CINDERELLA

Girls, departed for Chicago, and Travers and Van Bibber were left alone.

The annual ball was a month in the past when Van Bibber found Travers at breakfast at their club, and dropped into a chair beside him with a sigh of weariness and indecision.

"What's the trouble? Have some breakfast?" said Travers, cheerfully.

"Thank you, no," said Van Bibber, gazing at his friend doubtfully; "I want to ask you what you think of this. Do you remember that girl at that servants' ball?"

"Which girl?—Tall girl with red hair—did fancy dance? Yes—why?"

"Well, I've been thinking about her lately," said Van Bibber, "and what they said of her dancing. It seems to me that if it's as good as they thought it was, the girl ought to be told of it and encouraged. They evidently meant what they said. It wasn't as though they were talking about her to her relatives and had to say something pleasant. Lester thought she could make a hundred dollars a week if she had had six lessons. Well, six lessons wouldn't cost much, not more than ten dollars at the most, and a hundred a week for an original outlay of ten is a good investment."

Travers nodded his head in assent, and whacked an egg viciously with his spoon.

"What's your scheme?" he said. "Is your idea to help the lady for her own sake—sort of a philanthropic snap—or as a speculation? We might make it pay as a speculation. You see nobody knows about her except you and me. We might form her into a sort of stock company and teach her to dance, and secure her engagements and then take our commission out of her salary. Is that what you were thinking of doing?"

"No, that was not my idea," said Van Bibber, smiling. "I hadn't any plan. I just thought I'd go down to that hotel and tell her that in the opinion of the four people best qualified to know what good dancing is, she is a good dancer, and then leave the rest to her. She must have some friends or relations who would help her to make a start. If it's true that she can make a hit as a dancer, it seems a pity that she shouldn't know it, doesn't it? If she succeeded, she'd make a pot of money, and if she failed, she'd be just where she is now."

Travers considered this subject deeply, with knit brows.

"That's so," he said. "I'll tell you what let's do. Let's go see some of the managers of those continuous performance places, and tell them we have a dark horse that the Grahame Wests and Letty Chamberlain herself and

CINDERELLA

George Lester think is the coming dancer of the age, and ask them to give her a chance. And we'll make some sort of a contract with them. We ought to fix it so that she is to get bigger money the longer they keep her in the bill, have her salary on a rising scale. Come on," he exclaimed, warming to the idea. "Let's go now. What have you got to do?"

"I've got nothing better to do than just that," Van Bibber declared, briskly.

The managers whom they interviewed were interested but non-committal. They agreed that the girl must be a remarkable dancer indeed to warrant such praise from such authorities, but they wanted to see her and judge for themselves, and they asked to be given her address, which the impresarios refused to disclose. But they secured from the managers the names of several men who taught fancy dancing, and who prepared aspirants for the vaudeville stage, and having obtained from them their prices and their opinion as to how long a time would be required to give the finishing touches to a dancer already accomplished in the art, they directed their steps to the Hotel Salisbury.

"'From the Seventh Story to the Stage,'" said Travers. "She will make very good newspaper paragraphs, won't she? 'The New American Dancer, indorsed by Celestine Terrell, Letty Chamberlain, and Cortlandt Van Bibber.' And we could get her outside engagements to dance at studios and evening parties after her regular performance, couldn't we?" he continued. "She ought to ask from fifty to a hundred dollars a night. With her regular salary that would average about three hundred and fifty a week. She is probably making three dollars a week now, and eats in the servants' hall."

"And then we will send her abroad," interrupted Van Bibber, taking up the tale, "and she will do the music-halls in London. If she plays three halls a night, say one on the Surrey Side, and Islington, and a smart West End hall like the Empire or the Alhambra, at fifteen guineas a turn, that would bring her in five hundred and twenty-five dollars a week. And then she would go to the Folies Bergère in Paris, and finally to St. Petersburg and Milan, and then come back to dance in the Grand Opera season, under Gus Harris, with a great international reputation, and hung with flowers and medals and diamond sunbursts and things."

"Rather," said Travers, shaking his head enthusiastically. "And after that we must invent a new dance for her, with colored lights and mechanical snaps and things, and have it patented; and finally she will get her picture on

soda-cracker boxes and cigarette advertisements, and have a race-horse named after her,
and give testimonials for nerve-tonics and soap.
Does fame reach farther than that?"

"I think not," said Van Bibber, "unless they
give her name to a new make of bicycle. We
must give her a new name, anyway, and re-
christen her, whatever her name may be. We'll
call her Cinderella—La Cinderella. That
sounds fine, doesn't it, even if it is rather long
for the very largest type."

"It isn't much longer than Carmencita," suggested the other. "And people who have the
proud knowledge of knowing her like you and
me will call her 'Cinders' for short. And when
we read of her dancing before the Czar of All
the Russias, and leading the ballet at the Grand
Opera House in Paris, we'll say, 'that is our
handiwork,' and we will feel that we have not
lived in vain."

"Seventh floor, please," said Van Bibber to
the elevator-boy.

The elevator-boy was a young man of serious
demeanor, with a smooth-shaven face and a
square, determined jaw. There was something
about him which seemed familiar, but Van Bibber could not determine just what it was. The
elevator stopped to allow some people to leave

it at the second floor, and as the young man
shoved the door to again, Van Bibber asked him
if he happened to know of a chambermaid with
red hair—a tall girl on the seventh floor, a girl
who danced very well.

The wire rope of the elevator slipped less rapidly through the hands of the young man who
controlled it, and he turned and fixed his eyes
with sudden interest on Van Bibber's face, and
scrutinized him and his companion with serious
consideration.

"Yes, I know her—I know who you mean,
anyway," he said. "Why?"

"Why?" echoed Van Bibber, raising his eyes.
"We wish to see her on a matter of business.
Can you tell me her name?"

The elevator was running so slowly now that
its movement upward was barely perceptible.

"Her name's Annie—Annie Crehan. Excuse
me," said the young man, doubtfully, "ain't
you the young fellows who came to our ball
with that English lady, the one that sung?"

"Yes," Van Bibber assented, pleasantly.
"We were there. That's where I've seen you
before. You were there, too, weren't you?"

"Me and Annie was dancing together most all
the evening. I seen all youse watching her."

"Of course," exclaimed Van Bibber. "I remember you now. Oh, then you must know

her quite well. Maybe you can help us. We want to put her on the stage."

The elevator came to a stop with an abrupt jerk, and the young man shoved his hands behind him, and leaned back against one of the mirrors in its side.

"On the stage," he repeated. "Why?"

Van Bibber smiled and shrugged his shoulders in some embarrassment at this peremptory challenge. But there was nothing in the young man's tone or manner that could give offense. He seemed much in earnest, and spoke as though they must understand that he had some right to question.

"Why? Because of her dancing. She is a very remarkable dancer. All of those actors with us that night said so. You must know that yourself better than any one else, since you can dance with her. She could make quite a fortune as a dancer, and we have persuaded several managers to promise to give her a trial. And if she needs money to pay for lessons, or to buy the proper dresses and slippers and things, we are willing to give it to her, or to lend it to her, if she would like that better."

"Why?" repeated the young man, immovably. His manner was not encouraging.

"Why—what?" interrupted Travers, with growing impatience.

"Why are you willing to give her money? You don't know her."

Van Bibber looked at Travers, and Travers smiled in some annoyance. The electric bell rang violently from different floors, but the young man did not heed it. He had halted the elevator between two landings, and he now seated himself on the velvet cushions and crossed one leg over the other, as though for a protracted debate. Travers gazed about him in humorous apprehension, as though alarmed at the position in which he found himself, hung as it were between the earth and sky.

"I swear I am an unarmed man," he said, in a whisper.

"Our intentions are well meant, I assure you," said Van Bibber, with an amused smile. "The girl is working ten hours a day for very little money, isn't she? You know she is, when she could make a great deal of money by working half as hard. We have some influence with theatrical people, and we meant merely to put her in the way of bettering her position, and to give her the chance to do something which she can do better than many others, while almost any one, I take it, can sweep and make beds. If she were properly managed, she could become a great dancer, and delight thousands of people —add to the gayety of nations, as it were. She's

hardly doing that now, is she? Have you any
objections to that? What right have you to
make objections, anyway?"

The young man regarded the two young gentlemen before him with a dogged countenance,
but there was now in his eyes a look of helpless-
ness and of great disquietude.

"We're engaged to be married, Annie and
me," he said. "That's it."

"Oh," exclaimed Van Bibber, "I beg your
pardon. That's different. Well, in that case,
you can help us very much, if you wish. We
leave it entirely with you!"

"I don't want that you should leave it with
me," said the young man, harshly. "I don't
want to have nothing to do with it. Annie can
speak for herself. I knew it was coming to
this," he said, leaning forward and clasping his
hands together, "or something like this. I've
never felt dead sure of Annie, never once. I
always knew something would happen."

"Why, nothing has happened," said Van Bibber, soothingly. "You would both benefit by
it. We would be as willing to help two as one.
You would both be better off."

The young man raised his head and stared
at Van Bibber reprovingly.

"You know better than that," he said. "You
know what I'd look like. Of course she could

217

make money as a dancer—I've known that for
some time—but she hasn't thought of it yet,
and she'd never have thought of it herself. But
the question isn't me or what I want. It's
Annie. Is she going to be happier or not, that's
the question. And I'm telling you that she
couldn't be any happier than she is now. I
know that, too. We're just as contented as
two folks ever was. We've been saving for
three months, and buying furniture from the
instalment people, and next month we were
going to move into a flat on Seventh Avenue,
quite handy to the hotel. If she goes onto the
stage could she be any happier? And if you're
honest in saying you're thinking of the two of
us—I ask you where would I come in? I'll be
pulling this wire rope and she'll be all over the
country, and her friends won't be my friends
and her ways won't be my ways. She'll get
out of reach of me in a week, and I won't be in
it. I'm not the sort to go loafing round while
my wife supports me, carrying her satchel for
her. And there's nothing I can do but just
this. She'd come back here some day and live
in the front floor suite, and I'd pull her up and
down in this elevator. That's what will happen. Here's what you two gentlemen are doing." The young man leaned forward eagerly.
"You're offering a change to two people that

are as well off now as they ever hope to be, and they're contented. We don't know nothin' better. Now, are you dead sure that you're giving us something better than what we've got? You can't make me any happier than I am, and as far as Annie knows, up to now, she couldn't be better fixed, and no one could care for her more.

"My God! gentlemen," he cried, desperately, "think! She's all I've got. There's lots of dancers, but she's not a dancer to me, she's just Annie. I don't want her to delight the gayety of nations. I want her for myself. Maybe I'm selfish, but I can't help that. She's mine, and you're trying to take her away from me. Suppose she was your girl, and some one was sneaking her away from you. You'd try to stop it, wouldn't you, if she was all you had?" He stopped breathlessly and stared alternately from one to the other of the young men before him. Their countenances showed an expression of well-bred concern.

"It's for you to judge," he went on, helplessly; "if you want to take the responsibility, well and good, that's for you to say. I'm not stopping you, but she's all I've got."

The young man stopped, and there was a pause while he eyed them eagerly. The elevator-bell rang out again with vicious indignation.

CINDERELLA

Travers struck at the toe of his boot with his stick and straightened his shoulders.

"I think you're extremely selfish, if you ask me," he said.

The young man stood up quickly and took his elevator-rope in both hands. "All right," he said, quietly, "that settles it. I'll take you up to Annie now, and you can arrange it with her. I'm not standing in her way."

"Hold on," protested Van Bibber and Travers in a breath. "Don't be in such a hurry," growled Travers.

The young man stood immovable, with his hands on the wire and looking down on them, his face full of doubt and distress.

"I don't want to stand in Annie's way," he repeated, as though to himself. "I'll do whatever you say. I'll take you to the seventh floor or I'll drop you to the street. It's up to you, gentlemen," he added, helplessly, and turning his back to them threw his arm against the wall of the elevator and buried his face upon it.

There was an embarrassing pause, during which Van Bibber scowled at himself in the mirror opposite as though to ask it what a man who looked like that should do under such trying circumstances.

He turned at last and stared at Travers. "'Where ignorance is bliss, it's folly to be wise,'" he whispered, keeping his face toward his friend. "What do you say? Personally I don't see myself in the part of Providence. It's the case of the poor man and his one ewe lamb, isn't it?"

"We don't want his ewe lamb, do we?" growled Travers. "It's a case of the dog in a manger, I say. I thought we were going to be fairy godfathers to 'La Cinderella.'"

"The lady seems to be supplied with a most determined godfather as it is," returned Van Bibber.

The elevator-boy raised his face and stared at them with haggard eyes.

"Well?" he begged.

Van Bibber smiled upon him reassuringly, with a look partly of respect and partly of pity.

"You can drop us to the street," he said.

THE MAN WITH ONE TALENT

THE mass-meeting in the Madison Square Garden which was to help set Cuba free was finished, and the people were pushing their way out of the overheated building into the snow and sleet of the streets. They had been greatly stirred and the spell of the last speaker still hung so heavily upon them that as they pressed down the long corridor they were still speaking loudly in his praise.

A young man moved eagerly among them, and pushed his way to wherever a voice was raised above the rest. He strained forward, listening openly, as though he tried to judge the effect of the meeting by the verdict of those about him.

But the words he overheard seemed to clash with what he wished them to be, and the eager look on his face changed to one of doubt and of grave disappointment. When he had reached the sidewalk he stopped and stood looking back alternately into the lighted hall and at the hurrying crowds which were dispersing rapidly. He made a movement as though he would recall them, as though he felt they were still unconvinced, as though there was much still left unsaid.

THE MAN WITH ONE TALENT

A fat stranger halted at his elbow to light his cigar, and glancing up nodded his head approvingly.

"Fine speaker, Senator Stanton, ain't he?" he said.

The young man answered eagerly. "Yes," he assented, "he is a great orator, but how could he help but speak well with such a subject?"

"Oh, you ought to have heard him last November at Tammany Hall," the fat stranger answered. "He wasn't quite up to himself tonight. He wasn't so interested. Those Cubans are foreigners, you see, but you ought to have heard him last St. Patrick's day on Home Rule for Ireland. Then he was talking! That speech made him a United States senator, I guess. I don't just see how he expects to win out on this Cuba game. The Cubans haven't got no votes."

The young man opened his eyes in some bewilderment.

"He speaks for the good of Cuba, for the sake of humanity," he ventured.

"What?" inquired the fat stranger. "Oh, yes, of course. Well, I must be getting on. Good-night, sir."

The stranger moved on his way, but the young man still lingered uncertainly in the snow-swept corridor, shivering violently with the cold and stamping his feet for greater comfort. His face was burned to a deep red, which seemed to have come from some long exposure to a tropical sun, but which held no sign of health. His cheeks were hollow and his eyes were lighted with the fire of fever, and from time to time he was shaken by violent bursts of coughing which caused him to reach toward one of the pillars for support.

As the last of the lights went out in the Garden, the speaker of the evening and three of his friends came laughing and talking down the long corridor. Senator Stanton was a conspicuous figure at any time, and even in those places where his portraits had not penetrated he was at once recognized as a personage. Something in his erect carriage and an unusual grace of movement, and the power and success in his face, made men turn to look at him. He had been told that he resembled the early portraits of Henry Clay, and he had never quite forgotten the coincidence.

The senator was wrapping the collar of his fur coat around his throat and puffing contentedly at a fresh cigar, and as he passed, the nightwatchman and the ushers bowed to the great man and stood looking after him with the half-humorous, half-envious deference that the American voter pays to the successful politician. At the sidewalk, the policemen hurried to open the door of his carriage, and in their eagerness made a double line, through which he passed nodding to them gravely. The young man who had stood so long in waiting pushed his way through the line to his side.

"Senator Stanton," he began timidly, "might I speak to you a moment? My name is Arkwright; I am just back from Cuba, and I want to thank you for your speech. I am an American, and I thank God that I am since you are too, sir. No one has said anything since the war began that compares with what you said to-night. You put it nobly, and I know, for I've been there for three years, only I can't make other people understand it, and I am thankful that some one can. You'll forgive my stopping you, sir, but I wanted to thank you. I feel it very much."

Senator Stanton's friends had already seated themselves in his carriage and were looking out of the door and smiling with mock patience. But the senator made no move to follow them. Though they were his admirers they were sometimes sceptical, and he was not sorry that they should hear this uninvited tribute. So he made a pretense of buttoning his long coat about him, and nodded encouragingly to Arkwright to continue. "I'm glad you liked it, sir," he said with the pleasant, gracious smile that had won him a friend wherever it had won him a vote. "It is very satisfactory to know from one who is well informed on the subject that what I have said is correct. The situation there is truly terrible. You have just returned, you say? Where were you—in Havana?"

"No, in the other provinces, sir," Arkwright answered. "I have been all over the island; I am a civil engineer. The truth has not been half told about Cuba, I assure you, sir. It is massacre there, not war. It is partly so through ignorance, but nevertheless it is massacre. And what makes it worse is, that it is the massacre of the innocents. That is what I liked best of what you said in that great speech, the part about the women and children."

He reached out his hands detainingly, and then drew back as though in apology for having already kept the great man so long waiting in the cold. "I wish I could tell you some of the terrible things I have seen," he began again, eagerly, as Stanton made no movement to depart. "They are much worse than those you instanced to-night, and you could make so much better use of them than any one else. I have seen starving women nursing dead babies, and sometimes starving babies sucking their dead mothers' breasts; I have seen men cut down in

the open roads and while digging in the fields—
and two hundred women imprisoned in one
room without food and eaten with smallpox,
and huts burned while the people in them
slept——"

The young man had been speaking impetu-
ously, but he stopped as suddenly, for the senator was not listening to him. He had lowered
his eyes and was looking with a glance of mingled fascination and disgust at Arkwright's
hands. In his earnestness the young man had
stretched them out, and as they showed behind
the line of his ragged sleeves the others could
see, even in the blurred light and falling snow,
that the wrists of each hand were gashed and
cut in dark-brown lines like the skin of a mu-
latto, and in places were a raw red, where the
fresh skin had but just closed over. The young
man paused and stood shivering, still holding
his hands out rigidly before him.

The senator raised his eyes slowly and drew
away.

"What is that?" he said in a low voice,
pointing with a gloved finger at the black lines
on the wrists.

A sergeant in the group of policemen who
had closed around the speakers answered him
promptly from his profound fund of professional
knowledge.

"That's handcuffs, senator," he said importantly, and glanced at Stanton as though to signify that at a word from him he would take this suspicious character into custody. The young man pulled the frayed cuffs of his shirt over his wrists and tucked his hands, which the cold had frozen into an ashy blue, under his armpits to warm them.

"No, they don't use handcuffs in the field," he said in the same low, eager tone; "they use ropes and leather thongs; they fastened me behind a horse, and when he stumbled going down the trail it jerked me forward and the cords would tighten and tear the flesh. But they have had a long time to heal now. I have been eight months in prison."

The young men at the carriage window had ceased smiling and were listening intently. One of them stepped out and stood beside the carriage door looking down at the shivering figure before him with a close and curious scrutiny.

"Eight months in prison!" echoed the police sergeant with a note of triumph; "what did I tell you?"

"Hold your tongue!" said the young man at the carriage door. There was silence for a moment, while the men looked at the senator, as though waiting for him to speak.

THE MAN WITH ONE TALENT

"Where were you in prison, Mr. Arkwright?" he asked.

"First in the calaboose at Santa Clara for two months, and then in Cabañas. The Cubans who were taken when I was were shot by the fusillade on different days during this last month. Two of them, the Ezetas, were father and son, and the Volunteer band played all the time the execution was going on, so that the other prisoners might not hear them cry 'Cuba Libre!' when the order came to fire. But we heard them."

The senator shivered slightly and pulled his fur collar up farther around his face. "I'd like to talk with you," he said, "if you have nothing to do to-morrow. I'd like to go into this thing thoroughly. Congress must be made to take some action."

The young man clasped his hands eagerly. "Ah, Mr. Stanton, if you would," he cried, "if you would only give me an hour! I could tell you so much that you could use. And you can believe what I say, sir—it is not necessary to lie—God knows the truth is bad enough. I can give you names and dates for everything I say. Or I can do better than that, sir. I can take you there yourself—in three months I can show you all you need to see, without danger to you in any way. And they would not know me, now that

229

THE MAN WITH ONE TALENT

I have grown a beard, and I am a skeleton to what I was. I can speak the language well, and I know just what you should see, and then you could come back as one speaking with authority and not have to say, 'I have read,' or 'have been told,' but you can say, 'These are the things I have seen'—and you could free Cuba."

The senator coughed and put the question aside for the moment with a wave of the hand that held his cigar. "We will talk of that to-morrow also. Come to lunch with me at one. My apartments are in the Berkeley on Fifth Avenue. But aren't you afraid to go back there?" he asked curiously. "I should think you'd had enough of it. And you've got a touch of fever, haven't you?" He leaned forward and peered into the other's eyes.

"It is only the prison fever," the young man answered; "food and this cold will drive that out of me. And I must go back. There is so much to do there," he added. "Ah, if I could tell them, as you can tell them, what I feel here." He struck his chest sharply with his hand, and on the instant fell into a fit of coughing so violent that the young man at the carriage door caught him around the waist, and one of the policemen supported him from the other side.

THE MAN WITH ONE TALENT

"You need a doctor," said the senator, kindly. "I'll ask mine to have a look at you. Don't forget, then, at one o'clock to-morrow. We will go into this thing thoroughly." He shook Arkwright warmly by the hand and, stooping, stepped into the carriage. The young man who had stood at the door followed him and crowded back luxuriously against the cushions. The footman swung himself up beside the driver, and said, "Up-town Delmonico's," as he wrapped the fur rug around his legs, and with a salute from the policemen and a scraping of hoofs on the slippery asphalt the great man was gone.

"That poor fellow needs a doctor," he said as the carriage rolled up the avenue, "and he needs an overcoat, and he needs food. He needs about almost everything, by the looks of him."

But the voice of the young man in the corner of the carriage objected drowsily——

"On the contrary," he said, "it seemed to me that he had the one thing needful."

By one o'clock of the day following, Senator Stanton, having read the reports of his speech in the morning papers, punctuated with "Cheers," "Tremendous enthusiasm" and more "Cheers," was still in a willing frame of mind toward Cuba and her self-appointed envoy, young Mr. Arkwright.

Over night he had had doubts but that the

young man's enthusiasm would bore him on the morrow, but Mr. Arkwright, when he appeared, developed, on the contrary, a practical turn of mind which rendered his suggestions both flattering and feasible. He was still terribly in earnest, but he was clever enough or serious enough to see that the motives which appealed to him might not have sufficient force to move a successful statesman into action. So he placed before the senator only those arguments and reasons which he guessed were the best adapted to secure his interest and his help. His proposal as he set it forth was simplicity itself.

"Here is a map of the island," he said; "on it I have marked the places you can visit in safety, and where you will meet the people you ought to see. If you leave New York at midnight you can reach Tampa on the second day. From Tampa we cross in another day to Havana. There you can visit the Americans imprisoned in Morro and Cabañas, and in the streets you can see the starving pacificos. From Havana I shall take you by rail to Jucaro, Matanzas, Santa Clara, and Cienfuegos. You will not be able to see the insurgents in the fields—it is not necessary that you should—but you can visit one of the sugar plantations and some of the insurgent chiefs will run the forts by night and come in to talk with you. I will show you burning fields and houses, and starving men and women by the thousands, and men and women dying of fevers. You can see Cuban prisoners shot by a firing squad and you can note how these rebels meet death. You can see all this in three weeks and be back in New York in a month, as any one can see it who wishes to learn the truth. Why, English members of Parliament go all the way to India and British Columbia to inform themselves about those countries, they travel thousands of miles, but only one member of either of our houses of Congress has taken the trouble to cross these eighty miles of water that lie between us and Cuba. You can either go quietly and incognito, as it were, or you can advertise the fact of your going, which would be better. And from the moment you start the interest in your visit will grow and increase until there will be no topic discussed in any of our papers except yourself, and what you are doing and what you mean to do.

"By the time you return the people will be waiting, ready and eager to hear whatever you may have to say. Your word will be the last word for them. It is not as though you were some demagogue seeking notoriety, or a hotel piazza correspondent at Key West or Jacksonville. You are the only statesman we have, the

THE MAN WITH ONE TALENT

only orator Americans will listen to, and I tell
you that when you come before them and bring
home to them as only you can the horrors of
this war, you will be the only man in this country. You will be the Patrick Henry of Cuba;
you can go down to history as the man who
added the most beautiful island in the seas to
the territory of the United States, who saved
thousands of innocent children and women, and
who dared to do what no other politician has
dared to do—to go and see for himself and to
come back and speak the truth. It only means
a month out of your life, a month's trouble and
discomfort, but with no risk. What is a month
out of a lifetime, when that month means im-
mortality to you and life to thousands? In a
month you would make a half dozen after-
dinner speeches and cause your friends to laugh
and applaud. Why not wring their hearts instead, and hold this thing up before them as it
is, and shake it in their faces? Show it to them
in all its horror—bleeding, diseased, and naked,
an offense to our humanity, and to our prated
love of liberty, and to our God."

The young man threw himself eagerly forward and beat the map with his open palm.
But the senator sat apparently unmoved, gazing thoughtfully into the open fire, and shook
his head.

THE MAN WITH ONE TALENT

While the luncheon was in progress the young gentleman who the night before had left the carriage and stood at Arkwright's side had entered the room and was listening intently. He had invited himself to some fresh coffee, and had then relapsed into an attentive silence, following what the others said with an amused and interested countenance. Stanton had introduced him as Mr. Livingstone, and appeared to take it for granted that Arkwright would know who he was. He seemed to regard him with a certain deference which Arkwright judged was due to some fixed position the young man held, either of social or of political value.

"I do not know," said Stanton with consideration, "that I am prepared to advocate the annexation of the island. It is a serious problem."

"I am not urging that," Arkwright interrupted anxiously; "the Cubans themselves do not agree as to that, and in any event it is an afterthought. Our object now should be to prevent further bloodshed. If you see a man beating a boy to death, you first save the boy's life and decide afterward where he is to go to school. If there were any one else, senator," Arkwright continued earnestly, "I would not trouble you. But we all know your strength in this country. You are independent and fearless, and men of both parties listen to you. Surely, God has given you this great gift of oratory (if you will forgive my speaking so) to use only in a great cause. A grand organ in a cathedral is placed there to lift men's thoughts to high resolves and purposes, not to make people dance. A street organ can do that. Now, here is a cause worthy of your great talents, worthy of a Daniel Webster, of a Henry Clay."

The senator frowned at the fire and shook his head doubtfully.

"If they knew what I was down there for," he asked, "wouldn't they put me in prison too?"

Arkwright laughed incredulously.

"Certainly not," he said; "you would go there as a private citizen, as a tourist to look on and observe. Spain is not seeking complications of that sort. She has troubles enough without imprisoning United States senators."

"Yes; but these fevers now," persisted Stanton, "they're no respecter of persons, I imagine. A United States senator is not above small-pox or cholera."

Arkwright shook his head impatiently and sighed.

"It is difficult to make it clear to one who has not been there," he said. "These people and soldiers are dying of fever because they are forced to live like pigs, and they are already sick with starvation. A healthy man like yourself would be in no more danger than you would be in walking through the wards of a New York hospital."

Senator Stanton turned in his arm-chair, and held up his hand impressively.

"If I were to tell them the things you have told me," he said warningly; "if I were to say I have seen such things—American property in flames, American interests ruined, and that five times as many women and children have died of fever and starvation in three months in Cuba as the Sultan has massacred in Armenia in three years—it would mean war with Spain."

"Well?" said Arkwright.

Stanton shrugged his shoulders and sank back again in his chair.

"It would either mean war," Arkwright went on, "or it might mean the sending of the Red Cross army to Cuba. It went to Constantinople, five thousand miles away, to help the Armenian Christians—why has it waited three years to go eighty miles to feed and clothe the Cuban women and children? It is like sending help to a hungry peasant in Russia while a man dies on your door-step."

"Well," said the senator, rising, "I will let you know to-morrow. If it is the right thing

to do, and if I can do it, of course it must be
done. We start from Tampa, you say? I
know the presidents of all of those roads and
they'll probably give me a private car for the
trip down. Shall we take any newspaper men
with us, or shall I wait until I get back and be
interviewed? What do you think?"

"I would wait until my return," Arkwright
answered, his eyes glowing with the hope the
senator's words had inspired, "and then speak
to a mass-meeting here and in Boston and in
Chicago. Three speeches will be enough. Before you have finished your last one the American warships will be in the harbor of Havana."

"Ah, youth, youth!" said the senator, smiling gravely, "it is no light responsibility to
urge a country into war."

"It is no light responsibility," Arkwright answered, "to know you have the chance to save
the lives of thousands of little children and help-
less women and to let the chance pass."

"Quite so, that is quite true," said the senator.
"Well, good-morning. I shall let you know to-
morrow."

Young Livingstone went down in the elevator
with Arkwright, and when they had reached
the sidewalk stood regarding him for a moment
in silence.

"You mustn't count too much on Stanton,

you know," he said kindly; "he has a way of disappointing people."

"Ah, he can never disappoint me," Arkwright answered confidently, "no matter how much I expected. Besides, I have already heard him speak."

"I don't mean that; I don't mean he is disappointing as a speaker. Stanton is a great orator, I think. Most of those Southerners are, and he's the only real orator I ever heard. But what I mean is, that he doesn't go into things impulsively; he first considers himself, and then he considers every other side of the question before he commits himself to it. Before he launches out on a popular wave he tries to find out where it is going to land him. He likes the sort of popular wave that carries him along with it where every one can see him; he doesn't fancy being hurled up on the beach with his mouth full of sand."

"You are saying that he is selfish, self-seeking?" Arkwright demanded, with a challenge in his voice. "I thought you were his friend."

"Yes, he is selfish, and, yes, I am his friend," the young man answered, smiling; "at least, he seems willing to be mine. I am saying nothing against him that I have not said to him. If you'll come back with me up the elevator I'll tell him he's a self-seeker and selfish, and with

no thought above his own interests. He won't
mind. He'd say I cannot comprehend his motives. Why, you've only to look at his record.
When the Venezuelan message came out he
attacked the President and declared he was
trying to make political capital and to drag us
into war, and that what we wanted was arbitration; but when the President brought out the
Arbitration Treaty he attacked that too in the
Senate and destroyed it. Why? Not because
he had convictions, but because the President
had refused a foreign appointment to a friend
of his in the South. He has been a free-silver
man for the last ten years, he comes from a
free-silver state, and the members of the legis-
lature that elected him were all for silver, but
this last election his Wall Street friends got
hold of him and worked on his feelings, and he
repudiated his party, his state, and his con-
stituents, and came out for gold."

"Well, but surely," Arkwright objected, "that
took courage? To own that for ten years you
had been wrong, and to come out for the right
at the last."

Livingstone stared and shrugged his shoulders.
"It's all a question of motives," he said indifferently. "I don't want to shatter your idol; I
only want to save you from counting too much
on him."

THE MAN WITH ONE TALENT

When Arkwright called on the morrow Senator Stanton was not at home, and the day following he was busy, and could give him only a brief interview. There were previous engagements and other difficulties in the way of his going which he had not foreseen, he said, and he feared he should have to postpone his visit to Cuba indefinitely. He asked if Mr. Arkwright would be so kind as to call again within a week; he would then be better able to give him a definite answer.

Arkwright left the apartment with a sensation of such keen disappointment that it turned him ill and dizzy. He felt that the great purpose of his life was being played with and put aside. But he had not selfish resentment on his own account; he was only the more determined to persevere. He considered new arguments and framed new appeals; and one moment blamed himself bitterly for having foolishly discouraged the statesman by too vivid pictures of the horrors he might encounter, and the next, questioned if he had not been too practical and so failed because he had not made the terrible need of immediate help his sole argument. Every hour wasted in delay meant, as he knew, the sacrifice of many lives, and there were other, more sordid and more practical, reasons for speedy action. For his supply of money was running low and there was now barely enough remaining to carry him through the month of travel he had planned to take at Stanton's side. What would happen to him when that momentous trip was over was of no consequence. He would have done the work as far as his small share in it lay, he would have set in motion a great power that was to move Congress and the people of the United States to action. If he could but do that, what became of him counted for nothing.

But at the end of the week his fears and misgivings were scattered gloriously, and a single line from the senator set his heart leaping and brought him to his knees in gratitude and thanksgiving. On returning one afternoon to the mean lodging into which he had moved to save his money, he found a telegram from Stanton, and he tore it open, trembling between hope and fear.

"Have arranged to leave for Tampa with you Monday, at midnight," it read. "Call for me at ten o'clock same evening.—STANTON."

Arkwright read the message three times. There was a heavy, suffocating pressure at his heart as though it had ceased beating. He sank back limply upon the edge of his bed and, clutching the piece of paper in his two hands, spoke the words aloud triumphantly, as though to assure himself that they were true. Then a flood of unspeakable relief, of happiness and gratitude, swept over him, and he turned and slipped to the floor, burying his face in the pillow, and wept out his thanks upon his knees.

A man so deeply immersed in public affairs as was Stanton, and with such a multiplicity of personal interests, could not prepare to absent himself for a month without his intention becoming known, and on the day when he was to start for Tampa the morning newspapers proclaimed the fact that he was about to visit Cuba. They gave to his mission all the importance and display that Arkwright had foretold. Some of the newspapers stated that he was going as a special commissioner of the President to study and report; others that he was acting in behalf of the Cuban legation in Washington and had plenipotentiary powers. Opposition organs suggested that he was acting in the interests of the sugar trust, and his own particular organ declared that it was his intention to free Cuba at the risk of his own freedom, safety, and even life.

The Spanish minister in Washington sent a cable for publication to Madrid, stating that a distinguished American statesman was about to visit Cuba, to investigate, and, later, to deny the truth of the disgraceful libels published concerning the Spanish officials on the island by the papers of the United States. At the same time he cabled in cipher to the captain-general in Havana to see that the distinguished statesman was closely spied upon from the moment of his arrival until his departure, and to place on the "suspect" list all Americans and Cubans who ventured to give him any information.

The afternoon papers enlarged on the importance of the visit and on the good that would surely come of it. They told that Senator Stanton had refused to be interviewed or to disclose the object of his journey. But it was enough, they said, that some one in authority was at last to seek out the truth, and added that no one would be listened to with greater respect than would the Southern senator. On this all the editorial writers were agreed. The day passed drearily for Arkwright. Early in the morning he packed his valise and paid his landlord, and for the remainder of the day walked the streets or sat in the hotel corridor waiting impatiently for each fresh edition of the papers. In them he read the signs of the great upheaval of popular feeling that was to restore peace and health and plenty to the island for which he had given his last three years of energy and life.

THE MAN WITH ONE TALENT

He was trembling with excitement, as well as with the cold, when at ten o'clock precisely he stood at Senator Stanton's door. He had forgotten to eat his dinner, and the warmth of the dimly lit hall and the odor of rich food which was wafted from an inner room touched his senses with tantalizing comfort.

"The senator says you are to come this way, sir," the servant directed. He took Arkwright's valise from his hand and parted the heavy curtains that hid the dining-room, and Arkwright stepped in between them and then stopped in some embarrassment. He found himself in the presence of a number of gentlemen seated at a long dinner-table, who turned their heads as he entered and peered at him through the smoke that floated in light layers above the white cloth. The dinner had been served, but the senator's guests still sat with their chairs pushed back from a table lighted by candles under yellow shades, and covered with beautiful flowers and with bottles of varied sizes in stands of quaint and intricate design. Senator Stanton's tall figure showed dimly through the smoke, and his deep voice hailed Arkwright cheerily from the farther end of the room. "This way, Mr. Arkwright," he said. "I have a chair waiting for you here." He grasped Arkwright's hand warmly and pulled him into the vacant place at his side. An elderly gentleman on Arkwright's other side moved to make more room for him and shoved a liqueur glass toward him with a friendly nod and pointed at an open box of cigars. He was a fine-looking man, and Arkwright noticed that he was regarding him with a glance of the keenest interest. All of those at the table were men of twice Arkwright's age, except Livingstone, whom he recognized and who nodded to him pleasantly and at the same time gave an order to a servant, pointing at Arkwright as he did so. Some of the gentlemen wore their business suits, and one opposite Arkwright was still in his overcoat, and held his hat in his hand. These latter seemed to have arrived after the dinner had begun, for they formed a second line back of those who had places at the table; they all seemed to know one another and were talking with much vivacity and interest.

Stanton did not attempt to introduce Arkwright to his guests individually, but said: "Gentlemen, this is Mr. Arkwright, of whom I have been telling you, the young gentleman who has done such magnificent work for the cause of Cuba." Those who caught Arkwright's eye nodded to him, and others raised their glasses at him, but with a smile that he could not understand. It was as though they all knew something concerning him of which he was ignorant. He noted that the faces of some were strangely familiar, and he decided that he must have seen their portraits in the public prints. After he had introduced Arkwright, the senator drew his chair slightly away from him and turned in what seemed embarrassment to the man on his other side. The elderly gentleman next to Arkwright filled his glass, a servant placed a small cup of coffee at his elbow, and he lit a cigar and looked about him.

"You must find this weather very trying after the tropics," his neighbor said.

Arkwright assented cordially. The brandy was flowing through his veins and warming him; he forgot that he was hungry, and the kind, interested glances of those about him set him at his ease. It was a propitious start, he thought, a pleasant leave-taking for the senator and himself, full of good-will and good wishes.

He turned toward Stanton and waited until he had ceased speaking.

"The papers have begun well, haven't they?" he asked, eagerly.

He had spoken in a low voice, almost in a whisper, but those about the table seemed to have heard him, for there was silence instantly, and when he glanced up he saw the eyes of all turned upon him and he noticed on their faces the same smile he had seen there when he entered.

"Yes," Stanton answered constrainedly. "Yes, I—" he lowered his voice, but the silence still continued. Stanton had his eyes fixed on the table, but now he frowned and half rose from his chair.

"I want to speak with you, Arkwright," he said. "Suppose we go into the next room. I'll be back in a moment," he added, nodding to the others.

But the man on his right removed his cigar from his lips and said in an undertone, "No, sit down, stay where you are"; and the elderly gentleman at Arkwright's side laid his hand detainingly on his arm. "Oh, you won't take Mr. Arkwright away from us, Stanton?" he asked, smiling.

Stanton shrugged his shoulders and sat down again, and there was a moment's pause. It was broken by the man in the overcoat, who laughed.

"He's paying you a compliment, Mr. Arkwright," he said. He pointed with his cigar to the gentleman at Arkwright's side.

"I don't understand," Arkwright answered, doubtfully.

"It's a compliment to your eloquence—he's afraid to leave you alone with the senator. Livingstone's been telling us that you are a better talker than Stanton." Arkwright turned a troubled countenance toward the men about the table, and then toward Livingstone, but that young man had his eyes fixed gravely on the glasses before him and did not raise them.

Arkwright felt a sudden, unreasonable fear of the circle of strong-featured, serene, and confident men about him. They seemed to be making him the subject of a jest, to be enjoying something among themselves of which he was in ignorance, but which concerned him closely. He turned a white face toward Stanton.

"You don't mean," he began piteously, "that —that you are not going? Is that it—tell me —is that what you wanted to say?"

Stanton shifted in his chair and muttered some words between his lips, then turned toward Arkwright and spoke quite clearly and distinctly.

"I am very sorry, Mr. Arkwright," he said, "but I am afraid I'll have to disappoint you. Reasons I cannot now explain have arisen which make my going impossible—quite impossible," he added firmly—"not only now, but later," he went on quickly, as Arkwright was about to interrupt him.

Arkwright made no second attempt to speak. He felt the muscles of his face working and the tears coming to his eyes, and to hide his weakness he twisted in his chair and sat staring ahead of him with his back turned to the table. He heard Livingstone's voice break the silence with some hurried question, and immediately his embarrassment was hidden in a murmur of answers and the moving of glasses as the men shifted in their chairs and the laughter and talk went on as briskly as before. Arkwright saw a sideboard before him and a servant arranging some silver on one of the shelves. He watched the man do this with a concentrated interest as though the dull, numbed feeling in his brain caught at the trifle in order to put off, as long as possible, the consideration of the truth.

And then beyond the sideboard and the tapestry on the wall above it, he saw the sun shining down upon the island of Cuba, he saw the royal palms waving and bending, the dusty columns of Spanish infantry crawling along the white roads and leaving blazing huts and smoking cane-fields in their wake; he saw skeletons of men and women seeking for food among the refuse of the street; he heard the order given to the firing squad, the splash of the bullets as they scattered the plaster on the prison wall, and he saw a kneeling figure pitch forward on its face, with a useless bandage tied across its sightless eyes.

THE MAN WITH ONE TALENT

Senator Stanton brought him back with a sharp shake of the shoulder. He had also turned his back on the others, and was leaning forward with his elbows on his knees. He spoke rapidly, and in a voice only slightly raised above a whisper.

"I am more than sorry, Arkwright," he said earnestly. "You mustn't blame me altogether. I have had a hard time of it this afternoon. I wanted to go. I really wanted to go. The thing appealed to me, it touched me, it seemed as if I owed it to myself to do it. But they were too many for me," he added with a backward toss of his head toward the men around his table. "If the papers had not told on me I could have got well away," he went on in an eager tone, "but as soon as they read of it, they came here straight from their offices. You know who they are, don't you?" he asked, and even in his earnestness there was an added touch of importance in his tone as he spoke the name of his party's leader, of men who stood prominently in Wall Street and who were at the head of great trusts.

"You see how it is," he said with a shrug of his shoulders. "They have enormous interests at stake. They said I would drag them into war, that I would disturb values, that the business interests of the country would suffer. I'm under obligations to most of them, they have advised me in financial matters, and they threatened—they threatened to make it unpleasant for me." His voice hardened and he drew in his breath quickly, and laughed. "You wouldn't understand if I were to tell you. It's rather involved. And after all, they may be right, agitation may be bad for the country. And your party leader after all is your party leader, isn't he, and if he says 'no' what are you to do? My sympathies are just as keen for these poor women and children as ever, but as these men say, 'charity begins at home,' and we mustn't do anything to bring on war prices again, or to send stocks tumbling about our heads, must we?" He leaned back in his chair again and sighed. "Sympathy is an expensive luxury, I find," he added.

Arkwright rose stiffly and pushed Stanton away from him with his hand. He moved like a man coming out of a dream.

"Don't talk to me like that," he said in a low voice. The noise about the table ended on the instant, but Arkwright did not notice that it had ceased. "You know I don't understand that," he went on; "what does it matter to me?" He put his hand up to the side of his face and held it there, looking down at Stanton. He had the dull, heavy look in his eyes of

"You are like a ring of gamblers around a gaming
table."

a man who has just come through an opera-
tion under some heavy drug. "'Wall Street,'
'trusts,' 'party leaders,'" he repeated, "what
are they to me? The words don't reach me,
they have lost their meaning, it is a language
I have forgotten, thank God!" he added. He
turned and moved his eyes around the table,
scanning the faces of the men before him.

"Yes, you are twelve to one," he said at last,
still speaking dully and in a low voice, as though
he were talking to himself. "You have won a
noble victory, gentlemen. I congratulate you.
But I do not blame you, we are all selfish and
self-seeking. I thought I was working only
for Cuba, but I was working for myself, just
as you are. I wanted to feel that it was I who
had helped to bring relief to that plague-spot,
that it was through my efforts the help had
come. Yes, if he had done as I asked, I suppose I would have taken the credit."

He swayed slightly, and to steady himself
caught at the back of his chair. But at the
same moment his eyes glowed fiercely and he
held himself erect again. He pointed with his
finger at the circle of great men who sat looking up at him in curious silence.

"You are like a ring of gamblers around a
gaming table," he cried wildly, "who see nothing but the green cloth and the wheel and the

piles of money before them, who forget, in watching the money rise and fall, that outside the sun is shining, that human beings are sick and suffering, that men are giving their lives for an idea, for a sentiment, for a flag. You are the money-changers in the temple of this great republic; and the day will come, I pray to God, when you will be scourged and driven out with whips. Do you think you can form combines and deals that will cheat you into heaven? Can your 'trusts' save your souls—is 'Wall Street' the straight and narrow road to salvation?"

The men about the table leaned back and stared at Arkwright in as great amazement as though he had violently attempted an assault upon their pockets, or had suddenly gone mad in their presence. Some of them frowned, and others appeared not to have heard, and others smiled grimly and waited for him to continue as though they were spectators at a play.

The political leader broke the silence with a low aside to Stanton. "Does the gentleman belong to the Salvation Army?" he asked.

Arkwright whirled about and turned upon him fiercely.

"Old gods give way to new gods," he cried. "Here is your brother. I am speaking for him. Do you ever think of him? How dare you sneer at me?" he cried. "You can crack your whip over that man's head and turn him from what in his heart and conscience he knows is right; you can crack your whip over the men who call themselves free-born American citizens and who have made you their boss—sneer at them if you like, but you have no collar on my neck. If you are a leader, why don't you lead your people to what is good and noble? Why do you stop this man in the work God sent him here to do? You would make a party hack of him, a political prostitute, something lower than the woman who walks the streets. She sells her body—this man is selling his soul."

He turned, trembling and quivering, and shook his finger above the upturned face of the senator.

"What have you done with your talents, Stanton?" he cried. "What have you done with your talents?"

The man in the overcoat struck the table before him with his fist so that the glasses rang.

"By God," he laughed, "I call him a better speaker than Stanton! Livingstone's right, he *is* better than Stanton—but he lacks Stanton's knack of making himself popular," he added. He looked around the table inviting approbation with a smile, but no one noticed him, nor spoke to break the silence.

Arkwright heard the words dully and felt that he was being mocked. He covered his face with his hands and stood breathing brokenly; his body was still trembling with an excitement he could not master.

Stanton rose from his chair and shook him by the shoulder. "Are you mad, Arkwright?" he cried. "You have no right to insult my guests or me. Be calm—control yourself."

"What does it matter what I say?" Arkwright went on desperately. "I am mad. Yes, that is it, I am mad. They have won and I have lost, and it drove me beside myself. I counted on you. I knew that no one else could let my people go. But I'll not trouble you again. I wish you good-night, sir, and good-by. If I have been unjust, you must forget it."

He turned sharply, but Stanton placed a detaining hand on his shoulder. "Wait," he commanded querulously; "where are you going? Will you still——?"

Arkwright bowed his head. "Yes," he answered. "I have but just time now to catch our train—my train, I mean."

He looked up at Stanton, and taking his hand in both of his, drew the man toward him. All the wildness and intolerance in his manner had passed, and as he raised his eyes they were full of a firm resolve.

THE MAN WITH ONE TALENT

"Come," he said, simply; "there is yet time. Leave these people behind you. What can you answer when they ask what have you done with your talents?"

"Good God, Arkwright," the senator exclaimed, angrily, pulling his hand away; "don't talk like a hymn-book, and don't make another scene. What you ask is impossible. Tell me what I can do to help you in any other way, and——"

"Come," repeated the young man, firmly. "The world may judge you by what you do to-night."

Stanton looked at the boy for a brief moment with a strained and eager scrutiny, and then turned away abruptly and shook his head in silence, and Arkwright passed around the table and on out of the room.

A month later, as the Southern senator was passing through the reading-room of the Union Club, Livingstone beckoned to him, and handing him an afternoon paper pointed at a paragraph in silence. The paragraph was dated Sagua la Grande, and read:

"The body of Henry Arkwright, an American civil engineer, was brought into Sagua to-day by a Spanish column. It was found lying in a road three miles beyond the line of forts. Arkwright was surprised by a guerilla force while attempting to make his way to the insurgent camp, and on resisting was shot. The body has been handed over to the American consul for interment. It is badly mutilated."

Stanton lowered the paper and stood staring out of the window at the falling snow and the cheery lights and bustling energy of the avenue.

"Poor fellow," he said, "he wanted so much to help them. And he didn't accomplish anything, did he?"

Livingstone stared at the older man and laughed shortly.

"Well, I don't know," he said. "He died. Some of us only live."

AN UNFINISHED STORY

MRS. TREVELYAN, as she took her seat, shot a quick glance down the length of her table and at the arrangement of her guests, and tried to learn if her lord and master approved. But he was listening to something Lady Arbuthnot, who sat on his right, was saying, and, being a man, failed to catch her meaning, and only smiled unconcernedly and cheerfully back at her. But the wife of the Austrian Minister, who was her very dearest friend, saw and appreciated, and gave her a quick little smile over her fan, which said that the table was perfect, the people most interesting, and that she could possess her soul in peace. So Mrs. Trevelyan pulled at the tips of her gloves and smiled upon her guests. Mrs. Trevelyan was not used to questioning her powers, but this dinner had been almost impromptu, and she had been in doubt. It was quite unnecessary, for her dinner carried with it the added virtue of being the last of the season, an encore to all that had gone before—a special number by request on the social programme. It was not one of many others stretching on for weeks, for the summer's change and leisure began on the morrow, and there was nothing hanging over her guests that they must go on to later. They knew that their luggage stood ready locked and strapped at home; they could look before them to the whole summer's pleasure, and they were relaxed and ready to be pleased, and broke simultaneously into a low murmur of talk and laughter. The windows of the dining-room stood open from the floor, and from the tiny garden that surrounded the house, even in the great mass of stucco and brick of encircling London, came the odor of flowers and of fresh turf. A soft summer-night wind moved the candles under their red shades; and gently as though they rose from afar, and not only from across the top of the high wall before the house, came the rumble of the omnibuses passing farther into the suburbs, and the occasional quick rush of a hansom over the smooth asphalt. It was a most delightful choice of people, gathered at short notice and to do honor to no one in particular, but to give each a chance to say good-by before he or she met the yacht at Southampton or took the club train to Homburg. They all knew each other very well; and if there was a guest of the evening, it was one of the two Americans—either Miss Egerton, the girl who was to marry Lord Arbuthnot, whose mother sat on Trevelyan's right, or young Gordon, the explorer, who has just come out of Africa. Miss Egerton was a most strikingly beautiful girl, with a strong, fine face, and an earnest, interested way when she spoke, which the English found most attractive. In appearance she had been variously likened by Trevelyan, who was painting her portrait, to a druidess, a vestal virgin, and a Greek goddess; and Lady Arbuthnot's friends, who thought to please the girl, assured her that no one would ever suppose her to be an American—their ideas of the American young woman having been gathered from those who pick out tunes with one finger on the pianos in the public parlors of the Métropole. Miss Egerton was said to be intensely interested in her lover's career, and was as ambitious for his success in the House as he was himself. They were both very much in love, and showed it to others as little as people of their class do. The others at the table were General Sir Henry Kent; Phillips, the novelist; the Austrian Minister and his young wife; and Trevelyan, who painted portraits for large sums of money and figure pieces for art; and some simply fashionable smart people who were good listeners, and who were rather disappointed that the American explorer was no more sunburned than other young men who had stayed at home, and who had gone in for tennis or yachting.

The worst of Gordon was that he made it next to impossible for one to lionize him. He had been back in civilization and London only two weeks, unless Cairo and Shepheard's Hotel are civilization, and he had been asked everywhere, and for the first week had gone everywhere. But whenever his hostess looked for him, to present another and not so recent a lion, he was generally found either humbly carrying an ice to some neglected dowager, or talking big game or international yachting or tailors to a circle of younger sons in the smoking-room, just as though several hundred attractive and distinguished people were not waiting to fling the speeches they had prepared on Africa at him, in the drawing-room above. He had suddenly disappeared during the second week of his stay in London, which was also the last week of the London season, and managers of lecture tours and publishers and lion-hunters, and even friends who cared for him for himself, had failed to find him at his lodgings. Trevelyan, who had known him when he was a travelling correspondent and artist for one of the great weeklies, had found him at the club the night before, and had asked him to his wife's impromptu dinner, from which he had at first begged off, but, on learning who was to be there, had changed his mind and accepted. Mrs. Trevelyan was very glad he had come; she had always spoken of him as a nice boy, and now that he had become famous she liked him none the less, but did not show it before people as much as she had been used to do. She forgot to ask him whether he knew his beautiful compatriot or not; but she took it for granted that they had met, if not at home, at least in London, as they had both been made so much of, and at the same houses.

The dinner was well on its way toward its end, and the women had begun to talk across the table, and to exchange bankers' addresses, and to say, "Be sure and look us up in Paris," and "When do you expect to sail from Cowes?" They were enlivened and interested, and the present odors of the food and flowers and wine, and the sense of leisure before them, made it seem almost a pity that such a well-suited gathering should have to separate for even a summer's pleasure.

The Austrian Minister was saying this to his hostess, when Sir Henry Kent, who had been talking across to Phillips, the novelist, leaned back in his place and said, as though to challenge the attention of every one, "I can't agree with you, Phillips. I am sure no one else will."

"Dear me," complained Mrs. Trevelyan, plaintively, "what have you been saying now, Mr. Phillips? He always has such debatable theories," she explained.

"On the contrary, Mrs. Trevelyan," answered the novelist, "it is the other way. It is Sir Henry who is making all the trouble. He is attacking one of the oldest and dearest platitudes I know." He paused for the general to speak, but the older man nodded his head for him to go on. "He has just said that fiction is stranger than truth," continued the novelist. "He says that I—that people who write could never interest people who read if they wrote of things as they really are. They select, he says —they take the critical moment in a man's life and the crises, and want others to believe that that is what happens every day. Which it is not, so the general says. He thinks that life is commonplace and uneventful—that is, uneventful in a picturesque or dramatic way. He admits that women's lives are saved from drowning, but that they are not saved by their lovers, but by a longshoreman with a wife and six children, who accepts five pounds for doing it. That's it, is it not?" he asked.

The general nodded and smiled. "What I

said to Phillips was," he explained, "that if things were related just as they happen, they would not be interesting. People do not say the dramatic things they say on the stage or in novels; in real life they are commonplace or sordid—or disappointing. I have seen men die on the battle-field, for instance, and they never cried, 'I die that my country may live,' or 'I have got my promotion at last'; they just stared up at the surgeon and said, 'Have I got to lose that arm?' or 'I am killed, I think.' You see, when men are dying around you, and horses are plunging, and the batteries are firing, one doesn't have time to think up the appropriate remark for the occasion. I don't believe, now, that Pitt's last words were, 'Roll up the map of Europe.' A man who could change the face of a continent would not use his dying breath in making epigrams. It was one of his secretaries or one of the doctors who said that. And the man who was capable of writing home, 'All is lost but honor,' was just the sort of a man who would lose more battles than he would win. No; you, Phillips," said the general, raising his voice as he became more confident and conscious that he held the centre of the stage, "and you, Trevelyan, don't write and paint every-day things as they are. You introduce something for a contrast or for an effect; a red coat in a landscape for the bit of color you want, when in real life the red coat would not be within miles; or you have a band of music playing a popular air in the street when a murder is going on inside the house. You do it because it is effective; but it isn't true. Now Mr. Caithness was telling us the other night at the club, on this very matter——"

"Oh, that's hardly fair," laughed Trevelyan; "you've rehearsed all this before. You've come prepared."

"No, not at all," frowned the general, sweeping on. "He said that before he was raised to the bench, when he practised criminal law, he had brought word to a man that he was to be reprieved, and to another that he was to die. Now, you know," exclaimed the general, with a shrug, and appealing to the table, "how that would be done on the stage or in a novel, with the prisoner bound ready for execution, and a galloping horse, and a fluttering piece of white paper, and all that. Well, now, Caithness told us that he went into the man's cell and said, 'You have been reprieved, John,' or William, or whatever the fellow's name was. And the man looked at him and said: 'Is that so? That's good—that's good'; and that was all he said. And then, again, he told one man whose life he had tried very hard to save: 'The Home

AN UNFINISHED STORY

Secretary has refused to intercede for you. I
saw him at his house last night at nine o'clock.'
And the murderer, instead of saying, 'My God!
what will my wife and children do?' looked at
him, and repeated, 'At nine o'clock last night!'
just as though that were the important part of
the message."

"Well, but, general," said Phillips, smiling,
"that's dramatic enough as it is, I think.
Why——"

"Yes," interrupted the general, quickly and
triumphantly. "But that is not what you
would have made him say, is it? That's my
point."

"There was a man told me once," Lord Arbuthnot began, leisurely—"he was a great
chum of mine, and it illustrates what Sir Henry
has said, I think—he was engaged to a girl, and
he had a misunderstanding or an understanding
with her that opened both their eyes, at a dance,
and the next afternoon he called, and they
talked it over in the drawing-room, with the
tea-tray between them, and agreed to end it.
On the stage he would have risen and said,
'Well, the comedy is over, the tragedy begins,
or the curtain falls; and she would have gone
to the piano and played Chopin sadly while he
made his exit. Instead of which he got up to
go without saying anything, and as he rose he

upset a cup and saucer on the tea-table, and said, 'Oh, I beg your pardon'; and she said, 'It isn't broken'; and he went out. You see," the young man added, smiling, "there were two young people whose hearts were breaking, and yet they talked of teacups, not because they did not feel, but because custom is too strong on us and too much for us. We do not say dramatic things or do theatrical ones. It does not make interesting reading, but it is the truth."

"Exactly," cut in the Austrian Minister, eagerly. "And then there is the prerogative of the author and of the playwright to drop a curtain whenever he wants to, or to put a stop to everything by ending the chapter. That isn't fair. That is an advantage over nature. When some one accuses some one else of doing something dreadful at the play, down comes the curtain quick and keeps things at fever point, or the chapter ends with a lot of stars, and the next page begins with a description of a sunset two weeks later. To be true, we ought to be told what the man who is accused said in the reply, or what happened during those two weeks before the sunset. The author really has no right to choose only the critical moments, and to shut out the commonplace, every-day life by a sort of literary closure. That is, if he claims to tell the truth."

Phillips raised his eyebrows and looked carefully around the table. "Does any one else feel called upon to testify?" he asked.

"It's awful, isn't it, Phillips," laughed Trevelyan, comfortably, "to find that the photographer is the only artist, after all? I feel very guilty."

"You ought to," pronounced the general, gayly. He was very well satisfied with himself at having held his own against these clever people. "And I am sure Mr. Gordon will agree with me, too," he went on, confidently, with a bow toward the younger man. "He has seen more of the world than any of us, and he will tell you, I am sure, that what happens only suggests the story; it is not complete in itself. That it always needs the author's touch, just as the rough diamond——"

"Oh, thanks, thanks, general," laughed Phillips. "My feelings are not hurt as badly as that."

Gordon had been turning the stem of a wineglass slowly between his thumb and his finger while the others were talking, and looking down at it smiling. Now he raised his eyes as though he meant to speak, and then dropped them again. "I am afraid, Sir Henry," he said, "that I don't agree with you at all."

Those who had said nothing felt a certain

269

satisfaction that they had not committed themselves. The Austrian Minister tried to remember what it was he had said, and whether it
was too late to retreat, and the general looked
blankly at Gordon, and said, "Indeed?"

"You shouldn't have called on that last witness, Sir Henry," said Phillips, smiling. "Your
case was very good as it was."

"I am quite sure," said Gordon, seriously,
"that the story Phillips will never write is a
true story, but he will not write it because people would say it is impossible, just as you have
all seen sunsets sometimes that you knew would
be laughed at if any one tried to paint them.
We all know such a story, something in our own
lives, or in the lives of our friends. Not ghost
stories, or stories of adventure, but of ambitions
that come to nothing, of people who were rewarded or punished in this world instead of in
the next, and love stories."

Phillips looked at the young man keenly and
smiled. "Especially love stories," he said.

Gordon looked back at him as if he did not
understand.

"Tell it, Gordon," said Mr. Trevelyan.

"Yes," said Gordon, nodding his head in
assent, "I was thinking of a particular story.
It is as complete, I think, and as dramatic as
any of those we read. It is about a man I met

in Africa. It is not a long story," he said,
looking around the table tentatively, "but it
ends badly."

There was a silence much more appreciated
than a polite murmur of invitation would have
been, and the simply smart people settled themselves rigidly to catch every word for future
use. They realized that this would be a story
which had not as yet appeared in the newspapers, and which would not make a part of
Gordon's book. Mrs. Trevelyan smiled encouragingly upon her former protégé; she was
sure he was going to do himself credit; but the
American girl chose this chance, when all the
other eyes were turned expectantly toward the
explorer, to look at her lover.

"We were on our return march from Lake
Tchad to the Mobangi," said Gordon. "We
had been travelling over a month, sometimes
by water and sometimes through the forest, and
we did not expect to see any other white men
besides those of our own party for several
months to come. In the middle of a jungle
late one afternoon I found this man lying at the
foot of a tree. He had been cut and beaten
and left for dead. It was as much of a surprise
to me, you understand, as it would be to you
if you were driving through Trafalgar Square
in a hansom, and an African lion should spring

up on your horses' haunches. We believed we were the only white men that had ever succeeded in getting that far south. Crampel had tried it, and no one knows yet whether he is dead or alive; Doctor Schlemen had been eaten by cannibals, and Major Bethume had turned back two hundred miles farther north; and we could no more account for this man's presence than if he had been dropped from the clouds. Lieutenant Royce, my surgeon, went to work at him, and we halted where we were for the night. In about an hour the man moved and opened his eyes. He looked up at us and said, 'Thank God!'—because we were white, I suppose—and went off into unconsciousness again. When he came to the next time, he asked Royce, in a whisper, how long he had to live. He wasn't the sort of a man you had to lie to about a thing like that, and Royce told him he did not think he could live for more than an hour or two. The man moved his head to show that he understood, and raised his hand to his throat and began pulling at his shirt, but the effort sent him off into a fainting-fit again. I opened his collar for him as gently as I could, and found that his fingers had clinched around a silver necklace that he wore about his neck, and from which there hung a gold locket shaped like a heart."

AN UNFINISHED STORY

Gordon raised his eyes slowly from the observation of his finger-tips as they rested on the edge of the table before him to those of the American girl who sat opposite. She had heard his story so far without any show of attention, and had been watching, rather with a touch of fondness in her eyes, the clever, earnest face of Arbuthnot, who was following Gordon's story with polite interest. But now, at Gordon's last words, she turned her eyes to him with a look of awful indignation, which was followed, when she met his calmly polite look of inquiry, by one of fear and almost of entreaty.

"When the man came to," continued Gordon, in the same conventional monotone, "he begged me to take the chain and locket to a girl whom he said I would find either in London or in New York. He gave me the address of her banker. He said: 'Take it off my neck before you bury me; tell her I wore it ever since she gave it to me. That it has been a charm and loadstone to me. That when the locket rose and fell against my breast, it was as if her heart were pressing against mine and answering the beating and throbbing of the blood in my veins.'"

Gordon paused, and returned to the thoughtful scrutiny of his finger-tips.

"The man did not die," he said, raising his

273

head. "Royce brought him back into such form again that in about a week we were able to take him along with us on a litter. But he was very weak, and would lie for hours sleeping when we rested, or mumbling and raving in a fever. We learned from him at odd times that he had been trying to reach Lake Tchad, to do what we had done, without any means of doing it. He had had not more than a couple of dozen porters and a corporal's guard of Senegalese soldiers. He was the only white man in the party, and his men had turned on him, and left him as we found him, carrying off with them his stock of provisions and arms. He had undertaken the expedition on a promise from the French government to make him governor of the territory he opened up if he succeeded, but he had had no official help. If he failed, he got nothing; if he succeeded, he did so at his own expense and by his own endeavors. It was only a wonder he had been able to get as far as he did. He did not seem to feel the failure of his expedition. All that was lost in the happiness of getting back alive to this woman with whom he was in love. He had been three days alone before we found him, and in those three days, while he waited for death, he had thought of nothing but that he would never see her again. He had resigned himself to this, had given up all hope, and our coming seemed like a miracle to him. I have read about men in love, I have seen it on the stage, I have seen it in real life, but I never saw a man so grateful to God and so happy and so insane over a woman as this man was. He raved about her when he was feverish, and he talked and talked to me about her when he was in his senses. The porters could not understand him, and he found me sympathetic, I suppose, or else he did not care, and only wanted to speak of her to some one, and so he told me the story over and over again as I walked beside the litter, or as we sat by the fire at night. She must have been a very remarkable girl. He had met her first the year before, on one of the Italian steamers that ply from New York to Gibraltar. She was travelling with her father, who was an invalid going to Tangier for his health; from Tangier they were to go on up to Nice and Cannes, and in the spring to Paris and on to London for this season just over. The man was going from Gibraltar to Zanzibar, and then on into the Congo. They had met the first night out; they had separated thirteen days later at Gibraltar, and in that time the girl had fallen in love with him, and had promised to marry him if he would let her, for he was very proud. He had to be. He had absolutely nothing to offer her. She is very well known at home. I mean her family is: they have lived in New York from its first days, and they are very rich. The girl had lived a life as different from his as the life of a girl in society must be from that of a vagabond. He had been an engineer, a newspaper correspondent, an officer in a Chinese army, and had built bridges in South America, and led their little revolutions there, and had seen service on the desert in the French army of Algiers. He had no home or nationality even, for he had left America when he was sixteen; he had no family, had saved no money, and was trusting everything to the success of this expedition into Africa to make him known and to give him position. It was the story of Othello and Desdemona over again. His blackness lay from her point of view, or rather would have lain from the point of view of her friends, in the fact that he was as helplessly ineligible a young man as a cowboy. And he really had lived a life of which he had no great reason to be proud. He had existed entirely for excitement, as other men live to drink until they kill themselves by it; nothing he had done had counted for much except his bridges. They are still standing. But the things he had written are lost in the columns of the daily papers. The soldiers he had fought

with knew him only as a man who cared more
for the fighting than for what the fighting was
about, and he had been as ready to write on
one side as to fight on the other. He was a
rolling stone, and had been a rolling stone from
the time he was sixteen and had run away to
sea, up to the day he had met this girl, when he
was just thirty. Yet you can see how such a
man would attract a young, impressionable girl,
who had met only those men whose actions are
bounded by the courts of law or Wall Street, or
the younger set who drive coaches and who
live the life of the clubs. She had gone through
life as some people go through picture-galleries,
with their catalogues marked at the best pictures. She knew nothing of the little fellows
whose work was skied, who were trying to be
known, who were not of her world, but who
toiled and prayed and hoped to be famous.
This man came into her life suddenly with his
stories of adventure and strange people and
strange places, of things done for the love of
doing them and not for the reward or reputation, and he bewildered her at first, I suppose,
and then fascinated, and then won her. You
can imagine how it was, these two walking the
deck together during the day, or sitting side by
side when the night came on, the ocean stretched
before them. The daring of his present under-

taking, the absurd glamour that is thrown over those who have gone into that strange country from which some travellers return, and the picturesqueness of his past life. It is no wonder the girl made too much of him. I do not think he knew what was coming. He did not pose before her. I am quite sure, from what I knew of him, that he did not. Indeed, I believed him when he said that he had fought against the more than interest she had begun to show for him. He was the sort of man women care for, but they had not been of this woman's class or calibre. It came to him like a sign from the heavens. It was as if a goddess had stooped to him. He told her when they separated that if he succeeded—if he opened this unknown country, if he was rewarded as they had promised to reward him—he might dare to come to her; and she called him her knight-errant, and gave him her chain and locket to wear, and told him whether he failed or succeeded it meant nothing to her, and that her life was his while it lasted, and her soul as well.

"I think," Gordon said, stopping abruptly, with an air of careful consideration, "that those were her words as he repeated them to me."

He raised his eyes thoughtfully toward the face of the girl opposite, and then glanced past her, as if he were trying to recall the words the

278

man had used. The fine, beautiful face of the woman was white and drawn around the lips, and she gave a quick, appealing glance at her hostess, as if she would beg to be allowed to go. But Mrs. Trevelyan and her guests were watching Gordon or toying with the things in front of them. The dinner had been served, and not even the soft movements of the servants interrupted the young man's story.

"You can imagine a man," Gordon went on, more lightly, "finding a hansom cab slow when he is riding from the station to see the woman he loves; but imagine this man urging himself and the rest of us to hurry when we were in the heart of Africa, with six months' travel in front of us before we could reach the first limits of civilization. That is what this man did. When he was still on his litter he used to toss and turn, and abuse the bearers and porters and myself because we moved so slowly. When we stopped for the night he would chafe and fret at the delay; and when the morning came he was the first to wake, if he slept at all, and eager to push on. When at last he was able to walk, he worked himself into a fever again, and it was only when Royce warned him that he would kill himself if he kept on that he submitted to be carried, and forced himself to be patient. And all the time the poor devil kept saying how unworthy he was of her, how miserably he had wasted his years, how unfitted he was for the great happiness which had come into his life. I suppose every man says that when he is in love; very properly, too; but the worst of it was, in this man's case, that it was so very true. He was unworthy of her in everything but his love for her. It used to frighten me to see how much he cared. Well, we got out of it at last, and reached Alexandria, and saw white faces once more and heard women's voices, and the strain and fear of failure were over, and we could breathe again. I was quite ready enough to push on to London, but we had to wait a week for the steamer, and during that time that man made my life miserable. He had done so well, and would have done so much more if he had had my equipment, that I tried to see that he received all the credit due him. But he would have none of the public receptions, and the audience with the Khedive, or any of the fuss they made over us. He only wanted to get back to her. He spent the days on the quay watching them load the steamer, and counting the hours until she was to sail; and even at night he would leave the first bed he had slept in for six months, and would come into my room and ask me if I would not sit up and talk with him until daylight. You see, after he had given up all thought of her, and believed himself about to die without seeing her again, it made her all the dearer, I suppose, and made him all the more fearful of losing her again.

"He became very quiet as soon as we were really under way, and Royce an I hardly knew him for the same man. He would sit in silence in his steamer-chair for hours, looking out at the sea and smiling to himself, and sometimes, for he was still very weak and feverish, the tears would come to his eyes and run down his cheeks. 'This is the way we would sit,' he said to me one night, 'with the dark purple sky and the strange Southern stars over our heads, and the rail of the boat rising and sinking below the line of the horizon. And I can hear her voice, and I try to imagine she is still sitting there, as she did the last night out, when I held her hands between mine.'" Gordon paused a moment, and then went on more slowly: "I do not know whether it was that the excitement of the journey overland had kept him up or not, but as we went on he became much weaker and slept more, until Royce became anxious and alarmed about him. But he did not know it himself; he had grown so sure of his recovery then that he did not understand what the weakness meant. He fell off into long spells of sleep or unconsciousness, and woke only to be fed, and would then fall back to sleep again. And in one of these spells of unconsciousness he died. He died within two days of land. He had no home and no country and no family, as I told you, and we buried him at sea. He left nothing behind him, for the very clothes he wore were those we had given him—nothing but the locket and the chain which he had told me to take from his neck when he died."

Gordon's voice had grown very cold and hard. He stopped and ran his fingers down into his pocket and pulled out a little leather bag. The people at the table watched him in silence as he opened it and took out a dull silver chain with a gold heart hanging from it.

"This is it," he said, gently. He leaned across the table, with his eyes fixed on those of the American girl, and dropped the chain in front of her. "Would you like to see it?" he said.

The rest moved curiously forward to look at the little heap of gold and silver as it lay on the white cloth. But the girl, with her eyes half closed and her lips pressed together, pushed it on with her hand to the man who sat next her, and bowed her head slightly, as though it was an effort for her to move at all. The wife of the Austrian Minister gave a little sigh of relief.

"I should say your story did end badly, Mr. Gordon," she said. "It is terribly sad, and so unnecessarily so."

"I don't know," said Lady Arbuthnot, thoughtfully—"I don't know; it seems to me it was better. As Mr. Gordon says, the man was hardly worthy of her. A man should have something more to offer a woman than love; it is a woman's prerogative to be loved. Any number of men may love her; it is nothing to their credit: they cannot help themselves."

"Well," said General Kent, "if all true stories turn out as badly as that one does, I will take back what I said against those the story-writers tell. I prefer the ones Anstey and Jerome make up. I call it a most unpleasant story."

"But it isn't finished yet," said Gordon, as he leaned over and picked up the chain and locket. "There is still a little more."

"Oh, I beg your pardon!" said the wife of the Austrian Minister, eagerly. "But then," she added, "you can't make it any better. You cannot bring the man back to life."

"No," said Gordon, "but I can make it a little worse."

"Ah, I see," said Phillips, with a story-teller's intuition—"the girl."

"The first day I reached London I went to her banker's and got her address," continued

283

Gordon. "And I wrote, saying I wanted to see her, but before I could get an answer I met her the next afternoon at a garden-party. At least I did not meet her; she was pointed out to me. I saw a very beautiful girl surrounded by a lot of men, and asked who she was, and found out it was the woman I had written to, the owner of the chain and locket; and I was also told that her engagement had just been announced to a young Englishman of family and position, who had known her only a few months, and with whom she was very much in love. So you see," he went on, smiling, "that it was better that he died, believing in her and in her love for him. Mr. Phillips, now, would have let him live to return and find her married; but Nature is kinder than writers of fiction, and quite as dramatic."

Phillips did not reply to this, and the general only shook his head doubtfully and said nothing. So Mrs. Trevelyan looked at Lady Arbuthnot, and the ladies rose and left the room. When the men had left them, a young girl went to the piano, and the other women seated themselves to listen; but Miss Egerton, saying that it was warm, stepped out through one of the high windows on to the little balcony that overhung the garden. It was dark out there and cool, and the rumbling of the encircling city sounded as distant and as far off as the reflection seemed that its million lights threw up to the sky above. The girl leaned her face and bare shoulder against the rough stone wall of the house, and pressed her hands together, with her fingers locking and unlocking and her rings cutting through her gloves. She was trembling slightly, and the blood in her veins was hot and tingling. She heard the voices of the men as they entered the drawing-room, the momentary cessation of the music at the piano, and its renewal, and then a figure blocked the light from the window, and Gordon stepped out of it and stood in front of her with the chain and locket in his hand. He held it toward her, and they faced each other for a moment in silence.

"Will you take it now?" he said.

The girl raised her head, and drew herself up until she stood straight and tall before him.

"Have you not punished me enough?" she asked, in a whisper. "Are you not satisfied? Was it brave? Was it manly? Is that what you have learned among your savages—to torture a woman?" She stopped with a quick sob of pain, and pressed her hands against her breast.

Gordon observed her, curiously, with cold consideration. "What of the sufferings of the man to whom you gave this?" he asked. "Why not consider him? What was your bad quarter of an hour at the table, with your friends around you, to the year he suffered danger and physical pain for you—for you, remember?"

The girl hid her face for a moment in her hands, and when she lowered them again her cheeks were wet and her voice was changed and softer. "They told me he was dead," she said. "Then it was denied, and then the French papers told of it again, and with horrible detail, and how it happened."

Gordon took a step nearer her. "And does your love come and go with the editions of the daily papers?" he asked, fiercely. "If they say to-morrow morning that Arbuthnot is false to his principles or his party, that he is a bribe-taker, a man who sells his vote, will you believe them and stop loving him?" He gave a sharp exclamation of disdain. "Or will you wait," he went on, bitterly, "until the Liberal organs have had time to deny it? Is that the love, the life, and the soul you promised the man who——"

There was a soft step on the floor of the drawing-room, and the tall figure of young Arbuthnot appeared in the opening of the window as he looked doubtfully out into the darkness. Gordon took a step back into the

286

light of the window, where he could be seen, and leaned easily against the railing of the balcony. His eyes were turned toward the street, and he noticed over the wall the top of a passing omnibus and the glow of the men's pipes who sat on it.

"Miss Egerton?" asked Arbuthnot, his eyes still blinded by the lights of the room he had left. "Is she here? Oh, is that you?" he said, as he saw the movement of the white dress. "I was sent to look for you," he said. "They were afraid something was wrong." He turned to Gordon, as if in explanation of his lover-like solicitude. "It has been rather a hard week, and it has kept one pretty well on the go all the time, and I thought Miss Egerton looked tired at dinner."

The moment he had spoken, the girl came toward him quickly, and put her arm inside of his, and took his hand.

He looked down at her wonderingly at this show of affection, and then drew her nearer, and said, gently, "You are tired, aren't you? I came to tell you that Lady Arbuthnot is going. She is waiting for you."

It struck Gordon, as they stood there, how handsome they were and how well suited. They took a step toward the window, and then the young nobleman turned and looked out at the pretty garden and up at the sky, where the moon was struggling against the glare of the city.

"It is very pretty and peaceful out here," he said, "is it not? It seems a pity to leave it. Good-night, Gordon, and thank you for your story." He stopped, with one foot on the threshold, and smiled. "And yet, do you know," he said, "I cannot help thinking you were guilty of doing just what you accused Phillips of doing. I somehow thought you helped the true story out a little. Now didn't you? Was it all just as you told it? Or am I wrong?"

"No," Gordon answered; "you are right. I did change it a little, in one particular."

"And what was that, may I ask?" said Arbuthnot.

"The man did not die," Gordon answered.

Arbuthnot gave a quick little sigh of sympathy. "Poor devil!" he said, softly; "poor chap!" He moved his left hand over and touched the hand of the girl, as though to reassure himself of his own good fortune. Then he raised his eyes to Gordon's with a curious, puzzled look in them. "But then," he said, doubtfully, "if he is not dead, how did you come to get the chain?"

The girl's arm within his own moved slightly,

and her fingers tightened their hold upon his hand.

"Oh," said Gordon, indifferently, "it did not mean anything to him, you see, when he found he had lost her, and it could not mean anything to her. It is of no value. It means nothing to any one—except, perhaps, to me."

THE TRAILER FOR ROOM NO. 8

THE "trailer" for the green-goods men who rented room No. 8 in Case's tenement had had no work to do for the last few days, and was cursing his luck in consequence.

He was entirely too young to curse, but he had never been told so, and, indeed, so imperfect had his training been that he had never been told not to do anything as long as it pleased him to do it and made existence any more bearable.

He had been told when he was very young, before the man and woman who had brought him into the world had separated, not to crawl out on the fire-escape, because he might break his neck, and later, after his father had walked off Hegelman's Slip into the East River while very drunk, and his mother had been sent to the penitentiary for grand larceny, he had been told not to let the police catch him sleeping under the bridge.

With these two exceptions he had been told to do as he pleased, which was the very mockery of advice, as he was just about as well able to do as he pleased as is any one who has to beg

or steal what he eats and has to sleep in hall-
ways or over the iron gratings of warm cellars
and has the officers of the children's societies
always after him to put him in a "Home" and
make him be "good."

"Snipes," as the trailer was called, was determined no one should ever force him to be good
if he could possibly prevent it. And he certainly did do a great deal to prevent it. He
knew what having to be good meant. Some
of the boys who had escaped from the Home
had told him all about that. It meant wearing
shoes and a blue and white checkered apron,
and making cane-bottomed chairs all day, and
having to wash yourself in a big iron tub twice
a week, not to speak of having to move about
like machines whenever the lady teacher hit a
bell. So when the green-goods men, of whom
the genial Mr. Alf Wolfe was the chief, asked
Snipes to act as "trailer" for them at a quarter
of a dollar for every victim he shadowed, he
jumped at the offer and was proud of the position.

If you should happen to keep a grocery store
in the country, or to run the village post-office,
it is not unlikely that you know what a green-
goods man is; but in case you don't, and have
only a vague idea as to how he lives, a paragraph of explanation must be inserted here for

your particular benefit. Green-goods is the technical name for counterfeit bills, and the green-goods men send out circulars to countrymen all over the United States, offering to sell them $5,000 worth of counterfeit money for $500, and ease their conscience by explaining to them that by purchasing these green goods they are hurting no one but the Government, which is quite able, with its big surplus, to stand the loss. They enclose a letter which is to serve their victim as a mark of identification or credential when he comes on to purchase.

The address they give him is in one of the many drug-store and cigar-store post-offices which are scattered all over New York, and which contribute to make vice and crime so easy that the evil they do cannot be reckoned in souls lost or dollars stolen. If the letter from the countryman strikes the dealers in green goods as sincere, they appoint an interview with him by mail in rooms they rent for the purpose, and if they, on meeting him there, think he is still in earnest and not a detective or officer in disguise, they appoint still another interview, to be held later in the day in the back room of some saloon.

Then the countryman is watched throughout the day from the moment he leaves the first meeting-place until he arrives at the saloon.

THE TRAILER FOR ROOM NO. 8

If anything in his conduct during that time leads the man whose duty it is to follow him, or the "trailer," as the profession call it, to believe he is a detective, he finds when he arrives at the saloon that there is no one to receive him. But if the trailer regards his conduct as unsuspicious, he is taken to another saloon, not the one just appointed, which is, perhaps, a most respectable place, but to the thieves' own private little rendezvous, where he is robbed in any of the several different ways best suited to their purpose.

Snipes was a very good trailer. He was so little that no one ever noticed him, and he could keep a man in sight no matter how big the crowd was, or how rapidly it changed and shifted. And he was as patient as he was quick, and would wait for hours if needful, with his eye on a door, until his man reissued into the street again. And if the one he shadowed looked behind him to see if he was followed, or dodged up and down different streets, as if he were trying to throw off pursuit, or despatched a note or telegram, or stopped to speak to a policeman or any special officer, as a detective might, who thought he had his men safely in hand, off Snipes would go on a run, to where Alf Wolfe was waiting, and tell what he had seen.

Then Wolfe would give him a quarter or

293

more, and the trailer would go back to his post opposite Case's tenement, and wait for another victim to issue forth, and for the signal from No. 8 to follow him. It was not much fun, and "customers," as Mr. Wolfe always called them, had been scarce, and Mr. Wolfe, in consequence, had been cross and nasty in his temper, and had batted Snipe out of the way on more than one occasion. So the trailer was feeling blue and disconsolate, and wondered how it was that "Naseby" Raegen, "Rags" Raegen's younger brother, had had the luck to get a two weeks' visit to the country with the Fresh Air Fund children, while he had not.

He supposed it was because Naseby had sold papers, and wore shoes, and went to night school, and did many other things equally objectionable. Still, what Naseby had said about the country, and riding horseback, and the fishing, and the shooting crows with no cops to stop you, and watermelons for nothing, had sounded wonderfully attractive and quite improbable, except that it was one of Naseby's peculiarly sneaking ways to tell the truth. Anyway, Naseby had left Cherry Street for good, and had gone back to the country to work there. This all helped to make Snipes morose, and it was with a cynical smile of satisfaction that he watched an old countryman coming slowly up the street, and asking his way timidly of the Italians to Case's tenement.

The countryman looked up and about him in evident bewilderment and anxiety. He glanced hesitatingly across at the boy leaning against the wall of a saloon, but the boy was watching two sparrows fighting in the dirt of the street, and did not see him. At least, it did not look as if he saw him. Then the old man knocked on the door of Case's tenement. No one came, for the people in the house had learned to leave inquiring countrymen to the gentleman who rented room No. 8, and as that gentleman was occupied at that moment with a younger countryman, he allowed the old man, whom he had first cautiously observed from the top of the stairs, to remain where he was.

The old man stood uncertainly on the stoop, and then removed his heavy black felt hat and rubbed his bald head and the white shining locks of hair around it with a red bandanna handkerchief. Then he walked very slowly across the street toward Snipes, for the rest of the street was empty, and there was no one else at hand. The old man was dressed in heavy black broadcloth, quaintly cut, with boot legs showing up under the trousers, and with faultlessly clean linen of home-made manufacture.

"I can't make the people in that house over there hear me," complained the old man, with the simple confidence that old age has in very young boys. "Do you happen to know if they're at home?"

"Nop," growled Snipes.

"I'm looking for a man named Perceval," said the stranger; "he lives in that house, and I wanter see him on most particular business. It isn't a very pleasing place he lives in, is it— at least," he hurriedly added, as if fearful of giving offense, "it isn't much on the outside? Do you happen to know him?"

Perceval was Alf Wolfe's business name.

"Nop," said the trailer.

"Well, I'm not looking for him," explained the stranger, slowly, "as much as I'm looking for a young man that I kind of suspect is been to see him to-day: a young man that looks like me, only younger. Has lightish hair and pretty tall and lanky, and carrying a shiny black bag with him. Did you happen to hev noticed him going into that place across the way?"

"Nop," said Snipes.

The old man sighed and nodded his head thoughtfully at Snipes, and puckered up the corners of his mouth, as though he were thinking deeply. He had wonderfully honest blue eyes, and with the white hair hanging around his sunburned face, he looked like an old saint. But the trailer didn't know that: he did know, though, that this man was a different sort from the rest. Still, that was none of his business.

"What is't you want to see him about?" he asked sullenly, while he looked up and down the street and everywhere but at the old man, and rubbed one bare foot slowly over the other.

The old man looked pained, and much to Snipe's surprise, the question brought the tears to his eyes, and his lips trembled. Then he swerved slightly, so that he might have fallen if Snipes had not caught him and helped him across the pavement to a seat on a stoop. "Thankey, son," said the stranger; "I'm not as strong as I was, an' the sun's mighty hot, an' these streets of yours smell mighty bad, and I've had a powerful lot of trouble these last few days. But if I could see this man Perceval before my boy does, I know I could fix it, and it would all come out right."

"What do you want to see him about?" repeated the trailer, suspiciously, while he fanned the old man with his hat. Snipes could not have told you why he did this or why this particular old countryman was any different from the many others who came to buy counterfeit money and who were thieves at heart as well as in deed.

THE TRAILER FOR ROOM NO. 8

"I want to see him about my son," said the old man to the little boy. "He's a bad man whoever he is. This 'ere Perceval is a bad man. He sends down his wickedness to the country and tempts weak folks to sin. He teaches 'em ways of evil-doing they never heard of, and he's ruined my son with the others— ruined him. I've had nothing to do with the city and its ways; we're strict living, simple folks, and perhaps we've been too strict, or Abraham wouldn't have run away to the city. But I thought it was best, and I doubted nothing when the fresh-air children came to the farm. I didn't like city children, but I let 'em come. I took 'em in, and did what I could to make it pleasant for 'em. Poor little fellers, all as thin as corn-stalks and pale as ghosts, and as dirty as you.

"I took 'em in and let 'em ride the horses, and swim in the river, and shoot crows in the cornfield, and eat all the cherries they could pull, and what did the city send me in return for that? It sent me this thieving, rascally scheme of this man Perceval's, and it turned my boy's head, and lost him to me. I saw him poring over the note and reading it as if it were Gospel, and I suspected nothing. And when he asked me if he could keep it, I said yes he could, for I thought he wanted it for a

298

curiosity, and then off he put with the black bag and the $200 he's been saving up to start housekeeping with when the old Deacon says he can marry his daughter Kate." The old man placed both hands on his knees and went on excitedly.

"The old Deacon says he'll not let 'em marry till Abe has $2,000, and that is what the boy's come after. He wants to buy $2,000 worth of bad money with his $200 worth of good money, to show the Deacon, just as though it were likely a marriage after such a crime as that would ever be a happy one."

Snipes had stopped fanning the old man, as he ran on, and was listening intently, with an uncomfortable feeling of sympathy and sorrow, uncomfortable because he was not used to it.

He could not see why the old man should think the city should have treated his boy better because he had taken care of the city's children, and he was puzzled between his allegiance to the gang and his desire to help the gang's innocent victim, and then because he was an innocent victim and not a "customer," he let his sympathy get the better of his discretion.

"Saay," he began, abruptly, "I'm not sayin' nothin' to nobody, and nobody's sayin' nothin' to me—see? but I guess your son'll be around here to-day, sure. He's got to come before one, for this office closes sharp at one, and we goes home. Now, I've got the call whether he gets his stuff taken off him or whether the boys leave him alone. If I say the word, they'd no more come near him than if he had the cholera —see? An' I'll say it for this oncet, just for you. Hold on," he commanded, as the old man raised his voice in surprised interrogation, "don't ask no questions, 'cause you won't get no answers except lies. You find your way back to the Grand Central Depot and wait there, and I'll steer your son down to you, sure, as soon as I can find him—see? Now get along, or you'll get me inter trouble."

"You've been lying to me, then," cried the old man, "and you're as bad as any of them, and my boy's over in that house now."

He scrambled up from the stoop, and before the trailer could understand what he proposed to do, had dashed across the street and up the stoop, and up the stairs, and had burst into room No. 8.

Snipes tore after him. "Come back! come back out of that, you old fool!" he cried. "You'll get killed in there!" Snipes was afraid to enter room No. 8, but he could hear from the outside the old man challenging Alf Wolfe in a resonant angry voice that rang through the building.

"Whew!" said Snipes, crouching on the stairs, "there's goin' to be a muss this time, sure!"

"Where's my son? Where have you hidden my son?" demanded the old man. He ran across the room and pulled open a door that led into another room, but it was empty. He had fully expected to see his boy murdered and quartered, and with his pockets inside out. He turned on Wolfe, shaking his white hair like a mane. "Give me up my son, you rascal you!" he cried, "or I'll get the police, and I'll tell them how you decoy honest boys to your den and murder them."

"Are you drunk or crazy, or just a little of both?" asked Mr. Wolfe. "For a cent I'd throw you out of that window. Get out of here! Quick, now! You're too old to get excited like that; it's not good for you."

But this only exasperated the old man the more, and he made a lunge at the confidence man's throat.

Mr. Wolfe stepped aside and caught him around the waist and twisted his leg around the old man's rheumatic one, and held him. "Now," said Wolfe, as quietly as though he were giving a lesson in wrestling, "if I wanted to, I could break your back."

The old man glared up at him, panting.

"Your son's not here," said Wolfe, "and this is a private gentleman's private room. I could turn you over to the police for assault if I wanted to; but," he added, magnanimously, "I won't. Now get out of here and go home to your wife, and when you come to see the sights again don't drink so much raw whiskey." He half carried the old farmer to the top of the stairs and dropped him, and went back and closed the door. Snipes came up and helped him down and out, and the old man and the boy walked slowly and in silence out to the Bowery. Snipes helped his companion into a car and put him off at the Grand Central Depot. The heat and the excitement had told heavily on the old man, and he seemed dazed and beaten.

He was leaning on the trailer's shoulder and waiting for his turn in the line in front of the ticket window, when a tall, gawky, good-looking country lad sprang out of it and at him with an expression of surprise and anxiety. "Father," he said, "father, what's wrong? What are you doing here? Is anybody ill at home? Are *you* ill?"

"Abraham," said the old man, simply, and dropped heavily on the younger man's shoulder. Then he raised his head sternly and said: "I thought you were murdered, but better that than a thief, Abraham. What brought you here? What did you do with that rascal's letter? What did you do with his money?"

The trailer drew cautiously away; the conversation was becoming unpleasantly personal.

"I don't know what you're talking about," said Abraham, calmly. "The Deacon gave his consent the other night without the $2,000, and I took the $200 I'd saved and came right on in the fust train to buy the ring. It's pretty, isn't it?" he said, flushing, as he pulled out a little velvet box and opened it.

The old man was so happy at this that he laughed and cried alternately, and then he made a grab for the trailer and pulled him down beside him on one of the benches.

"You've got to come with me," he said, with kind severity. "You're a good boy, but your folks have let you run wrong. You've been good to me, and you said you would get me back my boy and save him from those thieves, and I believe now that you meant it. Now you're just coming back with us to the farm and the cows and the river, and you can eat all you want and live with us, and never, never see this unclean, wicked city again."

Snipes looked up keenly from under the rim of his hat and rubbed one of his muddy feet over the other as was his habit. The young countryman, greatly puzzled, and the older man smiling kindly, waited expectantly in silence. From outside came the sound of the car-bells jangling, and the rattle of cabs, and the cries of drivers, and all the varying rush and turmoil of a great metropolis. Green fields, and running rivers, and fruit that did not grow in wooden boxes or brown paper ones, were myths and idle words to Snipes, but this "unclean, wicked city" he knew.

"I guess you're too good for me," he said, with an uneasy laugh. "I guess little old New York's good enough for me."

"What!" cried the old man, in the tones of greatest concern. "You would go back to that den of iniquity, surely not,—to that thief Perceval?"

"Well," said the trailer, slowly, "and he's not such a bad lot, neither. You see he could hev broke your neck that time when you was choking him, but he didn't. There's your train," he added hurriedly and jumping away. "Good-by. So long, old man. I'm much 'bliged to you jus' for asking me."

Two hours later the farmer and his son were making the family weep and laugh over their adventures, as they all sat together on the porch with the vines about it; and the trailer was leaning against the wall of a saloon and apparently counting his ten toes, but in reality watching for Mr. Wolfe to give the signal from the window of room No. 8.

THE EDITOR'S STORY

IT was a warm afternoon in the early spring, and the air in the office was close and heavy. The letters of the morning had been answered and the proofs corrected, and the gentlemen who had come with ideas worth one column at space rates, and which they thought worth three, had compromised with the editor on a basis of two, and departed. The editor's desk was covered with manuscripts in a heap, a heap that never seemed to grow less, and each manuscript bore a character of its own, as marked or as unobtrusive as the character of the man or of the woman who had written it, which disclosed itself in the care with which some were presented for consideration, in the vain little ribbons of other, or the selfish manner in which still others were tightly rolled or vilely scribbled.

The editor held the first page of a poem in his hand, and was reading it mechanically, for its length had already declared against it, unless it might chance to be the precious gem out of a thousand, which must be chosen in spite of its twenty stanzas. But as the editor read, his interest awakened, and he scanned the verses again, as one would turn to look a second time at a face which seemed familiar. At the fourth stanza his memory was still in doubt, at the sixth it was warming to the chase, and at the end of the page was in full cry. He caught up the second page and looked for the final verse, and then at the name below, and then back again quickly to the title of the poem, and pushed aside the papers on his desk in search of any note which might have accompanied it.

The name signed at the bottom of the second page was Edwin Aram, the title of the poem was "Bohemia," and there was no accompanying note, only the name Berkeley written at the top of the first page. The envelope in which it had come gave no further clew. It was addressed in the same handwriting as that in which the poem had been written, and it bore the postmark of New York city. There was no request for the return of the poem, no direction to which either the poem itself or the check for its payment in the event of its acceptance might be sent. Berkeley might be the name of an apartment-house, or of a country place, or of a suburban town.

The editor stepped out of his office into the larger room beyond and said: "I've a poem here that appeared in an American magazine about seven years ago. I remember the date, because I read it when I was at college. Some one is either trying to play a trick on us, or to get money by stealing some other man's brains."

It was in this way that Edwin Aram first introduced himself to our office, and while his poem was not accepted, it was not returned. On the contrary, Mr. Aram became to us one of the most interesting of our would-be contributors, and there was no author, no matter of what popularity, for whose work we waited with greater impatience. But Mr. Aram's personality still remained as completely hidden from us as were the productions which he offered from the sight of our subscribers; for each of the poems he sent had been stolen outright and signed with his name.

It was through no fault of ours that he continued to blush unseen, or that his pretty taste in poems was unappreciated by the general reader. We followed up every clew and every hint he chose to give us with an enthusiasm worthy of a search after a lost explorer, and with an animus worthy of better game. Yet there was some reason for our interest. The man who steals the work of another and who passes it off as his own is the special foe of every editor, but this particular editor had a personal distrust of Mr. Aram. He imagined that these

THE EDITOR'S STORY

poems might possibly be a trap which some one
had laid for him with the purpose of drawing
him into printing them, and then of pointing
out by this fact how little read he was, and
how unfit to occupy the swivel-chair into which
he had so lately dropped. Or if this were not
the case, the man was in any event the enemy
of all honest people, who look unkindly on those
who try to obtain money by false pretenses.

The evasions of Edwin Aram were many,
and his methods to avoid detection not without
skill. His second poem was written on a sheet
of note-paper bearing the legend "The Shakespeare Debating Club. Edwin Aram, President."

This was intended to reassure us as to his
literary taste and standard, and to meet any
suspicion we might feel had there been no address of any sort accompanying the poem. No
one we knew had ever heard of a Shakespeare
Debating Club in New York city; but we gave
him the benefit of the doubt until we found that
this poem, like the first, was also stolen. His
third poem bore his name and an address,
which on instant inquiry turned out to be that
of a vacant lot on Seventh Avenue near Central
Park.

Edwin Aram had by this time become an ex-
asperating and picturesque individual, and the

editorial staff was divided in its opinion concerning him. It was argued on one hand that as the man had never sent us a real address, his object must be to gain a literary reputation at the expense of certain poets, and not to make money at ours. Others answered this by saying that fear of detection alone kept Edwin Aram from sending his real address, but that as soon as his poem was printed, and he ascertained by that fact that he had not been discovered, he would put in an application for payment, and let us know quickly enough to what portion of New York city his check should be forwarded.

This, however, presupposed the fact that he was writing to us over his real name, which we did not believe he would dare to do. No one in our little circle of journalists and literary men had ever heard of such a man, and his name did not appear in the directory. This fact, however, was not convincing in itself, as the residents of New York move from flat to hotel, and from apartments to boarding-houses as frequently as the Arab changes his camping-ground. We tried to draw him out at last by publishing a personal paragraph which stated that several contributions received from Edwin Aram would be returned to him if he would send stamps and his present address. The editor did not add that he would return the poems in person, but such was his warlike intention.

This had the desired result, and brought us a fourth poem and a fourth address, the name of a tall building which towers above Union Square. We seemed to be getting very warm now, and the editor gathered up the four poems, and called to his aid his friend Bronson, the ablest reporter on the New York ——, who was to act as chronicler. They took with them letters from the authors of two of the poems and from the editor of the magazine in which the first one had originally appeared, testifying to the fact that Edwin Aram had made an exact copy of the original, and wishing the brother editor good luck in catching the plagiarist.

The reporter looked these over with a critical eye. "The City Editor told me if we caught him," he said, "that I could let it run for all it was worth. I can use these names, I suppose, and I guess they have pictures of the poets at the office. If he turns out to be anybody in particular, it ought to be worth a full three columns. Sunday paper, too."

The amateur detectives stood in the lower hall in the tall building, between swinging doors, and jostled by hurrying hundreds, while they read the names on a marble directory.

"There he is!" said the editor, excitedly. "'American Literary Bureau.' One room on the fourteenth floor. That's just the sort of a place in which we would be likely to find him." But the reporter was gazing open-eyed at a name in large letters on an office door. "Edward K. Aram," it read, "Commissioner of ——, and City ——."

"What do you think of *that?*" he gasped, triumphantly.

"Nonsense," said the editor. "He wouldn't dare; besides, the initials are different. You're expecting too good a story."

"That's the way to get them," answered the reporter, as he hurried toward the office of the City ——. "If a man falls dead, believe it's a suicide until you prove it's not; if you find a suicide, believe it's a murder until you are convinced to the contrary. Otherwise you'll get beaten. We don't want the proprietor of a little literary bureau, we want a big city official, and I'll believe we have one until he proves we haven't."

"Which are you going to ask for?" whispered the editor, "Edward K. or Edwin?"

"Edwin, I should say," answered the reporter. "He has probably given notice that mail addressed that way should go to him."

"Is Mr. Edwin Aram in?" he asked.

THE EDITOR'S STORY

A clerk raised his head and looked behind him. "No," he said; "his desk is closed. I guess he's gone home for the day."

The reporter nudged the editor savagely with his elbow, but his face gave no sign. "That's a pity," he said; "we have an appointment with him. He still lives at Sixty-first Street and Madison Avenue, I believe, does he not?"

"No," said the clerk; "that's his father, the Commissioner, Edward K. The son lives at ———. Take the Sixth Avenue elevated and get off at 116th Street."

"Thank you," said the reporter. He turned a triumphant smile upon the editor. "We've got him!" he said, excitedly. "And the son of old Edward K., too! Think of it! Trying to steal a few dollars by cribbing other men's poems; that's the best story there has been in the papers for the past three months,—'Edward K. Aram's son a thief!' Look at the names—politicians, poets, editors, all mixed up in it. It's good for three columns, sure."

"We've got to think of his people, too," urged the editor, as they mounted the steps of the elevated road.

"He didn't think of them," said the reporter.

The house in which Mr. Aram lived was an apartment-house, and the brass latchets in the hallway showed that it contained three suites.

THE EDITOR'S STORY

There were visiting-cards under the latchets of the first and third stories, and under that of the second a piece of note-paper on which was written the autograph of Edwin Aram. The editor looked at it curiously. He had never believed it to be a real name.

"I am sorry Edwin Aram did not turn out to be a woman," he said, regretfully; "it would have been so much more interesting."

"Now," instructed Bronson, impressively, "whether he is in or not, we have him. If he's not in, we wait until he comes, even if he doesn't come until morning; we don't leave this place until we have seen him."

"Very well," said the editor.

The maid left them standing at the top of the stairs while she went to ask if Mr. Aram was in, and whether he would see two gentlemen who did not give their names because they were strangers to him. The two stood silent while they waited, eying each other anxiously, and when the girl reopened the door, nodded pleasantly, and said, "Yes, Mr. Aram is in," they hurried past her as though they feared that he would disappear in mid-air, or float away through the windows before they could reach him.

And yet, when they stood at last face to face with him, he bore a most disappointing air of every-day respectability. He was a tall, thin young man, with light hair and mustache and large blue eyes. His back was toward the window, so that his face was in the shadow, and he did not rise as they entered. The room in which he sat was a prettily furnished one, opening into another tiny room, which, from the number of books in it, might have been called a library. The rooms had a well-to-do, even prosperous, air, but they did not show any evidences of a pronounced taste on the part of their owner, either in the way in which they were furnished or in the decorations of the walls. A little girl of about seven or eight years of age, who was standing between her father's knees, with a hand on each, and with her head thrown back on his shoulder, looked up at the two visitors with evident interest, and smiled brightly.

"Mr. Aram?" asked the editor, tentatively.

The young man nodded, and the two visitors seated themselves.

"I wish to talk to you on a matter of private business," the editor began. "Wouldn't it be better to send the little girl away?"

The child shook her head violently at this, and crowded up closely to her father; but he held her away from him gently, and told her to "run and play with Annie."

THE EDITOR'S STORY

She passed the two visitors, with her head held scornfully in air, and left the men together. Mr. Aram seemed to have a most passive and incurious disposition. He could have no idea as to who his anonymous visitors might be, nor did he show any desire to know.

"I am the editor of ——," the editor began. "My friend also writes for that periodical. I have received several poems from you lately, Mr. Aram, and one in particular which we all liked very much. It was called 'Bohemia.' But it is so like one that has appeared under the same title in the —— *Magazine* that I thought I would see you about it, and ask you if you could explain the similarity. You see," he went on, "it would be less embarrassing if you would do so now than later, when the poem has been published and when people might possibly accuse you of plagiarism." The editor smiled encouragingly and waited.

Mr. Aram crossed one leg over the other and folded his hands in his lap. He exhibited no interest, and looked drowsily at the editor. When he spoke it was in a tone of unstudied indifference. "I never wrote a poem called 'Bohemia,'" he said, slowly; "at least, if I did I don't remember it."

The editor had not expected a flat denial, and it irritated him, for he recognized it to be the

316

safest course the man could pursue, if he kept to it. "But you don't mean to say," he protested, smiling, "that you can write so excellent a poem as 'Bohemia' and then forget having done so?"

"I might," said Mr. Aram, unresentfully, and with little interest. "I scribble a good deal."

"Perhaps," suggested the reporter, politely, with the air of one who is trying to cover up a difficulty to the satisfaction of all, "Mr. Aram would remember it if he saw it."

The editor nodded his head in assent, and took the first page of the two on which the poem was written, and held it out to Mr. Aram, who accepted the piece of foolscap and eyed it listlessly.

"Yes, I wrote that," he said. "I copied it out of a book called 'Gems from American Poets.'" There was a lazy pause. "But I never sent it to any paper." The editor and the reporter eyed each other with outward calm but with some inward astonishment. They could not see why he had not adhered to his original denial of the thing *in toto*. It seemed to them so foolish to admit having copied the poem and then to deny having forwarded it.

"You see," explained Mr. Aram, still with no apparent interest in the matter, "I am very fond of poetry; I like to recite it, and I often write it out in order to make me remember it. I find it impresses the words on my mind. Well, that's what has happened. I have copied this poem out at the office probably, and one of the clerks there has found it, and has supposed that I wrote it, and he has sent it to your paper as a sort of a joke on me. You see, father being so well known, it would rather amuse the boys if I came out as a poet. That's how it was, I guess. Somebody must have found it and sent it to you, because *I* never sent it."

There was a moment of thoughtful consideration. "I see," said the editor. "I used to do that same thing myself when I had to recite pieces at school. I found that writing the verses down helped me to remember them. I remember that I once copied out many of Shakespeare's sonnets. But, Mr. Aram, it never occurred to me, after having copied out one of Shakespeare's sonnets, to sign my own name at the bottom of it."

Mr. Aram's eyes dropped to the page of manuscript in his hand and rested there for some little time. Then he said, without raising his head, "I haven't signed this."

"No," replied the editor; "but you signed the second page, which I still have in my hand."

The editor and his companion expected some expression of indignation from Mr. Aram at this, some question of their right to come into his house and cross-examine him and to accuse him, tentatively at least, of literary fraud, but they were disappointed. Mr. Aram's manner was still one of absolute impassibility. Whether this manner was habitual to him they could not know, but it made them doubt their own judgment in having so quickly accused him, as it bore the look of undismayed innocence.

It was the reporter who was the first to break the silence. "Perhaps some one has signed Mr. Aram's name—the clerk who sent it, for instance."

Young Mr. Aram looked up at him curiously, and held out his hand for the second page. "Yes," he drawled, "that's how it happened. That's not my signature. I never signed that."

The editor was growing restless. "I have several other poems here from you," he said; "one written from the rooms of the Shakespeare Debating Club, of which I see you are president. Your clerk could not have access there, could he? He did not write that, too?"

"No," said Mr. Aram, doubtfully, "he could not have written that."

The editor handed him the poem. "It's yours, then?"

"Yes, that's mine," Mr. Aram replied.

"And the signature?"

"Yes, and the signature. I wrote that myself," Mr. Aram explained, "and sent it myself. That other one ('Bohemia') I just copied out to remember, but this is original with me."

"And the envelope in which it was enclosed," asked the editor, "did you address that also?"

Mr. Aram examined it uninterestedly. "Yes, that's my handwriting too." He raised his head. His face wore an expression of patient politeness.

"Oh!" exclaimed the editor, suddenly, in some embarrassment. "I handed you the wrong envelope. I beg your pardon. That envelope is the one in which 'Bohemia' came."

The reporter gave a hardly perceptible start; his eyes were fixed on the pattern of the rug at his feet, and the editor continued to examine the papers in his hand. There was a moment's silence. From outside came the noise of children playing in the street and the rapid rush of a passing wagon.

When the two visitors raised their heads Mr. Aram was looking at them strangely, and the fingers folded in his lap were twisting in and out.

"This Shakespeare Debating Club," said the editor, "where are its rooms, Mr. Aram?"

"It has no rooms, now," answered the poet. "It has disbanded. It never had any regular rooms; we just met about and read."

"I see—exactly," said the editor. "And the house on Seventh Avenue from which your third poem was sent—did you reside there then, or have you always lived here?"

"No, yes—I used to live there—I lived there when I wrote that poem."

The editor looked at the reporter and back at Mr. Aram. "It is a vacant lot, Mr. Aram," he said, gravely.

There was a long pause. The poet rocked slowly up and down in his rocking-chair, and looked at his hands, which he rubbed over one another as though they were cold. Then he raised his head and cleared his throat.

"Well, gentlemen," he said, "you have made out your case."

"Yes," said the editor, regretfully, "we have made out our case." He could not help but wish that the fellow had stuck to his original denial. It was too easy a victory.

"I don't say, mind you," went on Mr. Aram, "that I ever took anybody's verses and sent them to a paper as my own, but I ask you, as one gentleman talking to another, and inquiring for information, what is there wrong in doing it? I say, *if* I had done it, which I don't admit I ever did, where's the harm?"

"Where's the harm?" cried the two visitors in chorus.

THE EDITOR'S STORY

"Obtaining money under false pretenses," said the editor, "is the harm you do the publishers, and robbing another man of the work of his brain and what credit belongs to him is the harm you do him, and telling a lie is the least harm done. Such a contemptible foolish lie, too, that you might have known would surely find you out in spite of the trouble you took to——"

"I never asked you for any money," interrupted Mr. Aram, quietly.

"But we would have sent it to you, nevertheless," retorted the editor, "if we had not discovered in time that the poems were stolen."

"Where would you have sent it?" asked Mr. Aram. "I never gave you a right address, did I? I ask you, did I?"

The editor paused in some confusion. "Well, if you did not want the money, what did you want?" he exclaimed. "I must say I should like to know."

Mr. Aram rocked himself to and fro, and gazed at his two inquisitors with troubled eyes. "I didn't see any harm in it then," he repeated. "I don't see any harm in it now. I didn't ask you for any money. I sort of thought," he said, confusedly, "that I should like to see my name in print. I wanted my friends to see it. I'd have liked to have shown it to—to—well,

322

I'd like my wife to have seen it. She's interested in literature and books and magazines and things like that. That was all I wanted. That's why I did it."

The reporter looked up askance at the editor, as a prompter watches the actor to see if he is ready to take his cue.

"How do I know that?" demanded the editor, sharply. He found it somewhat difficult to be severe with this poet, for the man admitted so much so readily, and would not defend himself. Had he only blustered and grown angry and ordered them out, instead of sitting helplessly there rocking to and fro and picking at the back of his hands, it would have made it so much easier. "How do we know," repeated the editor, "that you did not intend to wait until the poems had appeared, and then send us your real address and ask for the money, saying that you had moved since you had last written us?"

"Oh," protested Mr. Aram, "you know I never thought of that."

"I don't know anything of the sort," said the editor. "I only know that you have forged and lied and tried to obtain money that doesn't belong to you, and that I mean to make an example of you and frighten other men from doing the same thing. No editor has read every poem that was ever written, and there is no protection for him from such fellows as you, and the only thing he can do when he does catch one of you is to make an example of him. That's what I am going to do. I am going to make an example of you. I am going to nail you up as people nail up dead crows to frighten off the live ones. It is my intention to give this to the papers to-night, and you know what they will do with it in the morning."

There was a long and most uncomfortable pause, and it is doubtful if the editor did not feel it as much as did the man opposite him. The editor turned to his friend for a glance of sympathy, or of disapproval even, but that gentleman still sat bending forward with his eyes fixed on the floor, while he tapped with the top of his cane against his teeth.

"You don't mean," said Mr. Aram, in a strangely different voice from which he had last spoken, "that you would do that?"

"Yes, I do," blustered the editor. But even as he spoke he was conscious of a sincere regret that he had not come alone. He could intuitively feel Bronson mapping out the story in his mind and memorizing Aram's every word, and taking mental notes of the framed certificates of high membership in different military and Masonic associations which hung upon the

walls. It had not been long since the editor
was himself a reporter, and he could see that it
was as good a story as Bronson could wish it
to be. But he reiterated, "Yes, I mean to give
it to the papers to-night."

"But think," said Aram—"think, sir, who I
am. You don't want to ruin me for the rest
of my life just for a matter of fifteen dollars,
do you? Fifteen dollars that no one has lost,
either? If I'd embezzled a million or so, or if
I had robbed the city, well and good! I'd have
taken big risks for big money; but you are going
to punish me just as hard because I tried to
please my wife, as though I had robbed a mint.
No one has really been hurt," he pleaded; "the
men who wrote the poems—they've been paid
for them; they've got all the credit for them
they *can* get. You've not lost a cent. I've
gained nothing by it; and yet you gentlemen
are going to give this thing to the papers, and,
as you say, sir, we know what they will make
of it. What with my being my father's son,
and all that, my father is going to suffer. My
family is going to suffer. It will ruin me——"

The editor put the papers back into his
pocket. If Bronson had not been there he
might possibly instead have handed them over
to Mr. Aram, and this story would never have
been written. But he could not do that now.

THE EDITOR'S STORY

Mr. Aram's affairs had become the property of the New York newspaper.

He turned to his friend doubtfully. "What do you think, Bronson?" he asked.

At this sign of possible leniency Aram ceased in his rocking and sat erect, with eyes wide open and fixed on Bronson's face. But the latter trailed his stick over the rug beneath his feet and shrugged his shoulders.

"Mr. Aram," he said, "might have thought of his family and his father before he went into this business. It is rather late now. But," he added, "I don't think it is a matter we can decide in any event. It should be left to the firm."

"Yes," said the editor, hurriedly, glad of the excuse to temporize, "we must leave it to the house." But he read Bronson's answer to mean that he did not intend to let the plagiarist escape, and he knew that even were Bronson willing to do so, there was still his City Editor to be persuaded.

The two men rose and stood uncomfortably, shifting their hats in their hands—and avoiding each other's eyes. Mr. Aram stood up also, and seeing that his last chance had come, began again to plead desperately.

"What good would fifteen dollars do me?" he said, with a gesture of his hands round the room. "I don't have to look for money as hard as that. I tell you," he reiterated, "it wasn't the money I wanted. I didn't mean any harm. I didn't know it was wrong. I just wanted to please my wife—that was all. My God, man, can't you see that you are punishing me out of all proportion?"

The visitors walked toward the door, and he followed them, talking the faster as they drew near to it. The scene had become an exceedingly painful one, and they were anxious to bring it to a close.

The editor interrupted him. "We will let you know," he said, "what we have decided to do by to-morrow morning."

"You mean," retorted the man, hopelessly and reproachfully, "that I will read it in the Sunday papers."

Before the editor could answer they heard the door leading into the apartment open and close, and some one stepping quickly across the hall to the room in which they stood. The entrance to the room was hung with a portière, and as the three men paused in silence this portière was pushed back, and a young lady stood in the doorway, holding the curtains apart with her two hands. She was smiling, and the smile lighted a face that was inexpressibly bright and honest and true. Aram's face had been lowered, but the eyes of the other two men were staring wide open toward the unexpected figure, which seemed to bring a taste of fresh pure air into the feverish atmosphere of the place. The girl stopped uncertainly when she saw the two strangers, and bowed her head slightly as the mistress of a house might welcome any one whom she found in her drawing-room. She was entirely above and apart from her surroundings. It was not only that she was exceedingly pretty, but that everything about her, from her attitude to her cloth walking-dress, was significant of good taste and high breeding.

She paused uncertainly, still smiling, and with her gloved hands holding back the curtains and looking at Aram with eyes filled with a kind confidence. She was apparently waiting for him to present his friends.

The editor made a sudden but irrevocable resolve. "If she is only a chance visitor," he said to himself, "I will still expose him; but if that woman in the doorway is his wife, I will push Bronson under the elevated train, and the secret will die with me."

What Bronson's thoughts were he could not know, but he was conscious that his friend had straightened his broad shoulders and was holding his head erect.

THE EDITOR'S STORY

Aram raised his face, but he did not look at the woman in the door. "In a minute, dear," he said; "I am busy with these gentlemen."

The girl gave a little "oh" of apology, smiled at her husband's bent head, inclined her own again slightly to the other men, and let the portière close behind her. It had been as dramatic an entrance and exit as the two visitors had ever seen upon the stage. It was as if Aram had given a signal, and the only person who could help him had come in the nick of time to plead for him. Aram, stupid as he appeared to be, had evidently felt the effect his wife's appearance had made upon his judges. He still kept his eyes fixed upon the floor, but he said, and this time with more confidence in his tone:

"It is not, gentlemen, as though I were an old man. I have so very long to live—so long to try to live this down. Why, I am as young as you are. How would you like to have a thing like this to carry with you till you died?"

The editor still stood staring blankly at the curtains through which Mr. Aram's good angel, for whom he had lied and cheated in order to gain credit in her eyes, had disappeared. He pushed them aside with his stick. "We will let you know to-morrow morning," he repeated, and the two men passed out from the poet's presence, and on into the hall. They descended the stairs in an uncomfortable silence, Bronson leading the way, and the editor endeavoring to read his verdict by the back of his head and shoulders.

At the foot of the steps he pulled his friend by the sleeve. "Bronson," he coaxed, "you are not going to use it, are you?"

Bronson turned on him savagely. "For Heaven's sake!" he protested, "what do you think I am; did you *see* her?"

So the New York —— lost a very good story, and Bronson a large sum of money for not writing it, and Mr. Aram was taught a lesson, and his young wife's confidence in him remained unshaken. The editor and reporter dined together that night, and over their cigars decided with sudden terror that Mr. Aram might, in his ignorance of their good intentions concerning him, blow out his brains, and for nothing. So they despatched a messenger boy up-town in post-haste with a note saying that "the firm" had decided to let the matter drop—although, perhaps, it would have been better to have given him one sleepless night at least.

That was three years ago, and since then Mr. Aram's father has fallen out with Tammany, and has been retired from public service. Bronson has been sent abroad to represent the United States at a foreign court, and has asked the editor to write the story that he did not write, but with such changes in the names of people and places that no one save Mr. Aram may know who Mr. Aram really was and is.

This the editor has done, reporting what happened as faithfully as he could, and in the hope that it will make an interesting story in spite of the fact, and not on account of the fact, that it is a true one.

www.ingramcontent.com/pod-product-compliance
Lightning Source LLC
Chambersburg PA
CBHW032232010726
47494CB00002B/461